COURAGE

Books by Dan Hayden

THE GAME WARDENS

THE GAME WARDENS, Book 2, Danger's Way

THE GAME WARDENS, Book 3,
The Game Warden's Bullet

TALL SHIP SAILOR

COURAGE

COURAGE

DAN HAYDEN

COURAGE

iUniverse books may be ordered through booksellers or by contacting:

iUniverse
1663 Liberty Drive
Bloomington, IN 47403
www.iuniverse.com
844-349-9409

Because of the dynamic nature of the Internet, any web addresses or links contained in this book may have changed since publication and may no longer be valid. The views expressed in this work are solely those of the author and do not necessarily reflect the views of the publisher, and the publisher hereby disclaims any responsibility for them.

Any people depicted in stock imagery provided by Getty Images are models, and such images are being used for illustrative purposes only. Certain stock imagery © Getty Images.

ISBN: 978-1-6632-5569-3 (sc)
ISBN: 978-1-6632-5570-9 (e)

Library of Congress Control Number: 2023917940

Print information available on the last page.

iUniverse rev. date: 09/20/2023

PREFACE

This book is written to provide a message to the parents and children that may be struggling with a childhood malady loosely referred to as a temporal lobe condition and some times more pointedly as petit mal. Most doctors that encounter a child that may be experiencing such a condition have been known to downplay the disorder for several reasons. If the child is young, the attending physician is most likely to be a pediatrician. The condition, if correctly diagnosed at the outset is considered a very mild form of epilepsy. However, in many cases the disorder may be confused with a multitude of other child maladies that may be general in nature and just part of the normal growing and maturation process.

By downplaying the condition, the doctor seeks to relax the parents and 'buy some time' in the child's growth cycle to determine if the condition is merely a phase, something transient that may be triggered by external influences, a general distraction from the moment, or a serious condition that could develop into a lifelong problem.

There is a multitude of reasons for, possibilities of, causes, and conditions that can be a part of, and take on the same form of the broad condition described above as epilepsy. A physician that chooses the 'wait and see' approach may be placing himself in poor position with the child's parents as he may come across as not considering the situation as serious as the parents do. On the other hand, the involved parents are very likely to consider a much more severe condition simply because they haven't been trained in the area of neurological disorders. For some reason, it is usually human nature to consider the worst situation and then stress over that, until after much pain, effort and money has been expended. Only after the condition or disorder has been defined, good or bad, will the inquiring parties be satisfied.

In the meantime, a lot of confusion and emotional distress is expended on areas that may not have deserved that kind of attention in the first place. Out of concern for the patient's good, outside sources as doctors, parents, and educators can have an influence on the child's growth in the social and physical sense. Because everyone is afraid of failure and embarrassment (those affected and those not affected), or labeling which leads to social ostracism, or physical trauma which can be an end result of a lack of focus, well intended care givers can retard the positive growth of an inflicted individual and influence any chances he or she has of moving out of his or her dilemma.

"The child will grow out it," many attending doctors will offer. In the very mildest of forms, this may be true. It has been found that most children that suffer from the disorder described above can, in most cases, live a normal life and normal life experiences, and given the opportunity, move in the same direction as a child who has never experienced any abnormalities.

It should be mentioned here, the child cannot accomplish this on his or her own. He or she must be allowed to make mistakes, be embarrassed, experience new things, and learn and forge forward with as much enthusiasm and confidence as possible. Being frightened will only help to stifle any progress. It is only in this way, that someone with such an affliction will have the chance to 'grow out of it.'

Dan Hayden
Author, COURAGE
August 2023

DEDICATION

This book is dedicated to Laurie, who entered my life at a very special time and unknowingly helped to mold the man I came to be.

COURAGE

Courage, it would seem, is nothing less
Than the power to overcome danger, misfortune,
fear, injustice,
While continuing to affirm inwardly that life
with all its sorrows is good;
That everything is meaningful
Even if in a sense beyond our understanding;
and that there is always tomorrow.

Dorothy Thompson

ACKNOWLEDGEMENTS

I would just like to mention that part of this novel was written within the confines of the home owned by famed writer Mark Twain, in Hartford, Connecticut.

As a birthday gift to me, my eldest son Dan made the reservations for the experience. The famous house was shut down for one night and only seven authors were invited to attend the experience of writing their novel in such a hallowed place. We could choose almost anywhere within the house to sit and write under the same conditions as the famous writer would have experienced at his time.

It was a cool September evening, and the rooms were lit by gas lighting as he would have used. There was no heat, and the fireplaces were yet unlit as September temperatures vary from cool to warm.

I found it difficult in the beginning to write where the famous Mark Twain once sat and did the same thing, but the surroundings, especially environmentally, also put an interesting spin on my concentration.

It was a unique experience, and something I am proud to say that I did…for me and this book.

CHAPTER 1

It was a Monday morning at Tobacco Valley Grammar School. A fourth-grade class was underway and sitting quietly in their seats doing 'seat work.' Talking among the students was prohibited.

Attendance already taken, fourth grade teacher Margaret Talbot sat at her desk at the front of the room and leafed through her in-basket and the morning mail. Every now and then, she looked up to keep a mindful eye on her class. Satisfied that everyone was quiet and busy, she turned her attention back to the mail scattered about the top of her desk.

Presently, Mrs. Talbot looked up at the large clock on the wall. It was time for arithmetic. The teacher rose from her desk, "Class! Arithmetic time! I have put addition problems on the chalkboard. When I call your name please go to the chalkboard and begin adding the numbers aloud so the class can hear each step in your addition."

Mrs. Talbot proceeded to take an empty seat at the side of the classroom and squeezed her rotund shape into the small desk and chair. "Okay, let's begin. Joseph! You're first." Joseph immediately experienced a queasiness in the pit of his stomach. His breathing quickened and his anxiety level began to escalate. Mrs. Talbot sat back in the tiny chair as a wicked, little smile crossed her face.

It wasn't Joseph's first time at the chalkboard for this exercise. He'd been through this routine several times before, all of which usually ended in the same fashion... embarrassment, sadness, and defeat. He approached the chalkboard and noticed long columns of double-digit numbers, six to eight rows tall, stacked one atop the other.

Joseph was nervous. He picked up the chalk from the chalk tray and pointed to the top number beginning with the right-most number of the double-digit pair...'the ones,' as referred to by educators of the time. Mrs. Talbot shouted from the side of the room, "Well, we're waiting."

Joseph looked at the column of numbers. Starting from the top, they were stacked one atop the other as 28, 34, 87, 43, 55, 86. He began to add aloud, "Eight plus four is twelve plus seven is...," Joseph paused. His nervousness in front of the class was getting the better of him.

Mrs. Talbot heard the pause and jumped at the opportunity, "Well, what is it? We're waiting. I want to know what the next number is." Joseph was frozen in his tracks with anxiety and embarrassment. He couldn't speak or move his hand that held the chalk. The teacher didn't let up. "What's the matter...can't you add? Just add the next number down...quickly...let's go." Joseph knew he had to give an answer, but his mind had now gone blank. His right hand, still holding the chalk, stayed glued to the chalkboard. In his mind, he knew he could add the column, but with the relentless barrage of ridicule from Mrs. Talbot, couldn't speak or think. He was intentionally being chastised in front of his class, and at the same time, asked to respond to the teacher's sarcasm as to what he was doing.

Then the inevitable happened. Mrs. Talbot started making comments to the class about Joseph's performance at the chalkboard. "Look at him up there. Is he asleep? Somebody go wake him up." Joseph stood there with his back to thirty-five of his peers, a mixed class of girls and boys, all the same age, anyone of which could be next to suffer before the expectant teacher. His hand that still held the chalk, at the third row of numbers, was frozen to the chalkboard. Joseph listened for any snickering or murmuring from the class. There wasn't any. The little boy just wanted the moment to end. He prayed for something to happen...anything...so he could get away from the chalkboard. Joseph was mortified.

Finally, in a disgusted tone, Mrs. Talbot said, "Sit down!" Joseph put the chalk back in its tray, turned around, and with his head down, marched back to his seat in shame. He sat in his chair, stared at the center of his desk, and waited for the awful moment to pass. Then, to add injury to insult, the teacher chose Joseph's best friend, Bobby to go up to the chalkboard and finish the addition for him.

It would seem the experience at the chalkboard could have marked or scarred Joseph in some way. After all, the victim was a mere boy of only 10 years old. One could ask if the teacher knew what she was doing when she chastised the child in front of an entire class, or was it something else? Was the teacher bringing personal problems to school with her, did she resent her job, or was she just abusive? Whatever it was, the child was verbally abused in such a way, and with such impact, at such a delicate age, the ordeal carried the potential to influence his future emotional and mental well-being. In any case, the threat was presented and carried out.

Now, the concern was about the child's inner strength and emotional stability. Joseph sat at his desk and tried to blot out the entire classroom, and everything in it, including people and sound. In the young lad's mind, he retreated to a place where he could feel safe until his embarrassment subsided. The need to feel confident that the students around him had forgotten about his performance at the front of the classroom was of utmost importance. Of course, he heard Bobby at the chalkboard adding the numbers, but it seemed far away and not a part of his focus at the moment. Normal classroom noise, like the chalk as it scraped the chalkboard, shuffling papers on student's desks, or random coughing sounds were not present in the boy's consciousness.

The boy's focus was on the center of his desk, although he didn't see what he stared at. His struggle was to get through the moment. Slowly, his respiration returned to normal, the heat he felt on his face subsided, and the awareness of his surroundings began to fill his conscious mind again. Joseph was ready to come back to the moment. He stared at the back of Bobby's shirt as he finished the arithmetic problem. Joseph met his friend's eyes as he returned to his seat.

Bobby's expression was sheepish as he met Joseph's forlorn gaze, but quickly turned away as he walked past. Joseph's feeling was that of inadequacy, in front of his friend, although he was grateful for Bobby's substitution.

Bobby sat down, and one by one, students were called to go to the chalkboard to complete one of the assigned problems. The exercise continued for another twenty minutes. Joseph watched the clock in desperation. Hopefully, arithmetic would be over soon and the chances of him getting called to the chalkboard again would be gone.

Arithmetic time was finally over and the remainder of the day passed routinely without further incident. Children are resilient and tend to deal in the present rather than dwell in the past. Soon everyone was watching the clock that hung on the wall above the chalkboard at the front of the room. It was five minutes to three in the afternoon. Mrs. Talbot rose from her desk, "Okay class, chairs on the desks." The children stood and obediently picked up their chairs, turned them upside down, and placed them on their desks with the chair legs facing the ceiling. "Line up! Mrs. Talbot walked to the classroom's entrance and stood by the door. The class formed a double line that extended from her position to the rear of the room. When the bell finally rang Mrs. Talbot led her procession of anxious fourth graders from the classroom and out of the school to the waiting buses. The day was over.

Joseph quickly scanned the filling bus for an empty seat near the window. If he was lucky, he could use the passing scenery outside the window as an excuse to ignore the raucous behavior that was about to take place among the rowdy children. It was behavior that generally took place whether the bus driver was looking or not.

He felt relieved that he was finally out of Mrs. Talbot's grasp, but now realized he was in a different situation with unruly fourth, fifth, and sixth graders that were trying to blow off steam from a tension packed day. Joseph wasn't the only student happy to be leaving the school.

The walk home from the bus stop was uneventful, and a short distance to Joseph's house. He was home now… away from that awful place and he began to relax. Joey could feel his real self, begin to return…the person he really was. He began to feel like Joey again.

The scenario he experienced that morning had been tucked into the back of his memory as just another day in Mrs. Talbot's class. It was becoming an expected thing, and the bus ride home with all of its distractions were a way for him to relinquish it to the back of his memory. When he walked into the house, his mom Virginia Hall was busy cleaning as usual. She looked up from her work and asked, "How was school?"

"Okay," Joey replied and went up to his room to change into his play clothes.

As five o'clock approached, Joey's dad, Frank came through the kitchen door, and all three siblings lined up at one end of the kitchen awaiting their turn to run and greet their father. One by one, they took turns as they ran toward him and jumped into his arms. Frank grabbed each child and with both arms and raised them into the air as he gave them a resounding hello. Virginia, or as Frank referred to her, Ginny, stood by her stove and watched the acrobatics with a smile. The family was reunited for another evening.

Awaiting dinner, the children lie on the floor and watched cartoons on television until their mother called everyone to the table. As they ate and passed different dishes around the table, each child was asked about his day and how it went. Frank asked Joey about his day while he cut up his pork chop, "…and how was your day, Joe?"

Joey began to talk about recess followed by a new subject the class was introduced to in social studies. The boy had been talking non-stop for a few minutes with so much zest and enthusiasm, Frank was compelled to look up from his dinner. As he watched the boy speak, he decided everything was normal because Joey was known to be a talker. The boy could go on and on when given the chance, so his dad went back to his pork chop and listened to his son's banter. All at once, in the middle of a sentence, Joey's excited dissertation of social studies stopped. The pause was obvious as it happened at an inappropriate place in the conversation and left an open ending. The pause caused his dad to look up at him once again. He found Joey staring at him, as if he was in deep thought, like he was looking for something to say.

Ginny stopped doing what she was doing, noticed the conspicuous situation, and said loudly, "Joey!" His brother and sister just went about their business and continued to eat their dinner.

A few seconds passed and Joey's dad spoke louder and more assertive, "Joey! Wake up! What are you doing?" Joey snapped out of his would-be trance and couldn't remember what he had been talking about.

Mr. and Mrs. Hall's eyes met. Both parents expressed a look of concern and bewilderment. What had just happened to their little boy? Was it a momentary distraction, a passing childhood anomaly, or something more serious? The parents let the situation go and decided to discuss it later, in private. Their feeling was to leave the boy out of it for now.

The evening passed without further incident and the children had long since gone to bed. Frank looked across the living room to his wife, "Ginny, what do you think that business with Joey was about...you know, at dinner...with the blank stare when he was telling me about his day?"

Ginny continued on with her knitting without looking up, "Oh Frank, it was probably nothing. You know kids... they get excited about things and can't get them out of their mouths fast enough. He probably just forgot what he was talking about or confused it with something else he was going to say. Besides, it's the first time I've seen him do it."

Frank stared at his wife for a moment digesting what she said, nodded his head and went back to watching television. A few minutes passed and Frank looked back at Ginny, "Do you think we should ask his teacher about it? I mean, it's the first time we've seen him do it, but how do we know what's happening when he's at school?"

Ginny looked up from her knitting. "If there was anything out of the ordinary happening, the school would be calling us...or at least sending a note home with Joey." Feeling relief and satisfaction in his wife's assessment, Frank turned back to the television and promptly fell asleep.

A few days passed and Wednesday morning found Joey Hall back at school. He had just gone through another one of Mrs. Talbot's tongue lashings at the chalkboard and was now experiencing some verbal bullying from a few of his classmates. It was recess and the kids were blowing off steam. Joey laughed it all off and joined in, laughing at himself as he did so. The boy was smart enough to know that laughing along with his peers was better than working against them. Inside, the boy was crushed. He had outwardly put a show on for his classmates, but inside the child was hurting.

As the days and weeks continued in the same fashion, Virginia and Frank Hall began to notice more and more of the little spells or, 'daydreams,' as his parents called them. At least, in their presence, it was obvious Joey was having more and more incidents. Each time a spell happened, either Virginia or Frank would instantly try to quell the problem by trying to shock Joey back into consciousness by loudly shouting, "Joey, you're doing it again." This scenario not only became very embarrassing for the boy, but aggravating at the same time.

Joey knew something was different. He didn't feel different. He just knew there was something different about him compared to his siblings and the kids in his class, and the kids on the bus, and every other kid he knew. The boy tried to push the problem to the back of his mind. The only thing he was sure about was that when it happened, when he had a spell, it made him feel sad and embarrassed. Not because of how he felt during the spell…he felt nothing when it was happening, but because of how everyone else reacted to it. Joey often thought, *Why do they have to get so mad? Why do they have to shout and embarrass me about what I was trying to say?*

The days turned into weeks, and weeks into months. Mrs. Talbot was really piling on the homework, especially in the area of arithmetic. It was the "new math," as they called it. The arithmetic was hard enough to understand at school and no one asked Mrs. Talbot to explain anything any further than what she had already offered for fear of being singled out. Joey was especially sensitive to asking anything more than he had to. He would satisfy himself by deciding to ask his dad about it that night after dinner. He knew his dad would know how to do it.

The irony of that thought was that at the back of his mind, Joey knew that homework sessions with his dad didn't always go very well either. His father, being from the 'old school,' was familiar with the old ways and would revert to them when he couldn't get Joey's homework problems to work out. The frustration levels of both child and parent would soon escalate, and more shouting and exasperation began to take place at the kitchen table where the two worked feverishly to complete Mrs. Talbot's homework.

Frank's patience would soon wane and frustration accompanied by anxiousness would begin to take over. It wasn't long before Frank was shouting at Joey to the point where the boy was so nervous, he was afraid to answer his father's questions. The chance for Joey to experience a spell at this point was imminent since extreme nervousness or excitement were one of the triggers guaranteed to instigate a spell. Of course, Frank had no idea that was part of the problem, or he'd have tried to express himself differently.

Then it would happen. Joey would experience a spell and Frank would be there in all his frustration to witness it. The occurrence would blow the lid off the entire homework session with Frank sometimes leaving Joey alone at the table to finish the homework by himself. Joey was at a loss. He couldn't control these spells, let alone know when they were going to happen. He wished people wouldn't get so angry.

Eventually, when Joey did something right, the whole situation changed with Frank saying, "Aha! See, you knew it all the time." The good humor was short lived until the two tackled the next problem and the whole scenario was repeated.

Joey accepted the way things were. In his ten-year old mind, he didn't understand what was going on and knew he couldn't do anything about it, so eventually he just dismissed the thought until it happened again.

CHAPTER 2

The end of fourth grade drew to an end. Joey was growing and gaining weight which is a normal consequence for children of that age. He still liked school, but was happy to be leaving Mrs. Talbot behind. He harbored no ill feelings for the teacher, but was ready for his summer vacation and nights without homework. The boy was ready to move on. His parents had bought a new house across town and the whole family would be leaving the little Cape Cod style house Joey loved so much.

Another happy thought was that because of the new house's location, Joey would be going to a different school for fifth grade. The new school was in the opposite direction of Tobacco Valley Grammar School and was situated in a more countryfied setting which Joey liked. He'd still have to take the bus to school but knew he had to tolerate it. The family had only one car and that was used to transport Frank to and from work or get Ginny to the grocery store, and whatever other errands were required to keep the family going.

The spells were still occurring and increasing in frequency, however the duration of the spells remained the same...about three to four seconds in length. Frank and Ginny were at their wits end. The boy seemed healthy enough, but was gaining weight. In one year, Joey had transformed from a slim ten-year old into an obese eleven-year old.

Frank and Ginny never spoke of 'the problem' in Joey's presence. That topic was reserved for a quiet time every night when the couple retired to their own bedroom. The distress and worry about their precious Joey became not only a concern but an obsession and was beginning to wear on their marriage.

One night after dinner, Joey was in the backyard and heard something around the front of the house. When he turned to look, he saw his mom and dad speeding away in the family station wagon. The haste of their exit seemed to be out of the norm for what the night's situation had offered. The boy was confused and went in the house to see who was still at home. His older brother Brian was sitting at the kitchen table. Joey walked in and asked, "Where did Mom and Dad go?"

Brian was looking at the funny papers (newspaper comics). He replied without looking up. "They went to see Doctor Smith about something."

Joey continued, "About what?"

Brian, still glued to the funnies replied, "Don't know. They were arguing about something, then got into the car and left."

Joey was concerned at first. It wasn't like his parents to just up and leave like that. He thought about it for a minute, shrugged his shoulders and went back outside.

What Joey wouldn't have known, is that the couple had

received another medical bill from Joey's pediatrician. The financial strain, coupled with the uncertainty about Joey's problem was becoming too much for the couple to handle. Frank was irate. "We're paying this guy a lot of money and we still don't know anything. The kid is getting worse. How do we know he doesn't have a tumor?

"Frank, calm down. He's a doctor. We have no choice but to trust in his judgement." Ginny looked as if she was pleading with her husband.

The physically and emotionally exhausted father was looking to place blame. The family's financial situation wasn't good and the other children had needs also. Frank was working sixty hours a week to make ends meet and felt he was being suffocated. He paced back and forth in the kitchen, and rose his arms in the air as he spoke. Finally, he stopped and said, "I'm going to see him right now! Right now…I'll get some answers." Frank threw open the kitchen door and headed for the car.

"Frank, wait!" Ginny ran after him and jumped into the passenger seat as Frank started the car.

Ginny only went along to keep Frank calm or at least keep him from doing something he might regret at a later date. She knew he was tired of hearing Doctor Smith refer to Joey's problem as minor. Frank repeated the doctor's words as he drove, "He'll grow out of in due time." To Frank, it was just the doctor's way of dismissing the Hall's concerns. Frank sped through the quiet streets of Johnsville. It was after dinner and Frank was determined to give that doctor a piece of his mind. His feeling was that the problem was now a reflection of Doctor Smith's laid-back attitude. He felt the doctor was taking the situation too lightly, and all Frank knew was that his boy was getting worse.

Ginny sat rigid in the front seat, her back pressed hard against the car's seatback and her feet stiff against the floor of the car. Her eyes were wide as she watched the traffic and scenery rush past, and she placed her hands firmly on the car's metal dash board. "Please slow down, Frank. His office doesn't close for another hour."

Frank ignored Ginny and stared at the road ahead as he continued his mad dash for the doctor's office. "That guy is going to give us some answers. He thinks we can't understand his fancy doctor lingo, so all he can say is, 'Ah, he'll get over it.' Well, he's going to do some talking now. We pay that guy good money for every visit. Money that we don't have…and he just blows us off by rolling his eyes and says, 'It's nothing.' Every damn time we go there." Frank flew into the doctor's parking lot and the car screeched to a halt, catching the attention of several happy couples taking a quiet after-dinner stroll along the sleepy, tree lined street.

Frank parked the family car and hurried for the entrance of Doctor Smith's office. Ginny struggled to keep up with her enraged and out of control husband.

Frank Hall was the typical hard-working dad who spent most of his time at the factory in town. He took whatever overtime he could…whenever he could get it, and never complained about having to go to work. The man was five foot eleven inches tall and slim, weighing in at one hundred seventy pounds. His sixty-hour work week and extra job on Saturday nights were part of the reason for Frank's physical appearance. The other was his responsibility around the house and his accumulated activities with the children.

Normally, he was a quiet man who kept to himself and hardly ever showed emotion, especially anger. It took an extreme circumstance to resurrect Frank's temper, but once that level was breached, Frank became someone that would be hard to reckon with.

He was a handsome man with black hair, brown eyes, and a wide smile when he let it appear. The most important thing in Frank's life was Ginny and the kids. He was the typical family man who worked hard all week and spent all of his off time with the family. His family was his sole purpose in life.

Ginny was the typical stay-at-home mom who took care of every aspect of the family's needs. She was a quiet woman who supported her husband's decisions, but inwardly had a way of steering Frank onto the right path without his realization that it was really her who had actually made the decision. Ginny stood her ground when appropriate, but was fiercely protective when it came to defending her family…sometimes to a fault. She was slightly shorter than her husband at five feet seven inches and attractive with long brown hair and a slender figure.

Frank burst through the doctor's office door with Ginny trailing close behind. "Frank, please get a hold of yourself. We need to talk about this first."

Frank walked straight up to the receptionist. "Get the doctor out here now! Tell him Frank Hall is here."

The receptionist smiled. "You're in luck, Mr. Hall. His last patient just left, so he is available. One moment please." Ginny held onto Frank's right arm as the receptionist paged the doctor. Frank stared down the hallway waiting for the physician to appear.

CHAPTER 3

Doctor Elliot J. Smith was a General Practitioner, as termed in the medical world, for a physician who diagnosed and treated medical problems that were of a general nature. He was one of three of the town's physicians who oversaw and attended to general health problems for the entire populace of Tobacco Valley. He attended to both young and elderly, and was generally responsible for bringing most of his younger patients into the world and some of their parents as well.

Most of his cases were more likely to have been involved with childhood diseases known as chickenpox, measles, and mumps. Stitching up cuts and lacerations, setting a broken arm, and diagnosing a sprained ankle were routine cases. The doctor treated scores of sore throats, colds, and the flu. Seasonal health problems like rashes due to contact with poison ivy in the summer months or bee stings were also common place. Intestinal disorders, stomach aches, and recurring headaches were all a part of the good doctor's responsibilities, and he acquired a reputation for being accurate in his diagnosis and treatments. Some of the older town folk referred to him as a horse doctor, but still chose his practice when they were sick.

The more serious health problems required treatment at a hospital from another kind of physician termed a specialist. Usually, it was Doctor Smith's call if he thought the patient's problem was out of his area of expertise.

Doctor Smith was a serious man who never seemed to smile. The man avoided direct facial contact and mumbled when he spoke, as if he was speaking to himself. He was a portly little man with his stethoscope hanging from his neck, and his head was bald with graying strands of hair on each side. He wore round, silver rimmed glasses which defined the old "spectacles" term. The glasses covered his gray eyebrows and exposed small but soft looking blue eyes. His white lab coat hung over round and slumped shoulders, tired from years of service to the community. He portrayed the stereotypical country doctor that so many Americans of the time willfully placed their families' welfare with.

Doctor Smith walked down the short hallway from his examining rooms and toward the reception area where Frank and Ginny waited. His head was down as he approached, as it always was. It was only when he was directly in front of the emotional couple, that he stopped and glanced quickly at Ginny. He began, "Hello, Virginia. I understand there is something you needed to discuss with me."

Ginny smiled weakly back at the doctor, and Frank interrupted the greeting. "Yeah, that's right, Doc. You know how concerned we are about our son Joey, and the only thing we ever hear from you is that, 'it's nothing…that he he'll grow out of it." Ginny squeezed Frank's arm as his voice was beginning to grow louder as he spoke. Doctor Smith continued to stare at some abstract point across the room as he listened. Frank's temper began to flare again as the doctor had not yet answered him. "Well, the kid is getting worse, but we still seem to be getting the medical bills from you."

Finally, Doctor Smith turned his head as if to look at a different corner of the room and answered. "What would you like me to tell you, Frank?"

Frank's voice grew even louder. "I want some answers. We're paying you good money for your services, and we still don't know anything…only that Joey is getting worse. It's only a matter of time before his peers notice it, and begin to pick on him."

The doctor now shifted his gaze to the floor directly in front of where Ginny and Frank stood. "Is that what you're worried about, Frank?"

Frank retorted, "What do you mean by that?"

The doctor replied in a calm tone, "Are you more concerned about what people think rather than what is really going on with your son?" The doctor's question was in line with Frank's statement, and appropriate for what the doctor knew about Joey's disorder, and the kind of questions Ginny and Frank had posed so far.

Frank's temper and blood pressure rose instantly. Frank took a step toward the unsuspecting doctor. "How dare you make an accusation like that!" Ginny grabbed Frank's arm and stifled Frank's advance while the doctor… surprised at such aggression, stumbled backward a few steps to avoid Frank.

The nurse in the reception area had been watching and rose from her chair. "Shall I call the police, Doctor?"

Doctor Smith raised his left hand and waved it up and down in her direction. "No, no. Thank-you, Joan. We're fine here. You may go home now."

The moment passed and both parties straightened up and collected themselves. Frank was breathing heavy and sweating profusely. Ginny dabbed at his forehead with a napkin. Dr. Smith smoothed the front of his lab coat, took a deep breath, and stepped back toward the two parents. "Frank, you are out of control. Before we talk any further, you're going to sit down and calm yourself. I'm going to get you some water and then listen to your heart...and take your pulse. It is only then that I will continue with this conversation. If you get out of line again, I'll have to send you home." Dr. Smith paused for an answer. Finally, Frank nodded his head in agreement.

After things had settled down and Dr. Smith had given Frank a quick wellbeing check, he sat back on his stool facing the emotional father. This time the doctor looked right into Frank's eyes. "You're going to have a heart attack if you keep up this line of worry and aggressive behavior." Frank started to say something but the doctor cut him off. "I know you think I'm not giving Joey's disorder the attention it deserves, but that can't be farther from the truth. This kind of thing happens in so many pre-adolescents that we have to wait and watch for some tell-tale signs. The first thing is that Joey has such a mild case of what I think is going on, that I know I'll never get you to believe it." The doctor paused and glanced through Joey's file. He nodded his head as he read the file and without looking up continued, "Joey just turned eleven, and at this point, the condition may just be a part of his maturing process as well as his emotional state. There are several things beginning to happen in an eleven-year old's body…and some of them are happening faster than others. Meanwhile, there is nothing dramatic going on with the boy. He is a happy, healthy kid that may just be experiencing a rough patch in his growth cycle right now."

Frank was embarrassed and stared at the floor in front of him for the moment. Ginny asked, "You mentioned 'a mild case of what you think is going on.' What were you referring to?"

The doctor looked at Ginny and said in an even, soothing tone. "I'm not a specialist in this area but if the disorder is other than just general growing pains, he may have a very mild form of epilepsy." Frank looked up in horror and Ginny's mouth dropped in disbelief. The doctor continued, "In Joey's case, it is very mild and is triggered by several outside stimuli, like nervousness, being overly excited, worry, being extremely tired, etcetera. You two have to watch the boy a little closer than before and see what may be happening around him that may be a little different than what he's used to. Once his life settles down a bit, the disorder may disappear."

Ginny asked, "What if it doesn't?"

"Then, we'll send him to see a specialist attached to one of the nearby hospitals that will put him through some very simple tests. But for right now, I need you two to stop worrying about other people or what it might be, and consider his environment and what might be bothering him. Once we get some good information, we can start outlining a plan. But, please stop worrying so much. Joey can pick up on that too. He already knows there is something different going on."

The Halls thanked the doctor for his time and Frank tried to apologize, but Doctor Smith patted him on the back and assured him that he understood. The three adults parted in a friendly way and the Halls left the doctor's office feeling a little better about the situation, but now were enlightened. Their education about what might be happening to their son was only beginning. Now, they had something to work with.

CHAPTER 4

The end of fourth grade finally came to an end, and the last day of school had arrived, otherwise known as Field Day. The special day was a celebration of the school year's end, 'no more teachers, no more books, and no more homework.' It was a day the entire school's population looked forward to. There would be grilled hot dogs and hamburgers… and soda. The students were allowed to 'dress down,' which meant to dress more casually, but to stay within the dress code. Short pants and blue jeans were allowed to accommodate the outdoor activities. These included games of skill like trying to lasso a stuffed animal perched on a pole, potato sack races, water balloon fights, and all kinds of sports. Running races were always popular and always attracted a lot of attention. It seemed as if the whole town was there…at least all the students and teachers, parents, and school administrators.

Joey was having a great day. He had already won a ribbon for throwing the most basketballs into the hoop in the allotted two-minute time period. The first running race was announced and would take place on the baseball field. Frank Hall had been following Joey around the field all morning and had heard the announcement. "Hey Joe, why don't you enter the race. You're pretty fast. You'll probably beat all those other kids." It was true, despite the weight Joey had gained, he was a naturally fast runner. Joey shrugged and looked back sheepishly at his father. The boy knew he had put on a few pounds and was a little sensitive about it. Frank remembered the conversation with Doctor Smith and encouraged Joey to run.

Joey, was having a fine time with all the fun stuff and really didn't care about the race. "Nah. I don't want to, Dad. Those other kids are all taller than me…skinnier too."

Frank wanted Joey to start building some confidence in himself. "You're going to be great, Joe. Come on, just go get on the starting line." Joey didn't want to make his dad angry, so as his father requested, walked over to the starting line.

The starter, which was one of the fifth-grade teachers, got everyone lined up. "Okay everyone. Stand behind the starting line." Joey bent forward in a crouch, left leg forward, head down, ready to run. The teacher waited for the runners to quiet down, "Ready…Set…" The next thing Joey was aware of were the sounds from the onlookers. He heard laughing and snickers in the crowd that surrounded the starting line area. What had happened? He was alone on the starting line, still in his starting pose, ready to run, but he was left standing there by himself. He looked up only to see the backs of his competitors as they ran down the field.

Joey knew what happened. He had experienced another spell. He stood up and felt his face getting red, and hot from embarrassment. Frank stepped forward and put his hand on his son's shoulder. "What happened, Joe? You could have beat all those kids."

Joey wanted to bury his face in his dad's chest...he was so embarrassed. "I didn't hear him say go, Dad." Joey knew the reason he hadn't heard the starter say go was because he had a spell just before the teacher gave the command.

Frank put his arm over the boy's shoulder and walked him away from the race area. Frank began to feel guilty. He knew from discussions with Doctor Smith that nervousness and excitement could be some of the triggers to bring on a spell. At the same time, he only wanted the best for his son and wanted him to take part in everything the other children were doing. "There will be other races, Joe. Forget about it. There will be a lot of these things coming up. You'll see." Joey's day was destroyed, and Frank knew it. The two walked off to their car and left for home. Not another word was said.

Dinner time at the Halls was routine and Joey's older brother Brian, spoke excitedly about his own performance during Field Day. Brian was a couple of years older than Joey and consequently attended a different school across town. The older boy continued with his excited dissertation about the day's occurrences and how he had personally excelled in every competition that he entered. Joey had always looked up to his older brother and tried to emulate him in some ways, but knew Brian was way ahead of him physically. The excited conversation was unusual for Brian and consequently drew the family's attention to the older brother. The boy was usually quiet and kept his opinions to himself and hardly ever offered conversation unless it was drawn out of him.

Joey listened, uninterested in his brother's achievements as he pushed his spaghetti around his dinner plate. Brian had no idea of what had happened at Joey's school or what he had experienced, so he continued to brag. Unfortunately, Brian's rare mood had the family's attention which removed any thoughts in everyone's mind about what Joey's day might have been about. The whole scenario made Joey sink deeper and deeper into a place of quiet despair.

Frank beamed at his oldest son as he bragged about his day and his winning performance. The father was so overcome with pride, he had completely forgotten about Joey's failed performance at the starting line. Frank went on to prompt more information from Brian and supported him with positive asides, as Brian spoke.

Finally, dinner was over, and Ginny was clearing the table. One by one, the family members got up from their seats and left the dinner table. Joey was last to get up. His little sister, Cheryl grabbed him by the arm. "Come on, Joey. Mom bought me a new board game today. Can you help me set it up?" Joey nodded his head and followed his sister into the living room.

The evening passed quietly. The children went to bed and Ginny and Frank were left alone in their usual places near the fireplace. "Frank, what went on at Joey's Field Day? Brian kind of monopolized the whole conversation."

Frank dropped his newspaper into his lap and looked up at the ceiling. "Oh, man, you're right! I was so happy to see that Brian was finally opening up to us, I forgot to talk to Joey about his Field Day." Frank shook his head in disgust.

Ginny stopped knitting and looked up at Frank. "Well, how did he do?"

Frank shook his head from side to side. "Ah, he entered a race and had one of those little daydreams he gets…"

Ginny cut him off, "Spells, Frank. They're called spells, not daydreams."

Frank paused and looked at Ginny for a moment as if to digest what she just said. "Yeah…, he had a spell. I guess because when the starter said go, he just stood there ready to run. Didn't move…just stood there like he was still waiting to hear the man say go."

"Oh my God, Frank! The poor kid. What happened?"

Frank shrugged, "Nothing. There was some snickering and some wise cracks aimed in his direction, but I just walked up to him and took him by the shoulders and walked him out of there. He was pretty embarrassed, so we went to the car and left."

Ginny paused a moment to gather herself. "Was that his whole Field Day experience? Didn't he do anything else?"

Frank felt as if he was to blame by the way Ginny posed her questions. "Wait a minute, Gin. I was there watching him the whole time and it was me who tried to get him in the race to begin with."

Ginny snapped back, "Frank! This is not about you. Did Joey have any fun at Field Day or was the race the only thing that happened?"

Frank quickly re-thought his position and explained that Joey had a fine day up until that time, and had participated in a lot of fun things, and tasted most of the free snacks that were offered. It had been a good day. However, Frank finally confessed that he felt guilty for having pushed the boy into entering the race, and if he hadn't done that, the incident would never have occurred.

Ginny looked at Frank with pursed lips and squinted eyes. "Frank! Like I said, this is not about you. Were you embarrassed by your son at the starting line?"

Frank thought for a moment. "My first thought was to ask him what he was doing, and then I was afraid someone was going to say something to embarrass him, so I got him out of there. I guess I was a little embarrassed too. After all, it was my son who was left standing there by himself."

Ginny took a deep breath. "Think about what Joey was feeling and try to keep your own feelings out of it. He needs to know we support him and that we don't think any differently of him...that we are not embarrassed of him, no matter what. You need to be more understanding than ever, or he won't ever get the strength and confidence to overcome this thing."

Frank nodded his head. There was going to be a lot to learn.

CHAPTER 5

Summertime had arrived. Everyone seemed to get up at the same time even though there wasn't any school to get ready for. Instead of having to rush off somewhere, breakfast was the highlight of the morning. Of course, there was always the backyard to go exploring or the possibility to take a trip down the street to call on a friend, but mostly it was always too hot to get any motivation going to do anything.

The move to the new house was finally over and everyone in the Hall family focused on making the adjustment to the new surroundings. The backyard abutted a forest and offered some interest as far as the exploration of unknown places, but the new neighborhood meant that friends were scarce and there were only a few candidates that lived nearby. It would be a while before there would be close friends. The emotional ache the children felt as a result of the move should have been shared by the companionship of children their own age. Those friends were now on the other side of town.

If a group of friends did collect at one or another's house, the scene was always the same. They would find a shady spot and hang around, lying in the grass or sitting on an unused picnic table. Then someone would say it, the old tired out phrase, "What do you want to do?"

And, someone else would respond, "I don't know, what do you want to do?"

The answer was always, "I don't know. It's too hot to do anything."

Another member of the group usually put in, "There's nothing to do. It's so boring around here." The conversation repeated itself as the hours droned on in the heat of the New England summer only to be interrupted by periods of silence and inactivity. Of course, there were the days that offered less humidity which the boys took advantage of. On those days, a baseball game might have been at least started down at the neighborhood sandlot if enough players could be scrounged up. This meant there were players of all ages. The game would be played with fervor until the heat of the day helped to influence the players' patience especially where rules or scores were a consideration. Soon an argument or fight would ensue, and the half-played game was over.

On their more creative days, someone usually suggested, "Hey, let's build a fort." The nearby forest offered a handy opportunity to create a structure of their own and a place where they were away from the watchful eye of the 'stay-at-home mothers.' As the fort took shape, which usually resembled a lean-to built from dead logs collected from the forest floor, there always seemed to be a need for someone to be the leader. Usually, it was the one who came up with the idea, or who picked the spot for the construction, or knew most about building the... fort. Mostly, it was the same person who chose all those items. Eventually, a disagreement about who really was the leader would present itself and consequently a mutiny would materialize, resulting in the destruction of the fort.

The trip to the local pond to float homemade toy boats proved to be a good pastime until those who didn't have one started to throw rocks at the boats that actually floated. Other boating activities included the construction of life size rafts intended to hold the weight of the soon to be fifth graders and were made of inner tubes with planks lashed to their top side. These were interesting and time-consuming activities devised by idle hands, looking for something interesting to do in an attempt to break free of the summer boredom. Such activities were 'against the law' according to the neighborhood moms who were constantly on watch while performing routine house chores. Historically, it was only a matter of time before someone fell into the pond and went home soaking wet with mud plastered all over their best jeans. The new-found activity would be cut short as the phone tree began to ring throughout the neighborhood and each mom was notified as to what the youngsters were up to.

Frank and Ginny Hall worried as the summer droned on. They knew that Joey's mental frame of mind was critical. All they could do was watch and observe as their son struggled through the summer doldrums with the few friends that he had made. The slow pace and unregulated schedule seemed to affect Joey's mental attitude in a different way than had the rigors of his school schedule. The frequency of spells had evened out, but he seemed to have less patience and was likely to 'blow up' when things didn't go his way.

Ginny watched Joey interact with one of his best friends one morning as they sat on the swings in the back yard. The old, 'what do you want to do' conversation came up, and suddenly Joey let loose on his best friend Rory. "I'm sick of this! You never want to do anything and when we do something, it's always something you want to do." Joey shouted these words at Rory while his friend just stared back at him with a bewildered look about his face. Ginny had been listening to the boys' conversation and knew there was no cause for Joey's outburst. She kept quiet and out of site, as she continued to observe the situation. Doctor Smith had instructed her and Frank to look for instances that were out of character for the boy, and if they observed such an instance, to look for any external stimulus that might have triggered it. Ginny watched and listened undetected for the better part of thirty minutes. There was no external influence that she could identify. Rory was a quiet, reserved boy that would just let such an incident pass. What could it be?

That night after the children had gone to bed Ginny and Frank discussed Joey's outburst that morning. Frank thought for a moment and then looked at his wife. "You say the boys have been pretty bored lately?"

Ginny nodded her head and said, "Well it has been pretty hot. Can't really blame them for being so lethargic."

Frank pursed his lips and considered the external stimuli to be boredom…no activity. "And, you say it's been for several days in a row?" Frank nodded his head as he put the information together in his head. "Hanging around doing nothing is eventually going to set anyone off. The Doc said to keep him busy mentally and physically."

Ginny was skeptical, "They had been building forts and going out to the pond in the woods, but all the moms got together and put a stop to that because it was too dangerous."

Frank raised his hands in the air. "They're eleven and twelve-year old boys for Pete's sake. Let them explore...let them do some wrong things."

Ginny softly replied. "Frank, I didn't see Rory acting the way Joey did. He's been exposed to the same boredom as Joey."

Frank cocked his head to one side. "Did you talk to Joey about it?"

Ginny nodded again as she said, "Yes, I did. I told him I had noticed a conversation between him and Rory this morning that seemed pretty tame until he lost his temper. He told me he had a headache at that time."

Frank looked concerned. "A headache...at his age? Do you think he could have a tumor?"

Ginny shook her head. "There you go again, thinking the worst. Doctor Smith said to keep it simple and look for signs. That's all we're doing right now."

Frank sat back in his chair again. "Your right, your right. So, what do we do now? If it's the heat causing the boredom and the non-activity...we can't control that. The lack of friends isn't helping either."

Ginny looked up at Frank and smiled. "Let's put in a swimming pool."

CHAPTER 6

The Halls scraped enough money together to buy a pool. It really wasn't in their budget but the project was for the children's benefit…especially Joey's. Installation would have to be a family affair since the allocated money only went so far. Frank dug out an area for the pool with the help of Brian and Joey. It was hot, tedious work but the boys just kept their minds set on the day they could fill it.

The pool was circular and twenty-four feet in diameter by four feet tall. Once the liner was in, it seemed an eternity before the pool was finally full. There was only one problem left. It would take a while before the sun could warm the cool pool water to a comfortable temperature suitable for swimming. Joey was the most eager to get into the new pool. He checked the temperature every day and even tried wading while the pool was filling. It was something unseen at this stage, but Joey's love for the water would later bring him success and notoriety as a young athlete, but right now just getting into the pool was a challenge.

Ginny watched Joey from the kitchen window. *That pool can't fill fast enough for him. He desperately needs the exercise.* She was concerned about the boy's weight gain. *He's getting so fat*, she thought. *His clothes are all stretched out and just hang on him.*

When Frank came home that night Ginny sat him down after dinner and pointed out she was not going to be the mother of a fat fifth grader, and he'd better do something about it.

Frank disagreed with his wife and calmly responded to her concerns. "Ginny, give the boy some room. They call that baby fat. In a couple of years that will be the stuff to help him shoot up. You'll see."

Ginny pursed her lips as if she was holding back what she really wanted to say. She didn't want another argument. Frank continued, "I'll keep him busy with chores around the pool. That'll keep him occupied for hours. Vacuuming the bottom, skimming the surface, cleaning the filter…and remember, some of that stuff he can do while he's in the pool, so it's not all work. Don't worry. It's going to be fine."

"What about the others?" Ginny stood with her arms crossed and her right hip cocked at a questioning angle. Don't you think he's going to be angry that you've got him doing all that work while the other kids sit around watching television or reading comic books?"

Frank replied, "Look, they are all old enough to be helping out around here. Brian can mow the lawn and do some of the general landscaping, and Cheryl can help you in the house."

Ginny nodded her head, "Okay. We'll give them the word in the morning after breakfast. They'll still have their 'off time' to do their own things, but I want them busy around here."

It was settled. Things were going to be different around the new house. The kids were going to be more involved with making the family routine a smoother experience, and be more productive at the same time.

CHAPTER 7

Joey's duties around the new pool were received matter-of-factly. He realized he'd be near the new pool and he would be the one in charge...not Brian, or his pesky sister.

It would be okay for now, Joey thought. It gave him a feeling of responsibility and satisfaction upon completion of the day's tasks. There was also a feeling of pride, which lent itself to a degree of confidence when he could see the fruits of his labor. He was especially proud on those days when the water clarity was abnormally clear, and it looked as though there was nothing between the pool bottom and the observer but air. The boy felt as if he had to show anyone who came within the backyard's limits what the pool looked like. He took special pride in taking the filter apart for cleaning. The real confidence showed when he got it all back together correctly to the point where the filter drew a suction and skimmed the pool's surface water like it was designed to do.

Joey was happy. He was taking care of something he cared about and could call his own. The best part of it was that he could actually use and enjoy the thing he was caring for. His parents noticed his temperament had calmed and there were fewer spells. He had more interest about what tomorrow would bring which fostered a new interest in the weather. Rain and wind were conditions that were directly associated with his pool efforts and distracted his thoughts toward the reactive consequences that affected his work.

Brian, on the other hand, was unhappy with the lawn work and began to show interest in sharing Joey's responsibilities with the pool. Of course, this was unacceptable to Joey resulting in a new anxiety to enter the formula that had been working so well. Joey had to learn that this was part of life, and compromise was a great virtue. He agreed to alternate jobs with his older brother, but what the boys didn't realize, was that the real key was keeping busy. Being active and focused on a specific activity was the key to motivation. The formula was critical for Joey's development and more of an obligation for Brian. Cheryl continued to help Ginny with the house and never was one to complain.

It seemed the Halls had found a way to make the temporary summer vacation work for everyone.

Frank was comfortable with the new regimen that buzzed about the new home. He swelled with pride when he came home for lunch on a given day and saw the children busy, all involved in a different activity. *Keeping them busy is the key*, he thought. *Maybe I should push this a little further. Ginny has been wanting a fence along the rear of the property. I'll pick up some wood and have the boys cut the pickets and construct the fence.*

Frank acquired a large pile of wood slats that would be used for the picket fence. One end of each slat would need to be cut into a point with a saw. Frank thought this would be good practice for the boys with a power tool. Tomorrow he'd get Joey in the garage and show him how to cut the pickets.

Frank and Joey stood in the garage near the concrete steps that led from the porch to the garage floor. He explained the operation of the jig saw to his son and emphasized safety over and over again. Finally, it was time for Joey to cut his first picket. An uncut wood slat was placed on the concrete steps on a flat place to hold the slat for cutting. Frank held the slat down while Joey operated the jig saw.

His father had instructed him to start about three inches from the end of the straight piece of wood and aim for the center of the picket's end. When the first cut was completed, he instructed Joey to turn the wood slat over and repeat the process on the opposite side forming a pointed end, completing the picket.

Joey was nervous. He knew his father had little patience, but when there was a chance of danger, there was even less. Frank held the wood for him and Joey began his first cut. There was no problem. The wood was pine and the jig saw cut right through it. Joey made a nice straight cut and Frank complemented him on it. Joey flipped the wood slat over and began the second cut to make the picket's pointed end. Again, no problem. The first picket was complete. Frank slapped his son on the back and Joey swelled with pride. He looked over at the uncut wood slats. A huge pile awaited their turn.

Joey and Frank continued to cut pickets. After a time, they fell into an almost rhythmic routine. They anticipated each other's moves and were cutting their way through the pile of wood slats. Father and son were bonding, but the process had become tedious to at least Joey. The nervousness was still present because Frank was still there. Joey felt he had to be perfect on every cut to keep the approval of his father. Then it happened. Joey had a spell. Was it because of the tedium of a repetitive process that lent itself to almost no conscious thought? Was it the nervousness Joey felt performing in front of his dad, or a combination of both? Whatever it was, Joey recovered from the spell and felt a warm sensation travelling down the inside of his right thigh. In horror, Joey's gaze shifted right to the scene of the sensation. He saw a long, thin, dark line that grew even longer and wider as it showed itself through his faded green jeans and approached his knee.

The jig saw was still on, and Joey was still cutting the wood slat. He knew his dad noticed the growing line of wetness but hadn't mentioned it yet. Frank stood on Joey's right side holding the wood with his head down at about Joey's hip level. Frank's face was only two feet from the boy's thigh. Joey began to panic. *He must see it! Should I stop the saw…Should I say something?* There were only a few inches of board left to cut. Joey decided to finish the cut.

Frank picked up the finished picket and threw it onto the pile with the rest of the completed pickets. He reached over to the pile of uncut wood slats, grabbed one, and placed it on the concrete stairs and said, "Okay, next one." Frank never made mention of what had just happened. He never even expressed a facial reaction.

Joey realized Frank was going to let it go at this point. He was saving the boy's pride. Joey said nothing but looked at his dad differently from that day on…and for the rest of his life for that matter.

What Joey had just experienced was the loss of bladder control during a spell. A common occurrence for his kind of disorder. The disorder allowed the person experiencing it to continue the activity using the motor skills he had begun with, but not with the same focus or intensity. That was a point that Joey would come to experience many times in future years, but was determined to play it out and deal with the situation as it occurred.

Although, this was the first time Joey had experienced the loss of bladder control during a spell, the boy was able to accept it as part of the problem and deal with it later. The embarrassment in front of his father was real but the incident would mark the first time the boy didn't feel he had to explain himself.

CHAPTER 8

The summer passed without further incident. The Halls' daily routine seemed normal and the family had adjusted to the new home. The end of summer had arrived with only one week left before the new school year began. Joey began to worry about what the new school would be like. A letter came to his parents announcing the name of his new teacher and what classroom he'd be assigned to. When Ginny read the letter to him, Joey remained silent. Ginny waited for Joey's response. "Aren't you excited Joey? A new school…new friends…a new classroom…there is so much to look forward to."

Joey managed a weak smile but inwardly worried about what the new teacher would be like. He didn't want another Mrs. Talbot. Would she be loud and abusive too? The boy kept his fears to himself. He'd just have to wait and see. There was still one week of summer left.

Ginny left the situation alone. She patted her son on the shoulder as she rose from the table, "It's going to be great, Joe." She smiled to herself as she left the room.

That evening as the two parents sat in the living room, Frank dropped his newspaper to his lap, and looked at his wife. "When are you going to tell Joey about the EEG?" Frank was a little nervous about what Joey's response might be.

Ginny sat in her usual soft chair by the fireplace. "I haven't told him yet. I want him to enjoy as much of his last week of summer as possible."

Frank cocked his head to the side as if to question her decision. "Gin, this is Monday and the test is on Friday. You're not going to just drop it on him the night before are you?"

Ginny shook her head. "I'm not going to make a big deal of it either, Frank. It's just a test, and it's not supposed to be painful. All they told me was to keep him up for most of the night before the test, so he'll be able to sleep during parts of it."

Frank was confused. "What does EEG stand for anyway?"

Ginny just kept knitting without looking up. "Electroencephalogram. They're going to glue a lot of electrodes to his head and read his brain waves."

Frank was leaning toward Ginny from his own chair. "That sounds awful! How can that not hurt? Is it like shock treatments?"

Ginny stopped knitting. "No Frank. It's nothing like that." Ginny took a deep breath. "I wish you'd take the time to read up on this a little more." She looked at Frank for a moment to make it sink in. "The brain gives off nerve impulses when a person is awake or asleep...all the time. It's just a function of the brain. They're going to record those impulses and compare them to a normal brain wave activity. They told me to ensure he's tired so he'll be able to sleep during some of the test, which is required."

Frank thought for a moment and tried to digest what Ginny had just described. "Well, what are they looking for? You told me not to worry about a tumor and now they're going to be measuring his brain waves. It sounds serious, Gin."

Ginny cocked her head to the side and pursed her lips together. "You have heard everything I have from the doctors. Hopefully, this test is going to help them get a little closer to the truth as to what is going on with him. No one is talking about tumors…just you, Frank."

Frank sat back in his chair and thought for a moment.

Ginny continued, "Hey, I'm scared too but every doctor he's seen so far has said the same thing…that it may be a very mild form of epilepsy, and if so, is treatable with medicine. They have also said that it is so mild that they aren't even sure what it is, or what is causing it. I have to trust in the doctors and what they are suggesting."

Frank looked away from Ginny, "Okay, but let's keep this to ourselves. No one else needs to know about it."

Frank looked straight ahead at the fireplace and said nothing. He knew it was their ignorance of the disorder that caused so much of their tension and anxiety. It was new territory for both of them. At the same time, his concern for his beloved son was paramount, and there were no answers yet. He hoped they were making the right decision. Frank told himself to trust Ginny and resigned himself to the fact she would tell Joey about the EEG on Thursday.

CHAPTER 9

Thursday morning, the day before Joey's EEG, came quickly. Ginny had dreaded this day all week. She so hated to ruin the boy's last week of summer. Everything had been going so well. It was late morning and the children had all gone about their regular routines for the day. Ginny looked out the kitchen window. Joey was busy vacuuming the pool. She watched him awhile and was amazed at how much attention he gave to his assigned task. He was so careful about the pool filter's operation, and how much suction the system drew. He moved the long aluminum shaft of the vacuum ever so slowly over the pool's bottom so as not to stir up too much of the bottom debris. Ginny smiled, *he's so meticulous. He really cares about what he's doing.*

Ginny stood at the window for some time just watching her son as he cleaned the pool. She stared at him, her arms folded in front of her, and was proud of the little boy she had brought into the world. She smiled as she watched her husky little twelve-year-old as he stood on the narrow wall of the pool. He used the long vacuum handle for balance.

He was the perfect, red blooded, American boy that got into trouble, liked to get dirty, and play rough. *If only he hadn't had to deal with this dilemma. What he must be thinking,* Ginny thought. *He never complains about it though. In fact, he never brings it up unless we catch him doing it or ask him questions about it. Hmmm.* Ginny caught herself in deep thought and pulled herself back to the moment. She cranked open the casement windows over the sink, "Joey. Take a break for a minute. I want to talk to you about something."

Joey looked back at the house in acknowledgement to his mother's call. He laid the long aluminum vacuum shaft on the side of the pool and tied it to the railing. When he was sure the shaft was secure, he climbed down and jumped onto the grass. Ginny came out of the house with a cold glass of lemonade and walked over to the picnic table where she set it down. Joey came over to join her. "Thanks, Mom. It's getting pretty hot. I think I'll go for a swim as soon as I finish the section I'm working on."

Ginny nodded her head in compliance and sat down across from where Joey stood. "Sit down, Joe. I want to tell you about something." Joey sat across the table from her and gulped the lemonade. Ginny began, "Tomorrow is the last day of summer vacation. School will be starting next Monday so we've got to start getting ready." Joey continued to watch her as he drank his lemonade and nodded his head. Ginny put her hand down on the table as if to make a point. "You've had a pretty good summer...got a new pool, some new friends." Joey nodded in agreement. Ginny was looking into the boy's eyes. "Well, we're going to have to shorten it by a day...okay? Today is your last full day of vacation because tomorrow we have to go see the doctor again. We have to be there for nine o'clock, so your last day off is going to get messed up a little."

Joey finished the lemonade. "It's okay, Mom. It's going to rain anyway. I don't care." He pushed the glass back in her direction. "Where are we going?"

Ginny explained that this time they were going to the hospital for a special kind of test and the hospital is the only place that has that kind of machine. She also mentioned that they would be meeting a new doctor called a neurologist that would be reading his test results.

Joey felt a little uncomfortable. "What kind of machine? Why do we need a machine? We usually just talk to the doctor…he asks me some questions, tests my reflexes, writes some things down, and then we go home."

Ginny leaned over the table toward the boy, "We need the machine so the doctor can read the signals your brain is giving us…like when Doctor Smith listens to your heart with his stethoscope."

Joey thought about that for a minute. "Is it going to hurt?" Joey was visibly upset.

Ginny realized his animosity and added, "Does it hurt when Doctor Smith listens to your heart?"

Joey looked away and shook his head as if to say no.

Ginny didn't want to make a big deal about it. She knew barely more than Joey about the test. "Joe, it's going to be fine. They're going to glue some wires to your head and see what your brain is telling them. In fact, they told me to keep you up late tonight so you can sleep through part of it."

Joey looked back at her. "Really?"

Ginny smiled, "Yup. So tonight, you and I are gonna' stay up late, watch all the late shows…and even some monster movies if you want, eat ice cream, and get you real tired."

Joey was confused. What kind of a test could this be? If

47

it involved staying up late and eating ice cream, it's probably nothing to worry about. He just didn't like being hooked up to a machine.

Joey was quiet for a minute and glanced at the pool. "Okay, can I go for a swim now?"

Ginny smiled and nodded her head. Joey ran off to the shed at the back of the yard to change into his swim suit.

He didn't let it show, but inside Joey was very uncomfortable with a new test. Moreover, a test that included a machine frightened him. He tried to put it at the back of his mind, but it kept coming back. He jumped into the cool water of the pool, but the test consumed his thoughts. He wasn't enjoying himself, so he climbed out of his beloved pool after only five minutes and went back to the shed to get dressed.

Ginny watched from the picnic table and knew the boy's day was ruined. Joey usually stayed in the pool for at least an hour. She looked down at the table and grimaced. *He's upset about that test and it's going to it bother him for the rest of the day. Maybe he'll get tired of thinking about it and just let it go until we get there tomorrow.* She got up from the table and walked back into the house.

Joey dried off and went for a walk in the woods behind his house. It was hot, but he wanted to be alone for a while. He went out to the path and just walked. He didn't think about anything except what was going on around him. In later years, the woods would become Joey's sanctuary. It would be the only place he could be himself and not have to worry about what people were thinking…or what they were expecting. It would become his place to go…his sanctuary.

"Come on Joe, it's only ten o'clock. You can't be getting sleepy yet."

Joey was tired from the day and was struggling to stay awake. He knew he had to make it to at least two AM. "I'm trying, Mom. My eyes keep getting so heavy."

Ginny got up from the couch and flipped through the television channels. "Maybe we can find an old war movie."

Finally, Joey couldn't watch television any longer. "Mom, the television is making me sleepier."

Ginny snapped off the TV. "Okay, let's just talk then." The boy and his mother had always had a special bond where they could sit for hours on a Saturday morning and talk about anything. Ginny asked him what he wanted to talk about.

Joey sat up straight and said, "I want to talk about the machine."

She explained that she didn't know much about it except that it measured activity from the brain. She explained what brain waves were and that everyone's brain emits them.

Joey tried to imagine what brain waves were and pictured radio waves from an antenna. "Is that what it's like, Mom…like a radio and antenna?"

Ginny knew Joey was an intelligent boy, but wasn't quite sure how to answer. "I really don't know, Joe. What I do know, is that they're invisible and everyone has them. Some people have brain waves that are a little different then what is considered normal. If they are a little different than normal, the doctor can treat the person with medicine and other ways."

The boy and his mother continued to talk about all

kinds of things, but eventually Joey would bring the conversation back to the machine again. Finally, Joey couldn't keep his eyes open any longer. He had made it to two-thirty AM. Ginny let him drift off to sleep and covered him with a blanket. She slept in the chair next to him.

CHAPTER 10

Joey lay on a flat clinical looking table in a small rectangular room. The walls were cinder block and painted olive green. To his left there was a half wall with a big glass window in the middle, and a chair positioned behind it. He stared at the ceiling above. There were different kinds of mechanical arms with large round lights at their ends that looked as if they could be moved out over his body. He wondered what those were for…and where was the machine that his mom told him about?

Joey tried to lie still on the table. It was flat with a little padding but very uncomfortable. At least there was a pillow for his head. He was getting nervous. He began to wonder when someone was going to come in and at least tell him what was about to happen? Joey began to shiver. It was cold in this small room. He looked to his right and saw what looked like an electrical console with a lot of wires coming out of it.

Suddenly the door opened from the far wall and a woman in a white coat came in. She went over to a chair behind the glass in the wall and began flipping switches and turning knobs. *The machine,* Joey thought. *She's turning on the machine.*

The woman looked through the glass and smiled. She finished moving around in front of the glass panel and disappeared behind the half wall. She came around the end of the wall and entered the room where he lay on the table. The woman came up to his side and put her hand on his arm. "Well, hello there, Joey. I'm Pamela and I'm you're technician for today. Let's get you all set up and then you can ask me any question you like." She smiled again and covered him with a white sheet. "This will keep you a little warmer. We like to keep it kind of cool in here."

The technician grabbed for the wires Joey had noticed earlier. "We're going to attach the ends of these wires to special places on your head, okay?" She showed him the ends of the wires. "These are called electrodes." Then she showed him a tube of glue. "I'm going to glue the electrodes to your scalp with this, so they'll stay on. Just be still and ask me anything you want."

Joey was getting more nervous. "Is this gonna' hurt?" He didn't look at the technician as he spoke. He kept his gaze on the ceiling above.

"Nope," the technician answered. She was busy rubbing something onto his head and then pushed something hard onto his scalp. She went on, "You won't feel anything. You'll hear me talking through that speaker over there and you're going to see a lot of pretty lights. Once in a while, I'll ask you to do some deep breathing, but that's about it." She looked down and gave him a reassuring smile. "Anything else?"

Joey asked, "Are you going to be able to read my mind?"

Pamela laughed, "No, Joey. We can't do that. They'll never build a machine that will be able to read anyone's mind...okay?" She looked back down at him and smiled. Joey was beginning to feel better.

The technician finished gluing the last electrode to Joey's head. "There. All done, Joey. That's the hardest part." Joey had twenty electrodes glued to various parts of his head. It didn't hurt but he knew they were there.

The technician left Joey for a moment and opened a door at the end of the room. It led to the hallway outside. In that brief opening of the door, Joey saw his mom in the hallway trying to get a glimpse of him before the door closed again. When Ginny saw the wires all over his head, she began to cry. The door closed as the technician went outside to speak to her.

Joey noticed she was crying...as if something was wrong...or about to go wrong. The door's hydraulic closer slammed the door shut and blocked any further view of the room again. Joey put the scene together in his mind. *The technician walked over to my mother and mom* was *crying. Why?* Joey began to get nervous again.

In a few minutes, the door opened and Pamela entered the room again. She disappeared behind the half wall that separated him from the glass window and sat down in the chair. He watched her as she moved her hands around in front of her. Joey couldn't see that she sat in front of a large control panel with many knobs and toggle switches and an equal number of meters and gauges. He watched her as she busied herself on the other side of the glass panel.

Pamela looked up to see the boy watching her. "Do you have any questions before we get started, Joey?"

Joey craned his head toward the glass window that Pamela sat behind. It hurt a little because the glue and wires pulled at his hair and felt like bumps against his head. "What are you doing behind that glass? It looks like you're turning things on."

Pamela smiled and looked back at him. "That is exactly what I'm doing, Joey. You are very observant. When we're done with the test, I'll bring you over here and you can take a look at it. It looks like a rocket ship control panel… it's really cool."

Joey smiled. "Is that for the machine?"

"Yup. I'm setting up all the things we're going to ask the machine to measure for us."

She saw Joey begin to relax as he turned his head back on the pillow. "Okay, Joey. Let's begin. Can you start taking some deep breaths for me? Just keep breathing until I tell you to stop." Joey complied.

The breathing exercise seemed to go on forever. Finally, Pamela asked him to stop. Joey felt a little light headed and exhilarated at the same time. Pamela was quiet for a while and then her voice came over the speaker mounted in the ceiling above him. "Okay, Joey. Keep your eyes closed. I'm going to flash a bunch of different colored lights above your head. You're going to see different colors and different shapes. It'll be pretty."

Joey watched the different colored light bursts as they flashed in front of his eyes. They seemed to come at differently timed intervals. Some of the bursts were brighter than others and some were shorter in duration than others. The only unpleasant part was the thrumming sound that accompanied the bursts of light.

Pamela continued the tests and mixed the bursts of light with more deep breathing. The only difference was the variation of how long the light bursts continued and how long the deep breathing exercise lasted. In between the light bursts and breathing she asked Joey to just relax and do nothing. Joey gave Pamela a quick glance. She seemed to be writing something down again. It almost looked as if she was scribbling. Finally, he heard her voice over the speaker. "Joey...now I'd like you to take a nap. I'll wake you up in a little while." Soon the boy was sound asleep.

After a time, Joey was awakened by the sound of Pamela's voice. "Okay Joey, wake up. You're all done. The test is over." Joey opened his eyes to see Pamela standing over him and smiling. "You did great! I'll get you some water and then we can go to work getting these electrodes off your head...and don't worry, I'll get most of the glue off so no one will notice what you just had done." In his young twelve-year old mind, he thought about that for a moment. *I hope she can get it all off. It would be awful if anyone knew about this.*

CHAPTER 11

The ride home from the hospital was anti-climactic. Joey was tired but didn't feel like sleeping. His mother seemed to be in a better mood now, and just drove the car. Joey noticed she didn't ask any questions. Not one question about the test. She smiled as she drove and finally said, "Let's go get some lunch. I'll bet you could go for a hamburger about now."

Joey brightened up. "Yeah, that would be great, Mom. Are you sure no one can see any of the glue in my hair?"

Ginny gave him a quick glance. "Can't see anything, Joe. No one will ever notice." Ginny parked the car and the two went into the restaurant for lunch.

Joey fell asleep on the way home and was still sleeping when Ginny pulled into their driveway. "Wake up, Joe. We're home." He opened his eyes and a view of the woods in his backyard and beloved pool, filled the windshield. *Yes, he was home*, he thought. Now to get to his favorite place.

"What are you going to do for the rest of the afternoon, Joe? Let the pool go for today. You earned some time off."

Joey looked back at his mom. "I'm going out in the woods for a while."

Ginny knew the woods were his favorite place to be besides the pool. "Okay, be home for supper. Dad is going to want to hear all about your adventure."

Joey nodded his head and went into the house to change his clothes.

Joey hurried outside. He ran to the wood line behind the Hall's house and jumped over the small trench that separated the family property from the forest. He immediately walked over to the path that led directly out and away from his backyard, and felt a calmness come over his body. He was out and away from everyone. There was no one watching him...no one judging him. In the woods, everything was the same..., everything was equal, and everything was simple. It just was what it was.

He watched the tree tops as they swayed ever so lightly in the gentle September breeze. There was creaking and rubbing sounds that accompanied the tree's activity that made him smile. These were the forest's sounds, like the familiar voice of an old friend.

Joey walked further into the woods until he reached the main path. He was in his safe place...the place he wanted to be...the place he went to when he needed to be alone. He turned east and kept walking. His house was now out of sight and out of earshot. Joey was engulfed in his favorite surroundings. The trees, the plants, the pines, the natural sounds of the forest. He began to smile. He was on his own turf. The place he understood so well. It always offered him what he needed, whether it be silence, solitude, or entertainment. He could always count on the woods. There were no expectations, no fees, no rules. He felt himself begin to grin.

Soon he passed one of his favorite areas...the pine forest. It was always dark in there, and a smile appeared on his face when thought about the secret tree fort that no one knew about. Joey started to run. He felt the soft forest floor as it gave cushion to his footsteps. He ran faster. The trees passed in a blur as he ran and he only noticed what his peripheral vision allowed. He looked straight ahead and ran faster. He jumped over small brooks that flowed silently through his treed sanctuary, and listened for their melodic gurgle. The sound of the slow-moving water made him smile and gave him motivation to run on.

Finally, Joey arrived at his secret place. A field that emerged out of nowhere. Surrounded by pine trees and undergrowth around its perimeter, the field was fairly hidden in the middle of the woods. He slowed down and walked over to a large pine tree. It was about thirty inches in diameter and about a hundred feet tall. A dry bed of pine needles formed a natural bed at its base and invited him to lie down.

He lay at the base of the giant tree and looked up into its branches. How small and insignificant he felt. The branches above seemed so strong and protective as they protruded into the air over him and the field. Such huge branches supported by nothing but the strong base he lay next to. Then he remembered something his dad had suggested one night while they were discussing his disorder. *Joey when you're feeling keyed up or angry at something, go to a special place. A place that is for you only...where no one else goes or knows about. Lay down and close your eyes. Blank out everything in your head and just focus on relaxing every muscle in your body. Start with one muscle and make yourself feel it loosen up. Then go to the next one. Imagine your body is so relaxed that it feels as if you're melting right into the ground.*

Joey looked around to see if anyone was watching. He closed his eyes and began the process his dad had explained. It was no use. He was too keyed up. He sat back up and leaned against the tree.

He began to consider the morning he had spent at the hospital and the test he had just taken. *Why me*, he thought. *How come I have to have this problem? My parents are so embarrassed of me. That's why they don't want anyone to know what I have. It must be something awful...even the lab tech Pamela, told me she'd get all the glue out of my hair so no one would know what I just had done. Are they that embarrassed?* Joey thought about that for a minute. *It's my problem and I wouldn't be embarrassed if everyone else wasn't.* He thought about the kids at school and how cruel they could be. *Maybe that's what everyone is so worried about. Can't have their little Joey getting labeled as an epileptic.*

Joey stared out into the field. It looked like it had witnessed a fair amount of activity at one time. Now, it appeared the field hadn't been used in years and had been abandoned for some time. The well-used and rutted dirt road that ran around the field's perimeter showed evidence that there had been a lot of movement around the area. Old and broken farm equipment that had been left to rot in the field's wood line were examples of human activity of times long past. *Someone worked real hard around here. I wonder what happened to them*. Whatever it was, he was glad he had this secret little spot to come and hide…and just be himself.

Gradually, his thoughts drifted back to his current situation. The more he thought about it, the angrier he became. *I'll show 'em…I'll show 'em all. I'll be better than all of them. I'll be the fastest, the smartest, and the most physically fit kid in school. I'll do what I have to do, but no one is ever going to be ashamed of me again!*

Joey began to feel good about his promise to himself. He felt determined. It gave him something to look forward to. It was a challenge that he himself could control and he didn't have to tell anyone about it. He would just let them wait and see. His thoughts went back to the test again. *What's going to happen now? Is there going to be more of these EEGs? I don't want to have to do that again.* His thoughts began to wander, *I'm so tired.* He continued to stare out into the field and could see the heat thermals as they rose off the field's bare dirt surface. Their motion was almost hypnotic. With that, Joey drifted off to sleep under the big pine tree.

CHAPTER 12

"The boy's test came out fairly normal." Doctor Horowitz (Doctor H as he would later come to be known) stared at the results of Joey's EEG test. "There were a few spikes here and there to indicate some abnormalities, but it all seems a very mild form of petit mal or even a condition we refer to as absence (pronounced absonce)." The doctor looked up at Ginny and Frank Hall, and smiled. "It's so mild we are not sure how to treat it yet."

Ginny and Frank looked at each other. It was a feeling of relief, yet of more confusion. Ginny leaned forward, as if to get a better description or meaning of what the doctor had just said. Doctor Ben Horowitz smiled back at her. A renowned neurologist at one of the largest hospitals in the region. He was a tall, but slim man that sported round, wire rimmed glasses on a thin face. He gave the impression of being an unassuming man, quiet and mild mannered, but very serious. He sat behind his desk and shuffled the EEG printouts.

"Well, what is causing our little boy's problem then?" Ginny's facial expression showed so much more concern than the doctor had expected.

Doctor Horowitz smiled back her, in a way that seemed almost condescending. "Mrs. Hall, your boy has such a mild form of petit mal that we aren't even sure what to call it yet. What I can tell you is that children who experience what your son has been going through generally have extremely high IQs." Ginny and Frank looked at each other and then back at the doctor. "That's right. In laymen's terms, the reason for the spell, or what is better described as a blackout of three to four seconds of conscious thinking, is a result of his subconscious mind racing so fast…so far ahead of his conscious mind, that his conscious mind short circuits due to the increased overload. Those three to four seconds of blackout are what it takes for his conscious mind to catch up." The doctor was smiling at the two concerned parents as he described the reason for the disorder. "You see, you have been blessed with an abnormally intelligent child and his immature mind is not yet ready to handle the thinking process he has been gifted with yet." Doctor Horowitz paused a moment while he scanned back through his notes regarding the EEG test. Then he continued, "He is on the verge of puberty which is also adding to the problem. It will get a little worse, the spells will occur more frequently as he begins to go through puberty, after which you'll see it begin to decline."

Frank sat back in his chair and was visibly relieved. "Well finally, some answers! We have been waiting for something…anything to latch onto."

Doctor Horowitz nodded his head to indicate that he understood. The doctor looked back up from his notes and smiled at the surprised couple. "He's going to grow out of this. Please allow him to push himself. He can do any of the extracurricular activities that will be coming his way. Encourage it!"

Ginny came back fast. "Oh! I don't know, Doctor. He's been talking about playing Pee Wee football this fall. What if he gets jumped on or knocked around?"

Doctor Horowitz smiled again, "Mrs. Hall. He is going to get jumped on and knocked around, and a lot of other things. You have to let him do this."

Frank piped up, "Hey Doc, he wants to play baseball too, and he's decided he wants to pitch. What if he's out there...all by himself on the mound...in front of everyone, and has one of these spells? He's liable to throw the ball anywhere besides the catcher's mitt. Or, what if someone throws the ball to him and he has a spell? He's liable to get hit right in the face. I mean, he's got to know what's going on around him all the time."

Doctor Horowitz sat back in his chair and shook his head. "He'll be fine, Frank. A disorder like this lends itself to continue the thought process that is present at the time the spell happens. That follows for any motor skills that may be in process at that time also. The difference is...that although he will continue the motor skill in process, the conscious thought is present, but not at the forefront of his thinking, so he will continue doing what he was doing, but not with the same focus or intensity. So relax, his mind's eye will see that baseball heading for his face and make him react to it."

Frank nodded his head and raised his eyebrows satisfied with the doctor's answer. His son would still be able to participate in all the same activities as all the other kids. What Frank and Ginny didn't realize, was that the lack of focus and intensity was going to play a negative role in Joey's performance, especially at the level Joey was intending to take his activities to. The parents were concerned that even if Joey had the inner strength to rise above any embarrassing situation, would he have the courage to face the same situation again, with the knowledge that it could repeat itself.

Horowitz continued, "There is something else folks. As the boy continues into his teens, hopefully with an active life style, his social life will be of utmost importance. He will need to feel secure in who he is, especially among his peers. His sense of belonging and acceptance will have a major effect on who he thinks he is and where he is going. That includes the opposite sex. When he settles on a girlfriend, you're going to see a huge difference in the frequency of the spells. They will become shorter in duration and less frequent. That will be one of the major areas to help him make the turn toward growing out of the disorder. I'm not saying to promote a girlfriend, but when you notice that he has chosen to spend more of his spare time with someone of the opposite sex, at least support him until he moves on to another. That will be an important part in the maturing process."

Ginny shook her head. "I'm confused. You're saying having a girlfriend is going to help Joey get better?"

Doctor Horowitz leaned forward again and smiled. "I used the word girlfriend, but that is to say, he will need someone special outside of his immediate family, that he knows cares for him and that he can return that same feeling to. Someone who he can share his innermost feelings with and not be ashamed or embarrassed. I am speaking of an intimate relationship where he can share half of the responsibility for its success or failure. It's all part of the maturing process and will have a huge impact on his emotional stability."

Frank and Ginny turned toward each other with concerned expressions. They didn't say it, but each parent thought, *The boy is only beginning fifth grade.*

Doctor Horowitz seemed to realize what might have been going through their minds. "Please understand. I'm talking about something that will probably take place in the middle of his high school career...as a natural course of events. It's not something to focus on at this point...only something to look forward to that will be good for him in many ways, and when that situation does present itself, you should think hard about supporting his interest."

The threesome began to end the conversation with closing comments and questions that might be discussed at the next meeting. Joey's parents had a huge burden lifted from their shoulders by what Doctor Horowitz had discussed and explained to them. They all shook hands and parted company. Joey rose from his seat, to say goodbye, but had not said a word throughout the entire meeting. He heard it all and filed it in a safe place at the back of his mind.

CHAPTER 13

The beginning of the school year arrived with its usual trials and tribulations. The nervousness of the first day was attributed to meeting the new teacher, and the unfamiliarity of a host of new classmates. The Halls were worried about how Joey would get through the experience. By now, they knew that one of the triggers for his spells was nervousness. Ginny mentioned her concern to Frank before he left for work that morning. Frank replied with a hard-line approach. "He has to face his fears, Ginny! He's going to be confronted with a lot of things in life that are going to make him nervous. The doctor said he'll learn from these experiences and figure out a way to deal with them. We can't worry about it, we just have to let him go do it."

Ginny was a wreck. Inside she knew Frank was right. She was a strong woman and kept her feelings locked up inside. Letting Frank know how she was feeling would only expose her weak side and probably instigate another argument.

Frank left for work and Ginny watched the clock until it was time for Joey to leave for the bus. "Okay, Joe. Have a great day. It must be so exciting! Going to your first day at a new school, new friends…and I hear this new teacher is really nice." Joey nodded his head and managed a little smile for his mother. He was very nervous but tried not to show it.

The first day passed without incident as did the second, third, and fourth. Joey had assessed the kids in his class, learned its scheduled routine, and found a place for himself. He was comfortable with everyone he had met and he liked the new teacher. Her name was Ms. Wattle. She was middle aged and quiet, but stern when she had to be, and gave the impression that she expected the right behavior from her students without having to demand it.

The weeks passed without incident. Joey was happy and enjoyed school. The spells still occurred but were normal in frequency and duration until one day when Ms. Wattle announced they were going to start having gym class. A new male teacher was going to be introduced to their school and for now the physical education program would be held in the library. All boys in the entire fifth grade would be taking the class at the same time and there would be a test on the first day, so the new gym teacher could assess everyone's abilities.

Joey was excited. Adding a sports program to his school schedule wasn't something he had figured on. This was going to be great. Ms. Wattle told her class their first gym class would be Wednesday…two days from now. He was a little nervous about the physical education test Ms. Wattle had mentioned, but would deal with that when it came up.

That night at dinner, Frank asked Joey about his day. Joey couldn't wait to talk about it. "We're gonna' start having gym class on Wednesdays…just the boys. Girls will be on a different day."

Frank looked up from his dinner and smiled. "Hey that's great, Joe. Do you know what they're going to have you doing yet?"

Joey sat back in his chair. It was obvious a little of his enthusiasm had disappeared. "Yeah. We have to have a physical education test first so the gym teacher can see what kind of shape we're in…I guess."

Frank looked over at Ginny who raised her eyebrows. Frank and Ginny were well aware of how Joey despised tests of any kind. "Well Joe, I can tell you right off, you're going to be as good as anyone else in that class. Probably better than most of 'em."

Joey's face brightened. "Really, Dad? You really think so?"

Frank nodded his head. "Of course. They're the same age as you and probably haven't had as much exposure to all the sports you have." Frank went on, "Remember, you usually play with your older brother Brian and his friends, so you've already been playing at a higher level."

Joey put his head down. "Yeah, but I'm always the last one to get picked for a team and they always call me fat."

Frank quickly put in, "The guys that call you names are only doing that because they know you're already better than they are and younger to boot. For Pete's sake, I saw you playing football with them the other day, and carrying half of them on your back while you crossed the goal line." Joey began to smile. Frank continued, "…and what about yesterday when you were playing baseball over at the sandlot and you got a home run when Brian's best friend threw his best fast ball trying to get you to strike out? Do you think any of those kids in your class could do that?"

Brian sat next to Joey at the table and rolled his eyes. "He was just lucky, Dad."

Joey elbowed Brian in the ribs. "Okay, knock it off," Frank cut Brian off quickly. "The point is, Joey plays a lot of sports with kids that are older than he is and can still do well. When he gets paired up against kids his own age... he's definitely going to have the advantage." Brian, smirked and went back to pushing the food around his dinner plate. Frank smiled at reassuringly at Joey, "You're gonna' be great, Joe. Just wait and see."

Wednesday morning finally came and Ms. Wattle marched her fifth-grade boys to the library for their first gym class and their physical education test.

As they turned the corner to the main hallway, they saw that the rest of the boys in the entire fifth grade stood in line, single file, in the hallway outside the school's library. There were four fifth grade classes of about fifteen boys in each class. The line seemed to go on forever. Joey tried to see if there was any end to it and stepped out of line to get a better view. The line continued down the main corridor and bent around a corner to the left. He knew the doorway to the library was about twenty feet down the hallway from there. Meanwhile the impatient fifth graders were slowly becoming unruly. They pushed and shoved each other and blew off their nervousness as they waited.

Finally, the doorway to the library was just a few feet

away. Everyone joked and speculated about what kind of test was taking place just around the corner of the door. Finally, Joey stood in the library's doorway and watched in horror as the fifth graders ahead of him took their turn with the new gym teacher. His name was Mr. Flanigan.

Mr. Flanigan looked like he was a big man. It was hard to tell because he appeared to be kneeling down on the floor holding a U-shaped block of wood about twelve inches tall. The testing student faced him in a prone position with hands placed on top of the block. It was a push-up test!

The line moved slowly. Joey was now inside the library. The room was stuffy and hot, and the air felt heavy. A continuous line of fifth grade boys continued to move toward the gym teacher and his block of wood. One by one, the boys took their turn in front of Mr. Flanigan.

The procedure was the same for everyone. The gym teacher asked for the boy's name, followed by the same instructions, "Get down on your knees and put your hands on top of the wood I'm holding." Once they were in position Mr. Flanigan instructed the boy to straighten out his legs behind him and begin doing pushups. The gym teacher counted the number of completed pushups and recorded the number next to the boy's name. Mr. Flanigan, would then look up and say, "Next," and the procedure began all over again.

Slowly, the line moved toward the gym teacher. Joey watched the scenario time after time. The result was always the same. The boy finished his pushups, and the teacher would shout, "Next." As Joey got closer, he thought Mr. Flanigan was kind of scary looking. He didn't have much hair on top of his head and sported dark black hair on either side. He wore a blue sweat suit with white stripes that ran down the side of his sweat pants and his shoulders were huge.

The gym teacher didn't smile and didn't talk except to say, 'next.' In fact, he looked kind of mean. All talking and giggling ceased as the pushup candidate got closer to the teacher. It was like standing in front of the executioner on the way to the gallows.

Joey was getting close and only two boys away from his turn. He was sweating and his heart was pounding. He looked to the back of the library where he had come from. The kids at the back of the room, still feeling safe, because of their distance from the teacher and the test, shouted wisecracks and made jokes about the boy performing for Mr. Flanigan.

Suddenly, it was Joey's turn. He got down on his knees and assumed the position. Mr. Flanigan hardly looked at Joey and said, "Get your legs out behind you and straighten your arms as you hold the top of the wood block. Do as many pushups as you can." The stoic gym teacher held the outside of the upright wood block to stabilize it. Joey began his pushups. He had had counted five when he found himself kneeling on the mat beneath him.

Joey immediately looked to see Mr. Flanigan looking exasperated and in an upward direction toward the ceiling. The teacher flatly said, "I said you're done! Can't you hear? Five pushups. Get up." Joey realized he had experienced a spell.

Quickly, he appealed to the brash teacher, "I can do more...really. Just let me continue."

Mr. Flanigan had lost what patience he had long ago.

He replied in an extremely loud manner, "I said...you're done! You only did five and knelt down on the mat." Joey was incredulous at the teacher's militant attitude and just stood there for a moment as if Flanigan was going to change his mind.

Suddenly, Flanigan seemed to lose his patience and raised his voice to Joey. "MOVE ON... NOW!"

The boys in the immediate area began to laugh and jeer. "Hey, Joey only did five pushups." Some of his classmates just pointed and snickered. Joey looked back into Mr. Flanigan's eyes and thought, *I can't even tell him why I stopped. Everyone will hear it.* In those few moments where he looked deep into the teacher's eyes, he felt disappointment and anger, but mostly frustration. *I'll show you Flanigan. If you're still a coach when I'm older, I'll show you.* Joey turned and walked out of the library.

There were more gym classes throughout the year. Flanigan seemed to always take notice of Joey. He always found areas to criticize, even if it was only the way Joey stood in the crowd as he listened to the teacher's instructions. Joey felt as if the man just didn't like him because he was a little heavier than most of the boys, so he decided he didn't like this man. In his fifth-grade mind, he sized up Flanigan as a teacher who hated his job.

The rest of the year included his band career and a parade on Memorial Day but no major upsets. Joey buried himself in his studies and returned to his beloved and safe woods every chance he got.

The boy's impression was that the adults he had met so far didn't understand anything but the normal, everyday child that came to school and didn't stick out from the general population. If the child was different because he was big or smart, or wore funny clothes, he was ignored. All they wanted to deal with were the kids who were of the norm. Kids that were of the right size for their age, were quiet, followed directions, and didn't require any extra attention or effort, were the children of choice, and were the ones who received acceptance.

The children that came across as a bit ahead of their age or showed an advanced intellectual level, seemed to be categorized very quickly and labeled as non-players. These were the children that questioned what they were being taught or may have required advanced application, especially in the physical realm.

Joey promised himself that he was not going to have any of this. He was old enough to have opinions and make judgements about right and wrong. The maturation process had begun.

The schoolyear passed without further incident. Joey tried to stay involved with all the extracurricular activities and enjoyed school immensely. His scholastic aptitude began to show, and Ms. Wattle called Ginny in for a meeting one afternoon. She began to sight the boy's mental abilities as exceptional for his age and thought Ginny and Frank should begin to plan the boy's college career. Ms. Wattle said she could envision Joey as a candidate for the naval academy at Annapolis or any of the higher-level institutes for higher learning when he came of age.

Ginny was of course, pleased to hear the news about

her son's academic abilities, but took those words from Wattle as only complimentary. She felt that Joey's affliction was going to impede any future opportunities that his scholastic abilities could help him achieve. He was still too young to consider the physical side, but there were signs that that his natural ability in sports might also someday be an advantage for him.

Ginny dismissed the future for at least the time being. The fear about how Joey would progress and the unknowns, as to whether he would someday outgrow the disorder, prevented her from considering his future in any way. She also worried about pushing him toward any far-reaching goal only to discover that after years of planning, that he would fail as an acceptable candidate. She satisfied herself with the present, and for now, her son was holding his own.

The months passed and finally spring presented itself with the usual outdoor activities and opportunities that warmer weather offered. Recess spent outside, and baseball games played during lunch time were among the first school activities to be a part of the new season.

The children welcomed Friday as the end of the school week. It was almost a holiday. It meant no teachers, books or homework. The only thing that could make it more special was that Friday afternoon was great. That started with recess and if the last recess of the week included a sunny, warm day accompanied by a special activity, it was considered the first step toward a great weekend, or at least a great ending for the week.

The fifth and sixth grades were marched outside promptly at noon time and the children were released for the next fifty-five minutes to do whatever they desired. "Hey, Joey." Tony, one of Joey's friends, shouted as he ran up to meet him. "We got a baseball game going in five minutes. It's all the guys in our class versus all the guys in Mr. Duggan's class. You're pitching, so get over to the ball field as soon as you can. Everyone is gonna' meet there." Tony ran off to collect more players and Joey headed for the school's only baseball diamond.

The day was a perfect June day. No wind, clear skies, and sunny. Joey walked out to the pitching mound and warmed up a little with another boy that had been designated as catcher. Someone shouted from the benches. "Okay, let's go! We've only got another forty-five minutes left to play. Come on…batter up!"

The catcher threw the ball back to Joey as he watched one of Mr. Duggan's boys walk up to the plate. Everyone started yelling and chanting as Joey put his right foot on the rubber in the middle of the pitcher's mound. "C'mon, Joe. Strike 'em out!" Another yelled, "Get him, Joe-he's got nothin." Shouts from the opposing side were just as loud and just as excited. "Pitcher has a rag arm." Another yelled, "He can't pitch," and another bellowed, "No pitcher out there…No pitch, no pitch."

Joey held the ball in his glove and sized up the batter. The kid looked like he could hit. The catcher raised his glove to the strike zone and signaled to Joey with a palm down move of his free hand across the open mitt. Joey looked to the side of the field. There were teachers, male and female, watching. Scores of students had come to watch and either sat or stood just outside the boundaries of the infield. He looked over at the opposing team's crowd.

Everyone just lingered to watch the activity. The fun was in the cat calls and to what extent they could rattle the pitcher. Joey looked back to the batter. Behind him and the catcher, another crowd of kids had collected to stare down the pitcher and also contributed with their own taunts and chants.

The crowd's actions and verbalizations usually didn't bother Joey as he was accustomed to the same treatment in a pee wee league that he played for during the week, but there were people in the crowd he felt he needed to impress. There were teachers and school friends who really didn't know him outside of school and he wanted to show them his other side.

Joey started to get nervous. He stood on the pitcher's mound, in the center of the infield by himself, subject to the attention of a hundred people. *I'll show 'em*, he thought.

Joey wound up and let the first pitch fly. It was a strike. The catcher never had to move his glove. Someone from Joey's team shouted. "That's it, Joe. Give 'em your fastball again." Joey smiled to himself. *That's all I really have.* He wound up again and tried to throw his best fastball.

Joey never heard the ball make contact with the bat, or even the action of catching the hot grounder that was hit back to him. When he came back to the moment, he had the ground ball in his glove and the batter was running to first base. His team shouted, "Throw him out, Joe! Throw the ball!" Joey had experienced a spell, but had reacted to the activity at hand without conscious thought. His first concern was if anyone had noticed, and then to throw the ball. In those first two seconds of play he was instantly embarrassed and flustered. He wondered what had happened in that small expanse of time. How had he reacted to the hit? In a panic, he threw the ball at the runner instead of the first baseman who had his glove poised and ready for the throw.

Joey had a good arm and when he threw at something, he usually hit it. The runner reacted with a painful, "Oww," and stumbled out of the base line almost falling over. Joey's throw had struck the runner right between the shoulder blades. The teacher officiating first base stopped play and tended to the stricken player. Once it was determined the runner was fit to continue, he raised his hand in the air and shouted, "Bad throw. Runner takes the base."

Joey's pride was saved. It looked as if it was only a bad throw, but Joey knew he had thrown the ball exactly where he wanted it to go, *Oh, good. They think it's a wild throw to first.* Joey walked back to the mound and had to listen to the other team comment about his throwing ability. The insults were a lot easier to accept than if they knew the real reason why he had hit the runner with the throw. At least the runner wasn't injured. Inside he felt embarrassed for himself and disappointed that he had done such a thing, in front of so many people.

Recess was finally over and it seemed as soon as the bell rang, there was more focus and concern about getting oneself back to his assigned class for the march back into the school. Joey's play at first base seemed to have been forgotten as well as the baseball game. It was just a last-minute pickup game at school recess. Joey thought about the importance of such a game in association with why the game was created and where it was. Why had he put so much importance on the game? It wasn't a league game...these weren't organized ball clubs...it was just a game in front of his peers and specific authority figures. Why couldn't he have realized it for what it was and just enjoyed the game. He knew he should always do his best, but now realized there was a definite difference between competitive play and playing just for fun.

The rest of the day continued without incident. It was already late spring and there was only another month of school left. Joey felt good that he had a good year compared to what he had tolerated in the past. Occasionally, the play at first base did enter his thoughts, but only served to remind him about the importance of different scenarios and what was worth worrying about and what wasn't.

CHAPTER 14

Eventually, the end of school arrived and another summer began. Joey and family busied themselves with the tedious work of opening the pool, attending baseball practices and games, and several other summer activities. Life continued as usual. The assignment of specific chores was reinstated by Ginny to guard against summer boredom and to instill a sense of responsibility and daily commitment for the Hall children.

Once again, Joey spent most of his time around the pool, mowing the lawn and going for long walks in the woods behind the house. The summer months droned on and the frequency of Joey's spells, or more accurately described by Doctor Horowitz as episodes, remained the same. The part Joey hated about his disorder most was when well-meaning family members tried to shock him out of an episode by shouting, "Joey, you're doing it again!" At first it was embarrassing, and with time, became intensely aggravating for the boy.

Joey realized everyone had his best interest at heart but inside, grew to resent any kind of sympathy or special treatment offered by anyone who had no concept of what was actually taking place.

The most shocking and exasperating scenario was when Joey overheard a conversation between Ginny and Frank. Ginny believed that Joey may be having these episodes because he was lacking for attention. He was astounded that his own mother could have believed such a thing. *It's like she really doesn't know me*, he thought. Joey's perception of the statement was also incorrect. Ginny was searching for a valid reason, one that she could identify with, to satisfy her concern for the problem her son was having. New, confusing tests, and proposed reasons for the disorder were beginning to wear on the emotionally exhausted mother. At night, she lay in bed thinking, *When will he grow out of this? When will it all come to an end? How will this affect his future?*

He'll grow out of it. Ginny refused to be comfortable with such a lame answer for what burdened her son. She searched for an answer worthy of her worry. Part of the problem was that there was a lack of comprehensive information available regarding Joey's disorder. It appeared the medical community had decided the severity of it didn't deserve in-depth attention and wasn't worthy of an information base.

Night after night, Ginny and Frank lay in bed considering the status of their son's malady. Sometimes they would discuss it, and other times silently considered the problem alone in the darkness, and in the privacy of their own minds, fearing the worst.

Joey was approaching his sixth year of school and the Halls had not noticed any improvement in two years. The situation seemed to remain without change, good or bad. The lack of knowledge on the Hall's part was probably their worst enemy. If they could have just accepted the status quo in their boy's development, life would have been so much easier, but people, especially parents, have always searched for the worst scenario.

The behavior of the distraught parents was in line with any couple that had to watch their child experience something daily, that might be considered abnormal to an accepted routine. In general, people naturally prefer to have something to defend against. Elaborate tests and fancy names for likely causes only complicated the understanding of the situation. For the Halls, there were so many unknowns, but what the they knew for sure, was that their son was getting older and would begin puberty soon.

CHAPTER 15

Doctor Horowitz sat in a conference room down the hall from his office. The hospital's quarterly meeting for the Neurology Department was about to convene. In attendance, were various neurologists from the northeast region of the United States. The Director and Chief of Neurology sat at the head of a long conference room table. Once everyone had settled into their chairs and the usual shuffling of paper and notebooks flopping open ceased, the director brought the meeting to order. Doctor Horowitz looked around the table. There were fifteen well known surgeons and five other reputable administrators of neurology in attendance.

The Director, Douglas Hoagland spoke first. "Ladies and gentlemen. Thank you for finding the time in your busy schedules to attend our quarterly meeting regarding the neurosciences and special projects, problems, and latest innovations. I know that several of you are involved in special projects outside the hospital's realm and related to your private practices. For those of you new to the hospital, it is the intention of these quarterly meetings to discuss specific problems or anomalies related to our associated science. This is merely a 'meeting of the minds' where group discussions on new...or old problems can be discussed, not only as an aid to the physician involved, but also as a learning tool for the rest of us. All discussions will be discrete and relegated to the confines of this room."

Doctor Hoagland looked around the room and smiled. "Okay, let's begin. Are there any new concepts, or questionable areas related to patients suffering from disorders that so far may have become commonplace for us as physicians to regard as routine treatment." There was an uneasy pause about the room. People shifted in their seats and Doctor Hoagland let the pause last for an uncomfortable period of time. He stood and addressed the room. "People! We have the best of the best sitting right here in our presence. If there are any questions about procedures, diagnoses, or confusion of symptoms...this is the time to speak. There is no competition here. Forget about titles and status for your patients' sake. This meeting is about sharing new problems, new observations...or un-defined disorders. Please don't hold any animosity about sharing this information. This is a meeting to make us better...better for our patients."

Once again, no one offered any information. Some of the doctors kept their eyes focused on their notebooks, some doodled on paper pads that lay in front of them, but no one made eye contact with Hoagland.

Finally, Doctor Horowitz raised his right hand with the slightest of gestures. Doctor Hoagland nodded at Horowitz, smiled and said, "Ben, please. What do you have to share with us?"

Doctor Horowitz remained seated as everyone at the

conference table turned their heads in his direction. He looked around the table and met the 'matter of fact' looks on their faces, opened his notebook and looked back up at Hoagland. "Sir, I have a patient that seems to fall into at least one of the categories you mentioned."

Hoagland smiled and nodded back at Ben.

Doctor Horowitz continued, "His name is Joey Hall…a boy of twelve years old. He has been in my care for a little over one year and has continued with my treatment after the EEG he took in September of 1960, his twelfth year of life. After reading his EEG results, and having met him and his parents, I have diagnosed him with a mild form of epilepsy related to petit mal." Horowitz looked up from his notes to see Hoagland nod at him. Hoagland showed no surprise, as petit mal was not a new disorder and was not a reason to express concern. The rest of the room reacted to Horowitz's statement in the same manner.

Everyone was familiar with petit mal and so far, hadn't heard anything out of the ordinary. It was common knowledge that the petit mal disorder was a very mild form of epilepsy and was extremely common in many young, as well as older patients, and sometimes disappeared on its own.

Horowitz looked back down at his notes and continued. "As I alluded to, the disorder seems related to a very mild form of petit mal, but has several anomalies connected to it which place it between that and something else." The statement got the attention of the room. Everyone was alert and focused on Horowitz. Usually, petit mal was fairly easy to diagnose, but disorders like Joey's were rare and difficult to identify. Horowitz looked up from his notes momentarily. Every doctor in the room was writing notes or awaiting more information with eager anticipation. "The 'something else,' I mentioned could be a temporal lobe condition or in the best possible case, maybe…a condition termed as "absence." Horowitz paused for effect and continued, "As you know, it's fairly rare and pronounced absonce."

The disorder, although extremely mild, was enough of a malady to be the beginning of something much more serious or at least serious enough to be a big enough handicap that could inhibit the patient's way of living.

Horowitz continued, "The boy is otherwise a very healthy, well-adjusted young man about to begin puberty which may cause the condition to worsen. I have chosen this patient as my research subject and would like to begin a medical log and living history of the boy including everything he does…or doesn't do, life changes he encounters…physically and mentally, accomplishments and disappointments, and an emotional history as well." Doctor Horowitz looked up at the group of neurologists with a serious face, "In short, everything he does or experiences."

Doctor Hoagland glanced at Resident Chief of Neurosurgery, Doctor Ronald Goldbloom, who had met his gaze with raised eyebrows. Hoagland looked back at Horowitz. "Doctor, this could be an extremely valuable and productive endeavor. Have you mentioned your plans to the boy's parents?"

Horowitz sat back in his chair and shook his head, "Not yet, sir. I plan on discussing my plan and its possibilities with them at the boy's next appointment."

Seated next to Horowitz were his partners in private practice, Doctors Howard Baldwin and George Petrillo. Baldwin was younger than Horowitz, and comes from a career in the Navy. He was short and balding with a brash personality. Petrillo, a quiet sort, was also younger than Horowitz. He was slim with graying hair, had past experience in only the best of hospitals in the United States, and enjoyed the best of life's comforts. He usually kept his opinions to himself unless pressed, and was usually quiet in nature but known to be calculating when there was an opportunity.

Baldwin gave Petrillo a glance to get his attention and slid a folded piece of note paper in front of him. Petrillo took the note as he met Baldwin's glance. Baldwin mouthed the word 'later' to suggest a time to discuss its contents. Petrillo nodded his head slightly to indicate that he understood.

The meeting continued as several of the other neurologists queried Horowitz on his plans and what his expectations might be. Finally, Doctor Hoagland asked, "Ben, are you willing to discuss the anomalies you've found in Joey's last EEG?"

Ben Horowitz's face flushed. "I'd rather not, Doctor. It's true, we are all physicians here, but because the disorder is so different, I would still like to classify the results as patient confidential until I and the boy's parents are more comfortable with what we have found and the course I plan to take. I hope no one is offended, but that is my prerogative as the boy's doctor."

Doctor Hoagland nodded his head as he raised both hands in the air with the palms facing outward. "You are correct Doctor, that is your prerogative. No harm done.

We hope to hear and share any results of your research at the next meeting."

The room became uncomfortably quiet with some garbled murmurs to indicate a distaste for Horowitz's decision. Hoagland then addressed the room and brought the meeting to a close. Baldwin whispered to Petrillo as they rose from their chairs. "In my office…thirty minutes."

CHAPTER 16

Doctor Howard Baldwin returned to his office, sat at his desk, and went back through the notes he had just taken. *Horowitz's project has every possibility of making us world renowned in the neuroscience world.* Baldwin hurriedly wrote down more notes and ideas about his plan to acquire at least his share of research information secured by Horowitz.

Baldwin's concentration was suddenly interrupted by a knock at the door. He looked up as if to see someone. "Yes?"

A muffled reply came from behind the thickness of the office door. "Ronald Goldbloom here. May I come in?" Doctor Goldbloom, Chief of Neurosurgery had made a chance stop at Baldwin's office.

Baldwin hurriedly closed his notes and placed them in his top drawer. He stood up from his desk and invited Goldbloom in. "Please come in, sir." The door opened and Goldbloom appeared in the doorway. "Come in...have a seat, sir. What can I do for you?"

Goldbloom approached the desk slowly and looked around the room. "Am I interrupting something?"

Baldwin sat back down and appeared as if he was hiding something. Goldbloom smiled and went on, "You don't usually have your door closed unless you are tending to a patient."

Baldwin smiled, "Oh no, it's nothing, Sir. Just writing some notes in the quiet of my office. What can I help with?"

Goldbloom sidled up to Baldwin's desk and looked down on the nervous doctor with a facial expression that appeared inquisitive. "I wanted to hear your take on Doctor Horowitz's announcement of his new research project."

Baldwin sat straight up in his chair. "It seems very interesting and may be productive toward our cause as neurologists."

Goldbloom pursed his lips while nodding his head in an affirmative way. "I expect Doctor Horowitz will get the confidentiality he requested at the meeting. I realize you and Doctor Petrillo share a practice with him, but I urge everyone to let Horowitz have his privacy on the matter. As you said, he has a rare opportunity to study and investigate an area we have been waiting on for a long time. His work could open many opportunities for involved patients as well as other doctors who have been struggling in similar areas."

Doctor Baldwin cocked his head to one side and asked. "If I may ask, Sir...why are you discussing Horowitz's request for project privacy with me? As you said earlier, I am one of his partners in private practice and under certain circumstances, are allowed specific privileges as well as other benefits that may result from the good doctor's efforts."

Doctor Goldbloom became very serious. "Doctor, do not lecture me on your rights or privileges with private practice or otherwise. I was watching you when Horowitz requested privacy on the matter and saw your aside to Doctor Petrillo. I have had the same discussion with him and expect nothing more than what I have already discussed with you. The possible outcome of Doctor Horowitz's endeavors are far too valuable to be influenced by the petty, self-serving ideas of anyone. I expect everyone on staff and otherwise, to respect my suggestion regarding the doctor's privacy."

Doctor Goldbloom turned to leave and almost bumped into Doctor Petrillo rushing into the office. "Oh, excuse me, Sir. I was a little late for a private discussion with Howard here…," Petrillo paused and glanced at Baldwin. Baldwin widened his eyes and shook his head from side to side to indicate silence.

Doctor Goldbloom stared blankly at Petrillo, nodded his head and walked out of the room.

CHAPTER 17

Joey's completion of sixth grade was once again, nothing out of the ordinary. It was always the same story. The attending teacher reported a well-adjusted male student with an extremely high IQ (Intelligence Quotient) yet the disorder was still present and continued to torment Joey as well as his parents.

Of course, there were the normal instances of happenstance that befall grammar school children. He had a couple of altercations with bullies that he refused to relent to. There was an instance where one of the larger, wilder boys in his class by the name of Big Mike, shot a spitball at him with a straw smuggled from the cafeteria. Joey considered the act one of disrespect and lashed out at his tormentor. Mike pointed at the short, husky Joey and publicly threatened him. "After school, Joey! I'm gonna' get you after school!"

Joey turned around to face the larger boy and accepted. "You got it. After school." Mike's face dropped, as he didn't think the quiet, studious Joey would have accepted the challenge.

Unfortunately, there was no time to settle the

disagreement before their teacher, Mister Hardy, walked back into the room. Mr. Hardy, unaware of the incident, immediately addressed the class, "Okay, take out your history books and turn to chapter five."

The afternoon proceeded quietly, but both boys secretly wished they had been allowed an opportunity to settle their problem before the teacher had returned to the classroom. Inside, Joey was seething, but really didn't want any trouble. He knew the stage had been set and his entire class was awaiting the outcome. He felt he had to go through with the challenge.

After school, Joey followed through and made good on his promise. As the students left the school for the waiting buses, Joey got Big Mike's attention and struck him in the eye, in full view of the attending teacher, Mr. Hardy. The fight was short lived, as Big Mike failed to retaliate and began to cry. Mr. Hardy had seen Joey deliver the punch and promptly grabbed him by the back of the neck ending any further consequence.

Both boys paid the price for their actions. Their parents were brought in for conferences after which the school routine continued normally. During Joey's parent/teacher conference, Joey sat at his desk and listened to his father speak to his teacher. Mister Hardy was highly put out by Joey's actions. He went on about how such an act was highly out of character for a boy of Joey's caliber and suggested to Frank that maybe the boy had an anger problem.

Frank smiled back at the academician and shook his head from side to side. "I don't think so, Mister Hardy. He's just being a boy...and we're done with this conversation.

He reacted as I would have wanted him to." Frank rose from his chair and collected Joey for the ride home.

The remainder of the school year was uneventful. Children seem to get over grudges easily and dismiss such things with more ease than adults. Mister Hardy had never forgiven Joey for stepping outside of the confines of the quiet, mild-mannered boy he had labeled as only intelligent and studious.

At such a vulnerable age, children cannot be labeled by parents, teachers, or peers. There is an inner spirit that is cultured by the child's perception of his everyday experiences...right or wrong. It is the child's make up that is at work balancing the outcome of behavior as maturity develops. Mistakes will be made, but that is all a part of the learning process. Hopefully, the reasoning between right and wrong prevails.

By the end of the school year, both boys were back on a friendly basis and sixth grade came to an end.

CHAPTER 18

Frank and Ginny Hall sat patiently in the waiting room for their turn with Doctor Horowitz. The sign on the main door read NEUROSURGEONS, Horowitz, Baldwin, and Petrillo. No one spoke. The anticipation of what was next always filled the young parent's thoughts. Joey busied himself with a sports magazine.

The office door opened, and Doctor Horowitz personally greeted the threesome. He nodded and smiled. "Good afternoon, folks. Come on in." Frank and Ginny stood and let Joey go first. When everyone was seated, Horowitz took a seat behind his desk. He was a quiet, unassuming man and shuffled through some papers before he pulled out Joey's folder. Doctor Horowitz leaned forward on his elbows smiling. "Mr. and Mrs. Hall, I have been studying Joey's entire file, his EEG tests, his school reports, and extracurricular activities that you have reported, and it is my intention to put an end to all of this for Joey and for both of you." Joey sat and watched the doctor. He liked Doctor Horowitz because of his quiet and easy-going manner. He always made him feel like everything would be alright.

The Halls smiled and nodded their heads eagerly. Horowitz continued, "I have been treating Joey for a few years now and as I told you from the beginning, Joey's disorder is, what we...at first thought, was merely a temporal lobe condition. After further investigation and several EEGs, symptoms seem to favor a very mild form of petit mal. My colleagues and I now agree that it is not even that." Horowitz paused so the parents could absorb the new information.

Frank took advantage of the short pause to interject. "Well, it's not nothing, Doc. He's still having the spells."

Doctor Horowitz raised his right hand as if to say stop, and continued. "We have defined this as a case of what we think is a condition called absence. It's pronounced absence."

Frank shifted in his seat and Ginny knew Frank was becoming irritated. "Look, Doc, we've been going through this a long time. We've been coming here to see you a long time as well. First, you call it one thing, then another. Now, after all these years, it's something else. I want to know what it is, so we can make it go away. If you guys can't make up your mind...maybe we're wasting our time here."

Doctor Horowitz waited for Frank to finish. Once again, the doctor smiled warmly at the confused parents. "I can appreciate how you feel, but remember...at the outset, I explained that this disorder is so mild that so many parents elect to let it go untreated...especially when they're told that he'll grow out of it. You guys have elected to stick with it and get to the bottom of it. Although mild, it is very troublesome, and in some cases...embarrassing. In later years, it could even be responsible for some very serious situations." Horowitz paused again waiting for comments from Frank or Ginny. There were none, so he continued. "Because of its nature, the disorder has been 'swept under the rug' by many professionals...and parents. That said, research on the disorder has been minimal at best. Identification of the cause, possibilities for the cure, and medications have been studied, but not much more has been addressed."

Ginny's expression became concerned as the doctor spoke. "I'm not sure where you're going with this, Doctor. You just said you were going to put an end to this."

Horowitz smiled, "And I intend to. I would like to give the disorder the attention it deserves. We have reached the point where it's time to dig in and look at everything. We have tried several medications and several combinations of medications, as well as dosages. Now, that we have a base line to follow and a medication that is showing some control, I'd like to go a little further."

Frank and Ginny both nodded their heads. "With your permission, I'd like to," and he paused a moment, "create a journal...a detailed medical log and living history on the boy. I want to know about everything he does, everything he's interested in, his accomplishments, failures... everything. I'd like to use Joey's case as a proving ground to finally get this thing under control...and for everyone else that suffers from it also."

Frank and Ginny turned to look at each other and simultaneously nodded their heads in agreement. Ginny looked back at the doctor. "Of course, but we still don't want this flaunted publicly...for Joey's sake."

Horowitz smiled, "Of course. Don't worry about that."

Joey watched as the adults made these decisions for him. He had no problem with what Horowitz wanted to do. In his twelve-year old mind, his part was easy. Just tell the doctor what he's been doing and what he wants do. It's the doctor's job to write everything down. *Whatever.*

CHAPTER 19

The fall was always a beautiful time in Tobacco Valley. August and September brought the cooler temperatures and Indian summer. It also brought about an American favorite pastime…football. Of course, new football teams were created and past teams lost older players, but in any case, the fall was the time of year where young men tried out for the team of their choice in hopes of becoming a player on one of the town's youth football teams.

Joey's best friend Nate had been pushing to Joey all summer to play tackle football on one of the town sponsored youth football teams. The age bracket was for eleven and twelve year-olds and Joey knew he was eligible. Nate would say, "C'mon, Joe. You're big enough to play. We could be on the same team together. I played last year, and with someone of your size and speed, you're sure to get put on the line…defense or offense."

Joey always answered by nodding his head. He knew his father was against those youth football teams because he believed the skeletal system of a twelve year old child had not matured enough for that kind of physical contact.

Joey definitely wanted to play, so once in a while he'd

answer Nate by saying," "I don't want to be on the line. I want to carry the ball. I want to be a halfback or a full back...I'm heavy, but I'm fast."

"Aww, forget that. Those positions are all taken. Even if you made the team as a "back," you'd probably end up being third string and sitting on the bench."

Finally, one night at dinner, Joey brought up the idea to his parents. It was immediately turned down because the idea of children playing such a rough sport at such an early age was unheard of. Frank and Ginny heard Joey out and listened to him talk about Nate and some of the other kids in the area, but were still skeptical.

Ginny looked at Joey's hopeful face and relented, "Frank, we did have a conversation about this with Doctor Horowitz once last year...the last time Joey had been interested, and he thought it would be fine. He said we should encourage Joey and support his interests...within reason of course."

Frank was quick to reply, "I know, but Joey isn't ready yet. He's big enough, but it all goes back to what a kid's bones are like at that age. I'm against it."

Ginny smiled at Joey and patted his arm. "Dad and I will discuss this later. Let us think about it. We'll see."

Frank shot an ugly glance at Ginny walked out of the room. Joey looked defeated and shook his head as he stared at the floor. "Everyone is gonna' think I'm scared or something."

Ginny smiled once more at her son. "We'll' see, Joe. We'll discuss this later and then all three of us will talk about it...okay?"

Joey nodded his head but knew how his dad felt. *I'm never gonna' get to play on one of those teams.*

A week passed and Frank took Joey for a walk. Every time Frank considered something the kids shouldn't take lightly, he took them for a walk to discuss it. "Joe, Mom thinks it's going to be okay for you to try out for this football team. I'm still not okay with it, but I know you'll do your best, so we're going to let you try it."

Joey looked up at Frank surprised and smiling. "Really?"

Frank stopped walking and looked Joey in the eyes with a serious glare. "I want you to be serious about this and focus on the sport. You can't get half way through the season and quit."

"I won't, I won't."

Frank added, "If you don't make first string and end up sitting on the bench, I expect the same. Once you're on the team...you're on the team."

Joey thanked his dad and they walked on awhile. Joey continued to go on about what it might be like to be a football player on an organized team, and Frank walked in silence.

Joey waited patiently all day for his dad to get home from work. When Frank finally pulled in to the driveway, Joey ran to the car. "C'mon dad! You gotta' eat quick. Tryouts are in forty-five minutes. Mom has your dinner on the table already."

Frank was dog tired and the last thing on his mind was going to watch a youth football practice. Frank had forgotten about tryouts and as he stared into Joey's eyes, and remembered what Dr. Horowitz had said, *Support him. Support his interests. Let him tryout for football...like the other boys.*

"Okay, Joe. Let me run into the house and say hi to Mom. I'll be right out."

Frank walked into the kitchen and Ginny had already put his dinner on the table. She looked at Frank with raised eyebrows, "Tonight's the night, Frank."

"I know. I forgot, but it might be kind of interesting. I'm interested to see how Joey takes to it."

In a few minutes, Joey and Frank were in the car and on their way to football tryouts. Frank began to counsel Joey on what the coaches might expect and urged him to do his best, "...and no matter what – don't give in. You can take whatever they have to dish out."

Joey had no idea of what to expect. He shrugged his shoulders, "Okay, Dad. I'll do my best."

The town's athletic fields were in a naturally formed hollow and surrounded by forest. It seemed as if half the kids in town were there. Frank got out of the car and found out where Joey's team was. "Your team is over there, Joe. Go ahead, go tell your coach who you are. He'll check your name off a list. I'll be right here. Good luck."

Once all the candidates were signed in, the coach told them they were going to pick only a few new players, so they better try their best. His name was Coach Dowd. "Okay everyone, we'll start by running the perimeter of the athletic field. Stay to the outside and no shortcuts. I'll be watching to see who comes in last."

Joey was one of the heavier kids but was still fast. *"Oh, it's gonna' be a race. Okay, Dr. Horowitz said to relax and just do it. I'm just gonna' run and stay in the middle of the pack… but I won't be last.*

The field of incumbent football players ran the perimeter of the field trying to impress the coach. When they returned, Dowd said, "That was kind of slow guys. Do it again, but pick up the pace a little."

Now, it was a race. The taller, leaner players were way out in front of the pack, fifty percent were bunched together in a tight group in the middle, and the heavier, slower kids were slogging along at the tail end. Joey was in the middle.

Out of breath, the player candidates finished in front of where Dowd was patiently waiting. Everyone was bent over trying to catch their breath. The coach gave them a minute and then announced, "Calisthenics! Jumping jacks first…begin." Dowd called out the repetitions and after they had done thirty, shouted "Stop!" He immediately followed with, "Squat thrusts, twenty of them…begin."

A squat thrust was performed by bending at the waist to a push up position, then the feet were brought back up under the body, allowing the performer to rise to a standing position. The process was repeated again as many times as the coach requested.

Joey heard something tear on his second repetition and felt cool air along the inside of his right thigh. He had ripped his pants from the crotch to his ankle, baring his entire right leg. He was mortified.

Joey looked around for his dad and finally found him in a group of waiting fathers, talking and enjoying their conversation. When Joey approached, Frank seemed surprised and embarrassed. "What is it, Joe? Why aren't you out there with the others?"

"I ripped my pants. We gotta' go home, so I can change."

Frank was visibly embarrassed in front of the other fathers who looked away as if they hadn't heard the boy. Frank ushered Joey to the car faster than one would expect, and started for home. As they drove away, Joey noticed his father seemed quiet and serious. "Don't worry, Dad. I got another pair in the closet. I'll just make a quick change and we can go back. It'll just take a minute."

Frank turned and looked at Joey. "We're not going back. You're cut now. You can't leave a tryout for anything. It's over...your cut."

Joey was crushed. "But, no one said that, Dad. I just ripped my pants. Please take me back there."

"You're done! Give Mom your pants when we get home. That's it."

No one ever said anything to Joey about the football tryout or what happened, but a few days later, Joey was outside when Ginny called him into the house. It was a warm evening and Joey had been in a tea shirt and jeans. "Joey, come on in for a minute please."

Joey ran into the house and Ginny seemed a bit agitated. "Go change that shirt for something that fits you better. That one makes you look fat."

Joey was shocked at his mother. She never spoke to him that way. He looked confused and turned to go to his room to change his shirt. As he walked away Ginny added, "We're going to do something about your weight. I'm not going to have a fat kid in my family. Start exercising or... something, but I do want you to start working on that."

The words broke the boy's heart. First, his father's reaction to the football tryout and now this. Joey pouted about it for a while, but really didn't know what to do except maybe eat less.

The next night Frank asked Joey and Brian to go to the store with him. "I've decided to get you guys a barbell set. You're both going to need to get into shape for the sports that are coming your way in the next few years, and I want you to be ready. There's one thing though...you can't tell anyone that you're lifting weights. They'll notice soon enough." Frank paused a moment and continued with, "You guys know my friend, Stan...the guy I go golfing with on Fridays? His son started lifting weights and Stan said it's made a difference in his studies as well as building him up. Mom and I decided we're going to have you guys try it. Okay?"

Brian remained silent but Joey was quick to reply, "Yeah, sure, Dad. Maybe it'll help me get into shape for football next year."

Frank stared into Joey's face and thought, *I can't believe he's not over that yet. After what happened at the tryouts and what I said in the car...he's still pushing the football. I'll let it go for now.*

The following night Brian, Joey and Frank set up the barbell set and began their first of what would be innumerable work outs for Joey. The program was designed to start light with one set of repetitions and increase weight and sets of the same repetitions as the boy progressed.

After a few weeks, Brian became more involved in what was going on at his own school and was getting his work outs from the high school's sports team. Joey continued to work out in his bedroom with his father...three times a week.

CHAPTER 20

⸻

Seventh grade, as everyone knows is a tumultuous time for most young teenagers. For many boys, it is the beginning of puberty when many changes occur, and sometimes, several of them at the same time. Emotional as well as physical changes are at the forefront of the child's life during this time of development and can cause the individual involved to exhibit severe behavioral patterns. The patterns can be out of character and noticeable, and sometimes invisible, as the individual experiencing the patterns, may elect or try to keep them hidden from would-be observers.

Many children, at this age are still carrying what adults call, 'baby fat.' A good number of children that enter puberty as short and plump, leave that phase as tall and slim. In Joey's case, he was 135 pounds and stood five feet, two inches tall. Ginny liked to call him husky, but Frank was concerned that the weight would continue to increase and affect his high school sports opportunities.

Generally, Joey was a happy thirteen-year-old now, a little overweight, and shy. The anxiety of entering junior high school coupled with the idea of going to a much larger school was a huge consideration…at least in Joey's mind. The number of attending students went from a few hundred in grammar school, to over a thousand, and he was expected to change classes and classrooms every hour. The unfamiliarity of the new school's layout was one thing, but now a new wrinkle had been added. There was a specified time limit of four minutes to get to the next class.

Since he no longer had his own desk to store his books, he was assigned a locker. The problem was that his locker was further from his assigned classes than it needed to be, and he never had time to go back to it to retrieve the required book for the next class. Tardiness to class authorized a detention, and detentions meant staying after school, so Joey began carrying most of his books under his arm to each class. There were just so many obstacles in this new way of schooling and so many more ways for him to get into trouble or to be embarrassed, usually in front of an entire class.

Joey's anxiety level had risen to a new height, and because of that, began to experience more spells. His peers were older now and more aware of what might be happening around them. They were also more in tune with what was considered normal behavior, at least by their standards. Because of this, Joey had to be extra careful in how he 'covered' for himself.

If he experienced a spell in public, his reaction time became a function of what he was doing, where he was, and to a greater extent...how many people were present. The idea that a child of such a young age was made to feel that he should hide his actions or shortcomings **is** very sad. The blame shouldn't be placed on anyone except society itself. Our culture tends to question anything that may be different, not of the accepted norm, or unknown altogether, and when it's something that isn't understood, that same society points fingers and labels the action, usually with derogatory results.

Anyone that has experienced such a condition would normally look for the quickest and most reasonable excuse for the disruption his behavior may have just caused. The trick was to disguise the behavior, and sometimes hide it in plain sight, either by not acknowledging it, or laughing it off. Joey became very adept at hiding what may have just happened or explaining it away. Graduating to the junior high school level, encouraged more maturity and required more responsibility, so Joey knew he'd have to find other ways to find solace in what could happen and then be able to justify his part in any activity. Part of that idea was to participate in activities he could do on his own, or find an interesting area of something he was expected to perform, and focus on that.

As time passed, the new school year had been so full of new and awkward scenarios, and unanticipated outcomes, Joey began to experience his worst year ever. Because he felt nervous about being 'pointed out,' the boy began to shy away from teen parties and large groups of teenagers. He felt it was safer to walk the extra mile home from school rather than take the bus. He spent most of his time after school in the woods behind his house with his dog Hunter, and going for long hikes. The woods were his sanctuary. If he wanted to be invisible…it was easy.

At school, Joey found comfort in Shop Class, now referred to as Industrial Education. He looked forward to putting the books aside for a while and working with wood. Joey saw the opportunity for making shelves for his books, and gifts for his parents. The school had provided the shop area with the latest in power equipment. There were radial arm saws, drill presses, power sanders, planers, and the like...machines that could easily remove a finger or limb in mere seconds. The shop teacher was careful to mention all the nasty things that could happen to anyone who inadvertently made a careless mistake or failed to use proper safety practices.

Joey seemed to be able to immerse himself in the shop's activities and it's carpentry projects, temporarily blocking out the rest of the school day. Everyone had their own projects to work on. He knew he could be in class, be active and still go unnoticed, as everyone was busy with their own machines and assignments. Shop Class was going well until one day, as the clock wound down to within five minutes before it was time to change classes.

The entire shop class was lined up by the shop's entrance under the watchful eye of the teacher, Mr. Willabe. The teacher was quietly watching the group of anxious seventh graders and set his gaze on Joey. Suddenly, without warning, without any kind of discretion, Willabe addressed Joey. "Hey Joe! Are you an epileptic?"

Joey was mortified. He could feel his face reddening and getting warm. He quickly shook his head as if he didn't know what the word meant and said in a questioning tone, "No." Joey made sure to wrinkle his eyebrows and look confused, as if he didn't understand why the teacher had asked him such a question.

Mr. Willabe was known to be a crass and insensitive man. He saw Joey's embarrassed reaction, but continued,

"Well, I can't have you around any of the machines if you are. Someone could get hurt." Just then the bell rang and Joey acted as if he didn't care what the teacher had just said, and followed the rest of the shop students as they left for the next class. Joey was totally humiliated.

The afternoon passed as one of Joey's worst. He felt low, embarrassed, and worried about what the rest of the shop class might still be thinking. Unbeknownst to Joey, anyone that had been paying any attention to the incident had forgotten about it almost as soon as it happened. To a self-conscious thirteen-year-old boy, it felt as if the entire school had heard of the incident.

Joey walked home, once again choosing to walk instead of riding the bus. He couldn't get the incident from shop class out of his mind. No one had mentioned anything to him that afternoon, but given the right circumstances, the incident could have been remembered and brought up instantly.

Joey continued to walk and think about the possible outcome. Finally, he decided there was no answer. He was very upset with Mr. Willabe, whom he had not been fond of to begin with, but considered the fall-out if he had told his parents about the incident. Joey finally decided, *I need to get home and go for a walk in the woods. I need to put all of this away for now.*

He began to run and continued running until he reached his house. Out of breath and sweating, Joey burst through the kitchen door surprising his mother at the sink. Ginny turned around with a start, "Oh! Hi, Joe. What's the rush?"

Joey, threw his books onto the kitchen table and

answered as he went to change his clothes. "Goin' out in the woods."

Ginny watched him go down the hallway. "You walked home again? You're all sweaty. Sit and talk with me for a minute."

Joey shouted from his bedroom. "Can't, Mom. It's gonna' be dark soon and I gotta' get out there."

Ginny leaned against the sink and watched as Joey grabbed his jacket and headed for the back yard. "Okay, be home for supper."

Joey trotted out to the woods until he reached the main path. He stopped to catch his breath and started walking. Finally, he reached his special place by the big pine tree. He sat down and leaned against it, closed his eyes and considered the shop teacher and what he had said in front of the class. After considering the pros and cons, Joey decided to tell his parents about the situation and what Mr. Willabe had said.

The Halls sat down to their dinner and Joey was unusually quiet. Everyone talked about their day and shared information about the different conversations. Ginny had been watching Joey and noticed he had been listening, but not offering anything about his day. She knew it was unusual behavior for a child who never needed prompting to speak. At an appropriate lag in the table discussions, Ginny quickly asked, "Hey Joey, you've been kind of quiet. How did your day go?"

Joey's face flushed red and he looked down at his plate

of food. "Uh, I didn't have too good a day. It's over and I just want to forget about it."

Frank and Ginny looked at one another. Frank nodded at Ginny to continue.

Ginny gently pressed Joey, "Well, I'd like to hear it anyway. Sometimes, getting it out into the open may make you feel better."

Frank leaned in the boy's direction, "Yeah, Joe. Tell us about it. Maybe we can help."

Joey took a deep breath and let it out. "Well, it was at the end of Shop Class." He paused a moment.

Frank prodded him, Go ahead, Joe. We're right here. It's okay."

Joey nodded before he continued, "Well, I don't want to get anyone in trouble."

Ginny came to the table and sat down putting her hand on the boy's arm. "Go ahead."

Well, we were waiting for the bell to ring and all of a sudden, Mr. Willabe asked me if I was an epileptic...right in front of everyone."

Frank slammed his hand down on the table and Ginny cupped her hands about her mouth. "Call the school department. I want this guy reported! Who does he think he is...saying things like that in front of strangers?"

Ginny was visibly upset. "How dare he say something like that!

Frank looked back over to Joey. "Joe, what happened? Why would he bring something like that up?"

Joey appeared scared. He shrugged his shoulders, "I don't know, Dad. We were just standing there waiting to change classes…waiting for the bell to ring, and he just looked at me and said it."

Frank glanced back at Ginny. "Call the school department in the morning. Report this teacher, and find out why he's even asking a question like that. This kind of thing shouldn't even be in his file. I mean they really don't even have a name for his disorder yet."

Ginny tried to calm Frank. "Frank, it's probably something one of Joey's teachers thought he recognized during school. Maybe Joey had a spell at some point and that teacher noticed it, and mentioned it to this guy. You know how the teachers all take breaks in the teachers' room. They talk about their students and something along those lines probably came up."

Frank began to calm down. "Maybe, but make sure this doesn't go in his file!"

Joey listened to his parent's outrage and thought, *Why is it so bad if it's in my file? I thought this was just a mild thing. Everyone's upset, and now they're gonna' get Mr. Willabe in trouble. I shouldn't have said anything.*

Early the next morning, Ginny Hall was on the phone with the town's school department. She demanded to speak with someone in the pupil services department about the incident and Joey's files. After being passed around to several different departments, she was put in touch with the assistant superintendent of schools, George Asher. Ginny explained Joey's disorder and the incident at the junior high school's shop class.

Asher was shocked and told Ginny he'd pull Joey's files immediately and call the junior high school's principal to get to the bottom of it all. He also promised Ginny a call back and what their plan of action would be.

Ginny was satisfied with Asher's attitude and concern, and hung up the phone. The parent's request to keep Joey's problem quiet until he could grow out of it became a struggle.

George Asher, assistant superintendent of schools, called Ginny before noon, as he had promised. It had taken a few hours to get to the source of what had happened, and Asher had demanded the boy' files on his desk immediately.

Ginny heard the phone and raced to pick it up. She was hopeful she would have an answer before Frank called. "Hello?"

"Hello, Mrs. Hall. This is George Asher. I feel we have gotten to the source and corrected the problem."

Ginny nodded her head and said, "Okay. What have you found?"

"Well, it appears that the school nurse had seen something on Joey's medical file from his last doctor's visit with Doctor Elliot J. Smith, a general practitioner here in town."

Ginny immediately retorted, "We never gave any permission to the doctor's office or anyone else for that matter, to give out any medical information about our son."

Asher was understanding and explained, "Unfortunately Mrs. Hall, the school department reserves the right to obtain that information from the child's doctor if he's involved in something that may put him in harm's way. In this case, Shop Class, where there are multiple kinds of power equipment the students would be personally operating."

Ginny was astonished, "Why weren't we advised about this? Why weren't we at least told what was going on? We would have had Joey take a different class rather have him embarrassed in front of his peers. This is just unacceptable!"

Asher concurred, "I agree with you Mrs. Hall. You should have been made aware of what was happening about the information transfer. Unfortunately, that phone call looks like it fell in a crack or was handled by someone merely on a clerical basis."

"That's not good enough Mr. Asher. This is a betrayal of student and patient trust. The boy's privacy has been compromised as well as his family's."

Asher tried to re-direct the conversation, "I understand Mrs. Hall, but let me get to the rest of the story and then we can figure out how to handle the problem."

There was silence on Ginny's side of the phone, so Asher began to explain. "It appears that the shop teacher, Mr. Willabe, was perusing all of his student's files prior to the beginning of this quarter's shop projects which included the introduction of power equipment. It's a normal thing for a shop teacher to do during this phase of that kind of class, merely from a safety standpoint." Asher paused to let that information sink in. Ginny was obviously upset. Asher continued, "Let me assure you Mrs. Hall, that Mr. Willabe had no motive or reason to seek out only Joey's file. It was merely procedure before entering into this particular phase of shop class that deals with power equipment."

Ginny interrupted, "But the man handled the entire situation incorrectly. He embarrassed Joey, put him at risk as far as peer labeling goes, and completely ruined the boy's day." Ginny was breathing hard into the phone. "We don't want 'epilepsy' mentioned anywhere in Joey's files, and I want that man to be reprimanded for his insensitive actions…and I want an apology from him, to us and Joey."

Asher chose his words carefully. "Again, Mrs. Hall, I apologize for how everything was handled, and you should have been notified of the information transfer. I personally feel very badly about Joey being embarrassed in front of his peers, but let me point out that kids of that age probably didn't even recognize the word and forgot about the whole event." Asher took a deep breath and continued, "Mr. Willabe is a shop teacher and most likely doesn't know the depth of the disorder, only the stereotypical description of what can happen if a seizure presents itself."

Ginny cut Asher off, "He doesn't have seizures, Mr. Asher. His episodes are so mild and infrequent that they are referred to as spells, and we don't want whatever this disorder is to follow him throughout his life and ruin any future opportunities he has in sports, college, or future occupations."

Asher remained calm and continued, "I will have a meeting with Mr. Willabe this afternoon, privately, in my office. I will have him call you and your husband and apologize for his outburst in front of Joey's classmates, but I cannot reprimand him for following safety procedures for his shop."

Ginny asked, "What about removing that word from Joey's file?"

Asher took another deep breath, "Unfortunately, Mrs.

Hall, we cannot change what is on the boy's medical report, so we cannot change what is now in his file."

Ginny was quiet for a moment and finally replied. "Well, we'll see about that! I can promise this though. If this incident goes on to affect Joey in any way, there will be consequences with everyone who had anything to do with his file." She paused, "I want to hear from Willabe this evening when my husband gets home after five o'clock."

Ginny hung up the phone and sat by the phone sobbing. Everything seemed to be working against her son and anything he enjoyed.

That evening, as Frank came through the kitchen door, the phone rang. Ginny went to pick up the phone, nodded to Frank, and signaled with her hand that this was probably the phone call from Willabe. "Hello?"

"Hello. Mrs. Hall, this is Charles Willabe, Joey's shop teacher.

Ginny nodded her head as she concentrated on Willabe's words. "Yes, Mr. Willabe. Thank you for calling."

Willabe continued, "I had a discussion this afternoon with Assistant Superintendent Asher regarding the incident in shop class yesterday. I apologize for being so ignorant of the fallout Joey's situation could have brought. I guess I was being too methodical and didn't consider the child when I was looking through his file…and that goes for the rest of the class. Please believe me that I never meant to put your son in an embarrassing situation or to make him feel less of a person."

Ginny said nothing for a moment. The teacher sounded sincere. "Well unfortunately, you did do all those things and the harm has been done. I hope you will think more about each and every one of your students from now on before you just blurt things out. It seems by the way everything was described to me by our son and your superintendent, that maybe you were a little too concerned about your responsibility in the shop class over the safety of each student."

Willabe continued to apologize to the irate mother and added that, although it doesn't help Joey's cause now, it was a wake-up call for him as to why he was looking over the students' files in the first place.

Frank declined the opportunity to speak with the teacher, but just shook his head as he listened to Ginny during the phone call. Ginny ended the call by telling the worried teacher that he should push to do what he could to get that word epilepsy, and any insinuation of it, removed from her son's file.

Finally, the call was over, and the Halls felt somewhat satisfied that they had made an institution as large as the school system realize they should be more focused on the children they serve, rather than the school's liabilities.

CHAPTER 21

Joey's shop class incident spurred a visit to Dr. Horowitz. The Halls were interested to see what the neurologist could do to push the school system to remove any inference to their son and the word epilepsy. They felt comfortable with the fact that the whole scenario was an accumulation of clerical errors and negligence but wanted the problem corrected.

"The doctor will see you now." Doctor Horowitz's receptionist poked her head through the waiting room door and smiled at the Halls.

Ginny leaned over and whispered to Joey. "Let's go, Joe. Dr. Horowitz is waiting."

The Halls walked into the same familiar office they had entered so many times before. The doctor rose from his chair, smiled, and greeted the parents. He sat down and looked across the desk at Joey as he pulled out his journal. "Hi Joe! Looks like you've grown since last September. What do you think about being in seventh grade…junior high school?"

Joey shrugged his shoulders and met the doctor's gaze. "It's awful! There are so many new rules and times I have to pay attention to…like getting from one class to another… classes change every hour. The new school is huge, and it took a while to figure out the shortest route to the next class. It seems like I never have a chance to catch up."

Dr. Horowitz chuckled as he noted Joey's responses. "That's all part of it, Joe. Your parents and I also had to get through that same year…all new stuff." The doctor stopped writing and looked at Joey, "Tell me, do all those new rules and time constraints…like getting to the next class on time, make you nervous?"

"Yeah. At first, it made me real nervous. If you're late, you get a detention."

Dr. Horowitz smiled and spoke in a very soothing tone. "Ah, don't let it bother you. Do your best, but try planning ahead. Planning ahead for the next few classes, or anything for that matter, can help to reduce the worry about where you have to go and what you need when you get there." The doctor continued, "How are your classes? Do you find them hard or challenging…or just boring?

Ginny interrupted, "He has a bad time with tests, Doctor…sometimes to the point where he gets so overwhelmed, he panics and just rushes through the test. All of his teachers have said that his test scores hardly ever reflect what he actually knows about the subject."

Horowitz looked back to Joey. "You know, no matter what you do as you get older, someone is going to want to test you…about something. Just remember, Tests are an old-fashioned way of trying to find out what someone knows or what they can do, but everyone knows they are not a true measure of anything."

Joey quickly put in, "I'm always worried that I won't finish in time."

Horowitz raised his eyebrows as he jotted that down. "Why are you afraid that you won't finish the test, Joe?"

"Because then, they won't know what I really know. They always have us doing speed tests and flash quizzes. I hate those! I like to think about it first...so I never finish."

Horowitz added, "So, would you rather take your time and get all the right answers, or rush through it and get all the wrong answers?" The doctor flipped open Joey's files, "You know, Joe. It says here that you have an IQ way above the normal child of your age...way above. That means you don't have to rush. You know the stuff. Just relax like you're doing homework and answer the questions. Remember what I'm telling you for the next test. Can you do that for me?"

Joey nodded that he would.

"Okay, what else?"

Ginny outlined the ordeal in shop class and her telephone call with the shop teacher, Mr. Willabe. "They did everything wrong, Doctor! And I don't want that label following him around through his career. Is there anything you can do to force the school system's hand?"

Horowitz nodded and said he'd make a few phone calls but then he paused and looked at the two concerned parents. "Why are you so concerned about the word epilepsy? What Joey has, is actually a very mild form of it...and we have to be grateful for that, but don't look at it like it's a bad word. It's just the name of a disorder."

Frank spoke up, "Well Doc, we know most people don't understand anything about that disorder and all the different levels it may manifest itself in. We're afraid that once someone or some report labels him like that, he'll be pushed aside for any future opportunities he may actually be eligible for."

Horowitz nodded his head, "I see. What I will tell you at this point, is that once you get past what the word infers and become comfortable with the fact your son has a mild form of it… you will begin to relax. Accept the word for what it is…just a name, nothing more." The doctor paused a moment and stopped writing notes. "If I told you how many famous people have a similar disorder to Joey's…and some are much worse…you would be shocked."

Ginny and Frank looked at each other with raised eyebrows.

Horowitz continued, "That's right. I mean newscasters, actors, politicians…and professional athletes. Those people didn't let it stop them. They challenged it, and that's how they got to where they are today."

The conversation continued with the doctor trying to get Joey to speak for long lengths of time and to see where his interests were, and to see if he could catch the boy having a spell. Joey went on and on about UFOs and all the sightings around the world. The boy talked for ten minutes before Horowitz stopped him.

The doctor smiled at Frank and Ginny. "You see, a lot of this has to do with the boy's comfort level, who he's speaking to, and how confident he is about what he's talking about. He just spoke to me for ten minutes without a spell."

Frank spoke up. "You mentioned confidence. How do we build that? I thought that was just something that developed on its own."

"Well, you can support him in things he talks about. Give him your full attention when he talks to you. Make him know you are interested in what he wants to tell you. If he wants to do something...support it. Don't just tell him no because it's not something you have the time for, or doesn't fit into the family schedule." The doctor paused. "He's thirteen now and sports are going to become more and more a part of his life...support that."

Ginny added, "Well, he's been talking about playing organized tackle football for his school again." She paused, "It'll be in a couple of years. The new school has a ninth-grade team. He tried out once before...about a year ago, for a league run by our town, and it ended before it got started."

Horowitz, nodded, "Let him try for it. Support his interest."

Ginny shrugged her shoulders as he placed her arms in front of her chest as if she just got a chill. "But, it's so violent! He could get tackled, or knocked around or even jumped on."

Horowitz sat back in his chair and chuckled, "He is going to get tackled, knocked around, and jumped on. That's okay. He's a healthy young boy...just like all the other boys that will be out there. Support it! One of the worst things you can do for Joey right now is to hold him back. Stop being so protective and go after what he's interested in. If he knows you're both behind him, he will excel. The best way for him to get through this is to challenge everything that brings it on...the worrying, the nervousness, the threat of failure, and judgement. He'll learn how to control these areas and the confidence he gains will cancel out any chances for failure."

Frank and Ginny looked at each other. It was obvious they were unsure about what the doctor had just suggested.

Horowitz interrupted the moment. "Folks, look at your son." Joey was beaming. "The doctor just said he should play football."

Before Horowitz ended the day's session, he asked the Halls for a few more minutes. "Mr. and Mrs. Hall, the confidence factor can be built in several ways. I think I've mentioned this before, but it's important and I'll just bring it up again as a reminder. Joey will soon be thinking about girls a lot more than usual. When he finds that first girl that he thinks he's in love with, you will see a dramatic change in him, as well as a decrease in the number of spells and their frequency. Support this behavior. Having someone from outside the family whom he knows cares for him in the same way as he cares for her, will be one of the turning points in his growth, and one of the great tools in neutralizing this disorder."

Ginny and Frank looked questioningly back at the doctor, nodded as if they understood, and left his office.

CHAPTER 22

Weeks passed, and then months. Joey was getting taller and slimmer. As the beginning of eighth grade approached, Joey began to transform into a different person, both physically and emotionally. When springtime approached, Joey returned to his beloved woods, except that now, he practiced running off the path. He purposely ran through areas where brush, trees and fallen logs were prevalent, so he'd have to dodge those obstacles or jump over them. As he got used to the new regimen, he intentionally increased his speed, sometimes colliding with a tree or stumbling over a pile of brush, but the boy was progressing. At the end of his work out, he retired to his big pine tree by the forgotten field, sometimes falling asleep.

The summer was approaching and along with it was the warm and humid New England weather. Frank had put together a harness arrangement that Joey could tie to a tree near the pool's perimeter and loop the other end around his feet. The arrangement allowed him to swim 'in place' in his pool. The boy was so distracted with the weight work outs, his runs through the woods, and in-place swims, he forgot about all the other things he had been focusing on for so long.

The eighth grader was getting into good shape, and soon that was where his biggest interest was. He took to carrying his football with him as he ran through the woods on his daily routine and was beginning to enjoy his life. The spells had stabilized, but occurred with less frequency. His demeanor had changed and the quiet, happy-go-lucky boy of years past, had left the scene.

Frank and Ginny noticed the transformation, but decided to be silent for now and just let it happen. The boy was making huge improvements. For the first time, in a long time, the Halls homelife was happy and serene.

Joey was slimming down and shooting up fast. His summer was full of activity. Among those activities included going to a nearby lake where he fished and canoed with his best friend, Nate. Sometimes they'd jump out of the canoe and swim around it while it drifted on the lake's calm water. At the end of the day Frank would drive over after work to pick the boys up. It was Joey's best summer yet.

The end of August approached and the idea of returning to the big school loomed ahead as a bad memory in Joey's mind. He dismissed the thought by thinking, *I'm a new person now, I'm bigger, better and I'm in good shape...I'll show 'em.*

CHAPTER 23

September arrived and so did Joey's annual EEG test. By now, the boy had been through three of them, and was looking forward to staying up late for it. He was also excited to make his new appearance at school. The boy had literally been transformed physically over the course of one summer...a very important summer in the growth process. Joey had gown five inches from May to September. His weight stayed the same at one hundred and thirty-five pounds, but he was slim at his new height and more muscular.

There were relatives that hadn't seen him over the summer and didn't recognize him as one of their own. Joey relished the experience. He'd hear someone say, "Oh, Joey? Is that you? What have you been doing? You look like a different person!"

Joey just smiled and sometimes offered, "Been working out."

The latest EEG came and went, requiring a follow up visit to Doctor Horowitz, or as Joey now referred to him, Doctor H. This time, it was only Frank and Joey that went to see the doctor. It was a Saturday and Frank had the day off from work. The two sat patiently before Doctor Horowitz while he read Joey's report from the last EEG. Finally, he looked up and slid his glasses to the end of his nose. He peered over their top at Frank. "Wow! This report is quite inspiring! Everything seems to have leveled out. The frequency and durations of the spells seem to have decreased and stabilized. According to the EEG findings, the spells are much milder than before and shorter in duration compared to previous tests."

Frank looked hopeful. "What does this mean, Doc?"

"It means that he has begun to make the turn we've been hoping for. He's getting older and according to the notes you've provided…has kept extremely busy, both physically and mentally, and has goals…specific sports goals in mind." The doctor paused as he glanced again at the Hall's notes. "It seems Joey has been much happier and is enjoying the new school year." He looked back at Frank, "Some of this is because you have given him a new look…same body but a more athletic looking appearance," the doctor turned toward Joey and winked, "and so much taller."

Joey was beaming. *Finally, some good news.*

Horowitz continued, "I think we'll keep his medication right where it is for a while. We'll just play it safe for now and see if we can start backing off on the meds by the end of the year."

Frank nodded his head, "Okay, what about the sports?"

Horowitz answered quickly, "Let him go for it. Encourage it. The sports are responsible for a good part of his progress." The doctor turned back to Joey, "Joe, get out there and try everything that you think interests you…not just sports either. Get involved socially. Go to dances. Try out for student counsel, get on school committees…it'll be fun, and you'll meet a lot of nice kids too."

Joey smiled and nodded his head. "I plan on it, Doctor. I'm not so sure about dances and stuff yet…and student council means you have to stand up in front of a lot of people and talk." The boy grimaced.

Horowitz quickly added, "Just do it, Joe! If it kind of scares you, then you need to do it. Try everything that's offered to you." Horowitz paused and sat back in his chair. "Be smart about what you choose to do… but have fun. Look forward to these things."

Once Joey and Frank left, Doctor Horowitz jotted down some notes from their meeting and stood from his desk. He walked over to his filing cabinet and slid the notes into Joey's medical log and living history file. *What good news*, the doctor thought. *Finally, after all these years we're making a turn for progress.* The doctor paused a moment and looked back at Joey's file. *Look at the size of that monthly log!* Horowitz pulled the log out of the file. *Almost three inches thick!* He nodded his head and smiled, *Well, if it's going to help the boy as well as other people, it's well worth the extra work and research.* The doctor flipped through the log. There was almost three years' worth of journaling, by date and in some cases, time of day and night to chronologize incidents. Horowitz smiled again and nodded favorably; *this compilation is going to finally give us a basis for treatment on a disorder we really never knew how to approach.* He shoved the medical log and living history back into Joey's file.

The ride home was a happy one. Both Frank and Joey came away from the meeting with Doctor Horowitz feeling positive and relieved. It seemed as if there was, after all, hope and an end to the nightmare they had all been living.

Joey's grades began to climb, especially in math and english. His teachers wrote letters home to the Halls describing their surprise with Joey's new scholastic performance. The Halls were pleased, and the entire family began to settle into a more relaxed atmosphere. Life was good. For once, the family lived without the uncertainty of what the future could bring.

The days and weeks passed and soon Joey began to shine in gym class. He began to excel in everything the gym teacher assigned, like endurance tests that required running the quarter mile for time. It seemed like a long way, but to Joey the distance's length description were only words. To him, it meant one lap around the track. The boy began with the entire class and soon pulled away from the pack without really trying, until he realized he was out in front by half a lap…and by himself. It was euphoric for the boy. He needed that special place…that recognition that he was better in something than everyone else.

To the regular eighth grader, accomplishments like the aforementioned, could possibly have encouraged the boy to become more arrogant than he had a right to be. But in Joey's case, the boy just enjoyed the result of his efforts and looked to the next challenge. In fact, he always felt bad for his competitor to the point where he was known to apologize for the outcome.

Whatever it was; wrestling, push up tests, climbing ropes, Joey became the new leader. He began to get a new reputation…and it spread around the school. The days of Mrs. Talbot's fourth grade class were in the past and in the back of Joey's memory, until one day when Joey came face to face with the boy who had bullied him back in sixth grade. The two boys stopped and sized each other up.

Joey recognized the bully right off. It was Burt Tuttle and although the bully had been huge as a sixth grader, now appeared as if he hadn't grown an inch. Joey stared down at him, and into his eyes, with confidence and amusement. The so-called bully was nothing to fear now, and Joey welcomed whatever was about to unfold. He looked at the bully and calmly said, "Hi Burt, I'm Joey Hall…remember me?"

Joey kept his eyes fixed on the squat looking boy and just smiled. The confidence and self-assuredness Joey exuded caused complete surprise as was obvious on the former bully's facial expression. Burt said nothing as his eyes widened and his jaw dropped.

Burt stepped backward as he remembered the former obese sixth grader he had tormented, turned around, and disappeared down the hallway. Joey didn't move. He just stood there and watched the former bully leave in shame. He never saw Burt again.

CHAPTER 24

Neurosurgeons Louis Baldwin, George Petrillo and Ben Horowitz sat in their private conference room leafing through their notebooks. It was time for their monthly meeting to discuss their personal practice and any related medical news or questions regarding procedures, disorders, or patient problems. Baldwin was first to speak. "Ben, it's been about a year since you mentioned your patient, Joey Hall and the medical log and living history you wanted to begin on him. Would you care to enlighten us as to how that is developing? We don't even know if the boy's parents approved journalizing his living history so others may benefit."

Ben was taken aback at Baldwin's sudden and pointed question regarding one of his patients. He cleared his throat and looked Baldwin in the eye. "Well, Doctor Baldwin, let me first say that I'm a bit surprised that you're asking about a specific patient...of mine, that at the outset...one year ago, I made perfectly clear that I would not discuss his case outwardly." Horowitz went on, "You said it yourself; it has been a year...and yes, I have received the required approval from the boy's parents. May I ask why you're bringing this up now?"

Baldwin's face began to redden, "Uh, forgive my brashness, Doctor. I guess I was a little too forward with that question, but I am interested in that patient's case, and to be frank...you seem to have been quite secretive about it."

Horowitz knew Baldwin well, and knew he was looking for information...not for the sake of science and other patients, but for what he could do with it. He smiled at Baldwin and turned his head toward Petrillo. "Is this something that is on your mind too, George?"

Petrillo's face reddened a bit as he looked up from his notepad. "Well, it is an interesting plan and research effort, considering the rarity of the disorder. Of course, I'd be interested in gleaning any information I can for the sake of future circumstances where my own patients are concerned."

Horowitz smiled, "I see, and do you plan on treating a patient with such a rare disorder any time soon?

"No, Ben. I'm just curious."

Horowitz cleared his throat, "Well, gentlemen. The information I have on Joey Hall," he paused and corrected himself, "it's actually Joe Hall now. The boy is growing up, and his history is still confidential per the parent's request. I can tell you I have a written history of everything he has done or wants to do. It's three inches thick at this time...a compilation of his life before he came to me and up to this point in time. It includes areas he's succeeded in, failed at, tried, future interests...everything." The doctor leaned forward over the conference table. "It's about everything that makes him Joe Hall. Included in all of those areas are worries, fears, an active imagination, emotions, goals, and regrets. The list goes on…a detailed living history of an entire person…detailed and exact. It shall remain," he shifted his gaze back to Baldwin, "secret…as you have already mentioned."

Howard Baldwin shot back quickly. "Let me remind you Doctor, that we are partners in a medical practice and should be privy to information as sensitive as what you describe."

Horowitz was already onto Baldwin. "When I am satisfied that I know exactly what I'm dealing with, and completely confident of the disorder's origin, its symptoms and its cure, I will make it known to the medical public as well as to the patients and/or their parents." He turned back toward Petrillo, "If either of you happen to come across a similar case, I'd be happy to offer my advice of what I know to this point, but Joe Hall's personal information will remain in my file cabinet."

An awkward and uncomfortable moment engulfed the room. Not a word was said until Horowitz was satisfied the two doctors were ready to move on. "Okay, I hope we're all on the same page now. Let's move on to some other concerns or questions.

Doctor Baldwin continued to be highly irritated and wasn't ready to move on. He felt as if Horowitz was holding back information that might be good for his future in neuroscience. He stared at his notepad and thought, *There are other ways of getting to that history. Horowitz has only a few years before retirement and then he has to pass that file on to Petrillo or me. I've got make sure it falls into my hands. I'll use Petrillo to leverage that in my direction.*

Dr. Horowitz saw the deep thought Baldwin was in. "Howard, are you with us? Is everything okay?"

"Oh, sorry. Yes, I'm fine. I was just considering some things that I'm not comfortable with that involve alliances with other neurology departments in the region."

Horowitz replied, "Okay, good subject. Let's discuss that."

The three doctors went on with their discussion regarding procedures and changing protocols for the next hour. Finally, it was time to bring the meeting to an end since all three doctors were due to meet patients.

Horowitz ended the meeting. "Okay, gentlemen. I think that will do it for this month. We covered a lot of ground and cleared the air about some things, but I feel it was a productive two hours. We all have other places to be, so let's adjourn to our offices...and remember, I am always open for advice or to share an opinion."

The doctors picked up their notes and left the conference room together.

CHAPTER 25

Eighth grade had been a wonderful year. Joey was growing up. His daily workouts with his dad continued and his positivity and multitude of interests continued to grow. It was time to open his beloved pool and continue his high-speed dashes through the woods with reckless abandon. Everything was falling into place with a lighter focus on his disorder. That fact alone relaxed the boy. He wasn't comfortable with other people, even family members, considering his personal problems on a continual basis... especially, if it was something that might be considered a weakness or a personal flaw.

Joey continued his private trips out to his favorite tree next to the abandoned field and thought about incidents that had long since passed but still plagued his memory. The time alone out in the woods allowed him to consider his plan for retribution. He thought about the people and unnecessary and embarrassing incidents in his past and what he could do to at least make himself be more accepting of what had happened. Memories of Mrs. Talbot...his fourth-grade teacher, Mr. Flanigan...the fifth-grade gym teacher, Burt Tuttle...the bully in sixth grade,

Mr. Willabe...his shop teacher, and some of the scenarios these people were responsible for initiating.

Should he continue to dwell on these unfortunate episodes in his past or should he forget them and consider the ignorance and unthinking behavior of these people. He looked into a clear blue sky as he considered every one of those incidents and every one of those people, and everything they did and said. He remembered the incidents as if they had happened yesterday. He thought, *I know they didn't know about my disorder or what it really was, but I'm still pissed at how they handled it.*

After a while, Joey came to the conclusion that the only person he really wanted to show what he was really made of was Coach Flanigan. He would write Mrs. Talbot off as a bad memory and an evil person. He figured she'd get her due someday. He had already faced off with sixth grade bully Burt Tuttle and shamed him, but Flanigan and Willabe would need to be shown the errors of their ways. Joey didn't want anything bad to happen to these people, but deep down, felt a need to show them who he really was and how wrong they were to do what they did.

The first person he considered was Coach Flanigan. The man had embarrassed him in front of the entire fifth and sixth grades during a push up test. Joey thought about who he was now and worked with that. *Hmmm, Flanigan is a big high school football coach now at our rival school in Montauk. He's getting pretty well known because his teams keep winning the conference title. Maybe, I can get good enough to take his team down when my team finally plays his. After freshman football, I've got three years to make first string on the high school team. Hmmm, that might be one way.* Joey smiled to himself and pictured the moment his team beat Flanigan's, and how he'd walk up to the brash coach and say, 'Nice try...I'm Joe Hall, remember me?'

His thoughts then turned to shop teacher, Mr. Willabe. Joe still felt a certain dislike for the man, but mostly because of his brash behavior with everyone. He finally concluded that he was just an ignorant man and never considered the effect of his actions on anyone he spoke to. He'd find out one way or another, but maybe someday when Joe was an adult, he could explain to the man what he had put him through. To embarrass him as an adult, face to face, with no one else present, might be the way to go. For now, Joey decided to let it be and do his best at everything he tried. He'd wait to see if he ever crossed paths with Tuttle or Willabe again, and then make a decision about how to handle it. For now, it was fun to think about what the possibilities were, and it was really up to him about what he could do about it.

Joe pushed the memories to the back of his mind and went back to considering the upcoming summer. There were going to be days at the lake swimming, fishing, sailing, and more workouts in the woods and in his pool. Of course, there was the other part...the work part. Mowing the lawn, vacuuming the pool, washing the cars...that would be there too. But there would be family picnics and days at the beach to look forward to.

He got up from under his tree and began to walk back through the woods. This time, he chose to walk along the old familiar path. Eventually, his thoughts drifted back to his recollections of the incidents and people he had just been considering, and suddenly realized, *Hey! I have always been in a group or with at least with one other person when I experienced a spell. I've never had a spell when I've been alone!*

This was a huge revelation. An individual with Joe's disorder always knew when they had just experienced a spell or episode, as the doctors now began to refer to them. The patient never had a warning as to when the episode was about to happen, but they always knew when they just had one. Joey in his young mind knew this was valuable information. *I gotta' get home and tell Mom and Dad so they can tell Doctor Horowitz. This is important!*

Joey broke into a run. He didn't know how it would help, but he knew it was something that none of the doctors had ever asked or talked about before.

It was just after five PM and Frank had just pulled into the driveway. Joey saw him as he neared the wood's tree line. He shouted to his father, "Hey, Dad! Wait."

Frank looked toward the woods and saw his son running toward him. He waited until Joey was right in front of him. "Just finishing up another workout, Joe?"

Joey was out of breath. "Yeah, kind of…I got some important news. Where's Mom?"

Frank smiled as he walked to the kitchen door. "Let's find out." The two walked through the kitchen door to find Ginny preparing dinner.

"Mom! We have to talk…right now."

Ginny turned to meet Joey with a startled look. She put down the pot she was drying and sat down at the table.

Frank remained standing, and Joey described his revelation to his concerned parents.

When Joey finished, they turned toward each other with confused expressions. Neither of them had ever considered what Joey was trying to tell them. They both felt like they had missed something they should have considered long ago.

Ginny put her hand on Joey's arm. "How did you come to think about such a thing, Joe? What were you doing when you realized this?"

Joey explained he had been thinking about some of the things that had happened in the past and something must have triggered that realization.

Frank finally sat down. "Well, how can you be sure, Joe? I mean…if you're by yourself. There's no one around that could tell you if you had one or not."

Joey felt frustrated at Frank's doubting attitude. "Dad, it's something I never thought about before…until today. I always know when I've had a spell. I never needed anyone to tell me that!" He paused as he looked into his father's eyes. "It's a clue as to what makes them happen…don't you see? I don't have them when I'm alone!"

Ginny smiled. She realized the importance of what Joey was saying. "I get it, Joe. I'm going to write this down in our notebook to bring to Doctor Horowitz for our next meeting.

That night, Joey laid in bed thinking about the afternoon, and what he'd discovered about himself as he considered the past and what he'd been through. *If I only have these episodes when I'm around other people, can it be that I'm not really comfortable around others? Do other people make me nervous?* Joey thought about that for a minute, and couldn't come up with an answer. *I never thought I was nervous around my buddies, Jeff or Nate. I always felt pretty calm around those guys. Is it that, I'm so worried about other people liking me...or that they won't like me, that I worry about losing them as a friend?* Then he thought about groups of people. *I think I'm always worried that I'm not going to fit in with everyone else.* He paused and nodded his head, *Yeah, so there it is...I'm not comfortable in a group.* Then Joey remembered how uncomfortable he felt taking the bus to and from school, and how he chose to walk home every day instead of being a part of the raucous behavior on the bus. *That must be what makes it happen. I'm so worried about not being accepted or teased if I'm not accepted, that I get myself all worked up.*

Joey nodded his head and smirked. *That's got to be it! That's why I'm so comfortable out in the woods...where no one can get to me...where no one can see me or judge me.* He thought a little more and came to a conclusion in his thirteen year-old mind. *Some of this is emotional! I should be able to control that! Now that I know, maybe I can work on that.* Then he realized, *It was also how I saw myself compared to other people! I have to build more confidence, and sports is one of the ways to do it.*

Joey considered that point for a while and remembered what Dr. Horowitz kept saying. *Confidence! He keeps talking about doing things to build my confidence. If I'm confident about what I'm doing, or where I am, or who I'm with...the problem will be less likely to happen.*

He thought about the past year and how working out had transformed his life and physical appearance. To many people, both family and friends, he had become unrecognizeable. His demeanor was different too. He had become more reserved and distant...especially in groups.

He lay back on his pillow and realized where his life was going...where it had to go, and that sports and exercise were going to be a part of his life from now on.

CHAPTER 26

Joey's eighth grade summer continued with all the exuberance it had begun with. Things were great, but on a different level than ever before. His spirits were up, his workouts were improving, and he enjoyed varying some of those sessions with other activities. All of his summer activities were at the forefront of his mind and he looked for new and interesting ways to perform them.

One day, Joey climbed into his above ground pool for a workout using the swimming harness his father made that enabled him to swim in place. He put it on and swam out to it's tether's extension and started his in-place swimming work out. As he swam, his thoughts drifted back to his new found revelation about his disorder and his plan to conquer it. Unconsciously, Joey began to swim harder. The power strokes were from his arms only, as his feet were secured to a rope line attached to a tree by the side of the pool. The more Joey thought, the harder he pulled against the water.

Joey's best friends, Jeff and Nate showed up unexpectedly and stood watching their friend as he swam. The boys were amazed as the tree attached to Joey's harness continued to bend inward toward the pool. The rope from the tree seemed so taught that the fibers looked as if they'd snap at any moment, and now exuded a light humming sound as they were stretched to their ultimate strength.

Jeff squinted and bared his teeth as if in pain, "Is he mad about something? I talked to him this morning and he seemed fine."

Nate answered without taking his eyes off the thrashing body in the pool. "I don't think so. I saw him after he finished his wild run through the woods about an hour ago. He just looked hot and out of breath."

Joey swam harder and harder as he considered the session of a few days ago by the abandoned field. Finally, the rope from his harness to the tree snapped and the bent tree whipped the broken line from the water and out of the pool. Joey, now untethered to a stationary object, shot forward and into the side of the pool. He stood up and shook the water from his head. He looked up to see Jeff and Nate. "Hey, guys. How long have you been standing there? You should have stopped me."

Jeff smiled, "Not a chance. You were thrashing that water so hard we knew something was gonna' give."

Joey grabbed the side of the pool and lifted himself from the water, swinging his legs over the pool's side.

He shook his head to the right one more time to shed the remaining water that dripped from his wavy brown hair. Jeff and Nate watched as a tanned, muscular body approached them...someone that looked and acted totally different only two years ago. Joe now stood at 5'-9 inches tall and weighed 135 pounds.

Nate shook his head as he watched Joey approach. "What happened to you, man? You're not the same person

I knew...even a year ago., and all you ever want to do is work out. What is goin' on?

Jeff saw his opportunity and added, "Yeah. Nate's right, Joe. It's like your obsessed with all this exercise stuff." He shot a finger out and poked Joey in the stomach. "Hard as a rock! What are you doing...trying out for the Olympics or something?"

Joey smirked and grabbed his towel that hung from a nearby tree branch. "Nope. I'm just getting into shape for ninth grade football next fall." He paused a moment and added, "There's going to be a swim team at the new high school too, but that's a couple of years off."

Nate nodded his head. "What's with that wild running routine you've been doing in the woods? I've never seen anyone do anything like that! You're gonna' slam into a tree or impale yourself on a stick. What's with that?"

Joe finished toweling off. "It's called 'extreme running.' Sometimes I do it while carrying my football. It's good for agility and balance at extreme speed. It'll also be good for track in the spring."

Nate chuckled, "So you are training for the Olympics.

"C'mon guys. I have the perfect set up here...right in my backyard. I'm just workin' out. When you guys aren't around, this is what I do." Joey paused and smiled, "Of course, you're welcome to join me, anytime."

Nate turned his head away and slapped the air in Joey's direction.

Jeff squinted at Joey and said, "I can't believe you. We have the whole summer off and you're spending all this time working out in the woods."

Joey shrugged his shoulders. "This is me now. You can

join me or we can get together at other times." He paused as he thought about last week. "Wait a minute, I played baseball with you guys twice last week and once the week before. What about that?"

Nate picked up on that, "Yeah, I meant to talk to you about that. I was on the receiving end of all those hardball pitches. You don't have to throw that hard. It's just sandlot baseball around here."

"Sorry, Nate. Guess I was just having a good day."

There was an awkward quiet for a few moments, so Joey took his wet towel, twisted it, and snapped it at Jeff, hitting him in the bare leg just above the knee.

"Oww! You asshole! Shit! Look at that welt!"

Joe wound up again and snapped his towel at Nate. Unfortunately, Nate turned just as Joey snapped it, and the towel struck him square in the back. "Damn it, Joe! That friggin' hurts!"

Joey accomplished what he set out to do. He had changed the subject and got their minds going in a different direction. Joey got into a defensive crouch and kind of danced around…his hands extended out toward Nate and Jeff. "Come on boys…come and get me." The two friends cocked their heads to one side as they considered Joey's invitation. Joey continued. "Come on. What're you go do now?" Joey snapped the towel at the two boys again.

Jeff and Nate started for Joey as he had anticipated. Joey turned and dove over the side of the pool, with Jeff and Nate in hot pursuit. They all wrestled in the water dunking each other, laughing, and threatening whoever had the advantage.

After Jeff and Nate had left for home in their wet clothes, Joey lay in the sun on a towel he had stretched out on the ground. He closed his eyes and smiled as he thought about his two friends and how he'd turned their serious conversation into fun. He smiled again as he realized that most of his friends that came to see him usually left his house soaking wet.

Eventually, his thoughts drifted back to his plan for the summer. His main focus was on making the junior high school's ninth grade football team in the fall, and track team in the spring. He also realized that he had begun to excel in math and in english last year, and he was developing an interest in outer space and astronomy. Reading was also on his mind, and for now couldn't get enough books that featured naval stories about World War Two. *I'm going to be something*, he thought. *I want to be good at a lot of things…not just one…like that former president, Thomas Jefferson.* He thought about his love for ships and the sea and wondered about the future. *I gotta' pick something for a career though and right now, I think I want to be on a ship…in the Navy.* Joey thought about that for a minute and suddenly became concerned. *First, I gotta' get over this petit mal thing… or whatever they're calling it now. Dad says they'll never take me if I've got something like that…no matter how good of shape I'm in or how smart I am.* Joey nodded his head as he lay there with his eyes closed. *I don't know if he's just worried about me leaving home or if he's just protecting me because he doesn't want to see me fail.* He thought about that for a moment and made up his mind. *Well, it's not about him…or Mom. It's my life and it's up to me to make it happen.*

At that moment in the sun, in the comfort of his own back yard, Joey made a promise to himself that he'd work as hard as he could to be want he wanted to be...despite his past or what others might want for him. He would do it his way.

CHAPTER 27

Joey's summer proceeded with occasional trips to the lake to go waterskiing and sailing, or visits to the river for a day of fishing, but always ended with a workout at night when the temperature was cooler. After an hour-long session with his loose weights, Joey ran through the neighborhood streets…sometimes with his father following close behind on a bicycle. The darkness, highlighted by the street lamps, was calming and the humid air rushing against his sweating body provided a natural cooling effect. He kept a good, steady pace breathing in on the first three steps and exhaling on the fourth. The oxygen entering his lungs was exhilarating and enticed him to go faster, but he focused on maintaining a steady pace. It was a peaceful time.

One June afternoon, Joey called a classmate he hadn't seen in a while and asked if he was interested in going to the annual town fair. "Hey, Mike. It's Joey Hall. How's your summer going?"

"Hey, Joe. It's been kind of boring so far…kinda' slow."

Joey continued, "Want to go to the Fourth of July Fair on Saturday night? Everybody in town will probably be there. There's going to be a lot of game booths, an arcade, music, and lots of food. There'll probably be some girls from school there too. Might be fun."

Mike agreed to Joey's offer and the two planned to meet at the corner of Mike's street and walk the remaining two miles to the fair. Joey ended the call, "Okay, see you at 6:30 by Tanglewood Lane and Maple Street." He hung up the phone and smiled. *Maybe we'll bump into some of our friends from school.*

It was Saturday night July 2nd and Joey and Mike entered the town's fairgrounds. The fairgrounds were packed with town folk of all ages. The boys immediately scanned the area for people they knew, but it was too congested to pick anyone out yet. The sun was setting, and the fair's Italian lights began to light up, increasing the festive atmosphere. As the boys walked through the gate, they passed the beer tent. There was a lot of loud talking and laughing accompanied by expletives of all kinds. Joey looked at Mike. "Seems kind of rowdy in there. Why do those people have to drink so much? They just get rowdier and until all they want to do is fight."

"I don't know, Joe. They're just celebrating in their own way, I guess."

Joey suggested they take a spin around the fair to see who or what was around. The boys passed some of the game booths and watched as some of the booth attendants conned innocent people into going another round, and smiled greedily as they took the patrons' money. Soon, the boys passed the rides and vowed they'd be back to spend some time there. Finally, they reached the far end of the fair and began to cross the grassy field to start down the fair's other end. There were no booths, and consequently, the area was darker than what they had just experienced, with only a few people that also passed between the fair's two ends of tents and game booths.

Joey walked with his head down, listening to Mike as he spoke about the fireworks scheduled for later that night. Suddenly, Joey was jolted backward by a violent and aggressive shove against his chest. He caught his balance and looked up to see an intoxicated Spanish looking man threatening him with his bared fists. "C'mon man! Let's go...you and me. Let me see what you got."

The man appeared to be in his mid-twenties, had a mustache, and glared at Joey, as if he had done something wrong. The man continued, "I'm gonna' kick your ass. C'mon. Come and get me."

Joey looked around and noticed Mike was gone. He was alone and encircled by more of the attacker's gang, obviously, every one of them drunk. They all began to taunt Joey and urge him to fight. Outside of the group of attackers were another group of onlookers with their children or dates. Everyone just stared at Joey. No one moved or said anything. His mind raced. He knew had to make a decision quickly...and it had to be the right one.

Joey raised his arms in a semi-protective manner and asked himself, *We were just crossing the field to the other side of the fair. What happened? What happened to Mike? He was just here.*

The drunken attacker continued to jeer Joey and the group around him began to close in on him. Joey looked beyond the circle of aggressors and noticed a middle aged man holding a little boy's hand. He seemed to have positioned himself deliberately behind the man that threatened Joey, and stared into Joey's eyes. His face seemed to give him a message. Joey looked back at his group of assailants...the meanness apparent in their eyes and taunts. He thought, *I can take this skinny drunk easily, but as soon as I do, his buddies around me are going to pounce on me, and I can't fight all of them at once.* He looked back at the man holding his son's hand. He seemed to be saying something like, *Don't do it*, although Joey couldn't hear all of it.

Joey made his decision. He turned and walked away from the group of angry drunks. Once he was well clear of the circle of aggressors, he began to look for Mike. As he scanned the fairgrounds, he began to question what had happened. The last thing he remembered was that he and Mike were crossing the field between the rows of fairground tents and Mike was right by his side. There was a sudden and violent shove, almost knocking him off his feet by someone who wanted to fight...and Mike was nowhere to be found. He began to question his own actions, *Did I have an episode as we crossed the field? Did I do something to piss those guys off? Could I have crossed in front of them and cut them off, or unknowingly walked through their group?*

Joey considered those thoughts for a moment and then dismissed them. He realized he always knew if he had experienced an episode and he also knew the episodes only lasted for about three seconds, so what could he have done that was so bad in such a short period of time. Joey came to the conclusion nothing had happened. It was just an unfortunate circumstance where he was suddenly confronted with a group of intoxicated guys looking for a fight. Mike must have somehow got clear of the angry group and fled the scene when he detected a bad situation.

Eventually, Joey spotted Mike by a game booth watching people throw darts at colored balloons. "Hey, Mike! What happened? Where did you go?"

"Uh, what do you mean? I've been standing here for a while waiting for you."

Joey gave Mike a questioning glance and pointed toward the end of the fairgrounds. "We were crossing from one side of the fair to the other and you were telling me about that girl you're interested in, and suddenly you were gone."

Mike's face flushed, "I don't know, Joe. I guess we got separated in the crowd."

Joey stared at Mike for a moment and said nothing. *He's covering up for leaving me with that gang of drunks. Okay, I guess I can't depend on this guy. This'll be the last time I go anywhere with him. I'll let it go for now.*

After Mike's reply and obvious desertion, the night didn't matter anymore. The boys walked over to the music area and listened to the band for a while, but both boys knew the night was over. It was obvious Mike was embarrassed about leaving Joey with an angry gang. And on the other hand, Joey felt let down. He believed in friendships and trust. How could there be any alliance with someone who could leave a friend in time of trouble.

"Ah, I've had enough, Mike. Let's get out of here."

Mike was quick to reply, "Yeah, me too. I'm out of money anyway."

The boys walked through the fair's gate and began

their walk home. Neither had much to say. When they reached Tanglewood Lane, Joey just kept walking, waved his hand in the air and said, "See ya.' Have a nice summer."

Mike stopped and stood by the side of the road surprised by Joey's insensitive departure, and watched him walk away. He understood why, but couldn't find the strength to admit what he'd done or apologize for it.

Joey walked home in the darkness, alone with his thoughts and disillusioned by his friend's behavior.

In the morning, Joey sat at the kitchen table eating cereal and stared out the window. He thought of how his friend had left him the night before, and when confronted with it, never said a word about it...like it never happened. He went back through the entire scenario, beginning when they had reached the end of the long line of game booths and attractions and started to cross the vacant field to begin their walk down the other side of game booths. Mike had been talking about a girl he liked, and Joey was walking alongside him with his head down. The lights of the fair were in his peripheral vision as well as all the normal sounds of the fair and distant 'people noise', like laughing and shouting. It was dark, but dimly illuminated by the distant fairground lighting. Suddenly, he was surprised by a violent shove to his upper chest. Someone had approached him and forcefully pushed him backward. He felt the force against his chest muscles and struggled to keep his balance as he stumbled backward. The fair and its associated attributes had never left his conscious mind. As he regained his footing and looked up, he experienced further surprise to see an angry, intoxicated Spanish man with fists bared, ready to fight. What had happened? Was it just an unfortunate meeting with an unruly gang of intoxicated guys causing Mike to show his true colors and flee in the presence of danger? Was Mike really a coward? Did he misjudge his friend and should he judge a friend under such terrible conditions? Joey also questioned his own actions and decision. Did he do the right thing by walking away from the angry gang and crowd of onlookers?

Then something occurred to him. He had done nothing to provoke the situation. The behavior of an unruly group of intoxicated guys were causing him to question who he was and what he really was about.

Joey went through the scenario in his mind several more times. He had been completely cognizant of his surroundings and his current situation. He considered everything that could have happened, as he had been concentrating on Mike's presence and what he had been saying.

His mom came in from sweeping the garage breaking his concentration. "Hi, Joe. Did you have fun last night?"

"Uh, it was okay. You know…same old thing."

Ginny stopped and raised her eyebrows. "Well, there'll be a lot more of them to come and someday you'll be bringing a girlfriend. That will make it seem like a whole different thing. You'll see."

Joey nodded his head as he continued to stare out the window.

CHAPTER 28

July passed and Joey eventually put the fair behind him. It was time to get on with his summer. The situation at the fair had not left him, but he relegated himself to the idea that he had made the right choice and it was just an unfortunate circumstance that he experienced.

Soon, Joey was back to his regular summer routine, working out, playing baseball, enjoying morning runs through the forest and nightly jogs through the neighborhood. His dad had replaced the broken swimming harness allowing him to continue his workouts in the pool. Life was back to normal.

Finally, fall arrived. Joey was going back to the big junior high school that had taken on a different association in his mind. It was no longer a place to be wary of. It was a place to see his friends, study some of the subjects that he yearned for, and a place to play organized sports.

Ginny reminded Joey as the first week of school approached. "Remember, Joe. We have an appointment with Doctor Horowitz next week. He's going to want to talk about your summer and what you discovered that day about not having episodes when you're by yourself. I think he'll be so happy to hear that kind of information...and you know that will be important enough to put down in your medical history file."

Joey nodded his head but said nothing. His thoughts were on the try outs for the ninth-grade football team. *I hope that appointment doesn't interfere with any of my football tryouts. I don't even know when they'll be yet.*

The week passed slowly, and Joey found himself back at the junior high school. The first week was more of the usual getting used to a new class schedule, teachers, and friends.

Finally, the first scheduled gym class came. Joey rushed down to the locker room and changed for class. Coach Murray walked in and leaned against the far set of lockers. "Hey, Joe. Looks like you've been working out. How was your summer?"

"It was great coach. I used my loose weights every other night...except for weekends." Joey looked up from tying his sneakers and gave the coach a sheepish smile. "Did a lot of running and swimming too."

"It shows, Joe. I want to see you out there for football tryouts next week...okay?"

"Joey nodded his head and smiled. "I'll be there, Coach."

It was Saturday and Joey woke up to his mother's voice. "Come on, Joe. Time to get up. We have to meet with Doctor Horowitz at 10:00 o'clock. You have an hour to wash up and eat breakfast."

Joey stared at the ceiling for a moment. *Oh yeah. Doctor H, at ten. Shit! Saturday morning too! Oh well, at least it won't interfere with football tryouts this week.* He rolled over and out of bed. *Let's get this over with.*

Soon Joey and his mom were sitting before Doctor Horowitz. The aging surgeon looked up from his desk and smiled. "Good morning, folks. I'm just finishing up on some of the notes attached to Joey's file. It'll only be a minute." He smiled again and nodded at Joey. It was obvious he was happy to see the boy.

Joey watched the doctor's hands as he read his file and wrote notes in the margin. The man still used a pencil with an eraser. He seemed to be an 'old school' sort of guy, but very gentle and down to earth. Joe liked him a lot and identified with his short gray hair, hollow cheek bones and wire rimmed glasses. He hadn't changed in all the years Joey had been going to him.

Finally, Doctor Horowitz looked up at Joey. "Well, Joe. It says here that you've made a sort of a...discovery. It's something that even the best doctors around didn't know about these...episodes." The doctor squinted at Joey and pursed his lips. "We still don't know a lot about this disorder, so I'm told we are once again changing its name. Now, we are referring to what we called spells or episodes, as seizures."

Joey quickly interrupted the doctor, "But Doctor H, I don't have seizures. I just have kind of a...short daydream. Nothing happens except for a short period of staring."

"I know, Joe...I know. I just have to refer to it that way in the current medically approved and acceptable terminology, so the rest of the medical society...and by that, I mean anyone reading your medical file will know what I'm referring to."

The doctor sat back in his chair and took his glasses off. "You know Joe, the name of something is not to be feared or ignored. It's just a description...a label. It's got nothing to do with what your disorder is or how it behaves. You've got to learn that. Don't let the medical profession's names for things get you down."

Ginny added, "I agree with Joey, Doctor. For something as mild as what Joey has, it seems to be a harsh...label."

Horowitz nodded his head. I agree, but it's not up to me. It just goes to show you how much they don't know about it yet."

Doctor Horowitz cleared his throat and glanced back at Joey's file. He looked back at Joey and smiled warmly. "Joe, tell me about how you came to realize the fact that you are never alone when you experience a...seizure."

Joey went through the entire scenario of that day out in the woods, by his favorite tree, and how he had been considering some of the incidents over the past years, and how some of the people had reacted to his situation. It became apparent to the boy that in every instance, he had been in a group situation or accompanied by at least one other individual.

Doctor Horowitz smiled and wrote down what Joey had just described. "You know Joe, what you have described is, in fact, one of the missing links to this disorder. We know some of the triggers for a seizure are nervousness, excitability, anxiety, and sorrow...but no one has ever thought to consider the patient and what he experiences when he's alone. This is valuable information! It opens a lot of avenues for us. "I'm going to have to study it and see how it fits into several areas. Although, the disorder is not completely emotion based, this information will get us closer to controlling the triggers. Thank you." Doctor Horowitz reached across the desk and shook Joey's hand.

Ginny interrupted, "Sooo, does this mean we should isolate him from groups of people and public events, and things where he could become nervous or anxious?"

Joey shot his mother a quick glance. The doctor noticed the boy's reaction and quickly answered. "Absolutely not! Not in the most remote way. He is coming through this thing quite well, and that in part, has a lot to do with his new sports interests which include large groups of people… either audiences or team mates. In fact, I get the feeling that Joe has got to the point where he may be thinking he can't, or doesn't want to spend the time thinking about this… disorder anymore."

Ginny and the doctor turned their attention to Joey. Ginny dipped her head in a questioning way and said, "Joey?"

Joey nodded his head in agreement to what the doctor had just explained. "He's right mom. I'm sick of the whole thing. I just want to go out and do whatever I want to do without having you and dad wondering whether I should because of this thing…or if I'm gonna' get hurt because of it. I can do anything any other kid my age can do…and I'm going to."

Doctor Horowitz nodded and smiled broadly at the boy as he sat back in his chair. "He's on the road to beating this problem. Let him be."

CHAPTER 29

It was the second week of the new school year. Joey was in the ninth grade and eligible to play freshman football. He passed by the gym every day to see if tryouts had been posted yet. Finally, one day at the beginning of history class, his best friend Jim Fulton burst into the class just before the bell rang. "Hey Joe! They've posted sign-ups for football. They're on the wall by the locker rooms. You're gonna' do it …right?"

Joey smiled broadly. "Really? That's great! I'll go down there next period."

Jim was excited and smiled as he spoke. "What position are you going for? I'm trying out for Center.

Joey nodded his head, "Halfback. I'm going for halfback."

Jim smiled and slapped Joe on the shoulder. "We're finally gonna' get to do it!" Suddenly, Jim's face became serious. "You realize, there's gonna' be cuts. I hear Coach Murray is pretty tough."

Joey nodded his head and suddenly felt vulnerable. *Aww crap. I forgot about cuts. What if I don't make it? It'll be like Youth Football all over again. My dad will be so embarrassed.*

Jim was waiting for Joey to answer. Finally, Joey looked into his friend's eyes, "Cuts...huh? Crap, I forgot about that." His face had suddenly become serious.

Jim saw the change in Joey's face. "Ah, you've got nothing to worry about. Just do your thing out there. You're faster and stronger than anyone I know going for a 'back' position."

The bell rang and Jim had to take his seat in the class. "Okay, we'll talk later."

Joey looked down at his desk, *Damn it! Why do they have to have cuts anyway? It's not like the whole school is trying out. I hate this competition thing.* The boy's afternoon was ruined. He spent the afternoon worrying about making the team and he knew worry and anxiety were two of the triggers that initiated his episodes.

That evening as the Hall family sat down to dinner everyone noticed that Joey was quieter than usual. Frank got Ginny's attention and nodded his head in Joey's direction in a questioning manner. Ginny nodded back to indicate her awareness.

"Hey, Joey! Did they post football tryouts yet?" Frank gave the boy a quick glance and went back to cutting his pork chop.

Joey looked up at his dad and smiled. "Oh, yeah. I signed up for tryouts after history class. I'm on the list. Tryouts are Wednesday after school."

Frank gave Ginny another glance and then back to Joey. "Well, finally! You must be excited about that?"

Joey didn't look up. He just nodded his head as he looked down at his plate. "Yup!"

Frank glanced back at Ginny wondering if he should

pursue the issue and Ginny shook her head slightly and mouthed, *not now*. They let the subject drop for the time being, knowing it would surface again.

Later that night, Joey was unable to sleep as he thought about Wednesday's tryouts. The room was dark, as he stared at the ceiling above with his hands folded behind his head. *Everyone says it should be easy for me....that I should make it with no problem.* He thought about his dad's comment after dinner, *"You've got no worries! For Pete's sake, you've been working out hard every day for three years now! Do you think any of those other guys having been doing that? I'm tellin' ya' Joe, you don't have a problem. Just go in there, do what they tell you, do your best, and you'll be on the team."*

Meanwhile, Ginny and Frank sat in the living room discussing Joey's concerns. They knew their son, and realized he was stressing about making the team. Frank shrugged and shook his head from side to side. "He still hasn't got any confidence...still, after all the progress he's made. Hell, just picture him against the regular ninth grader...there's no comparison."

Ginny was more concerned about his emotional aspect. "I know he has the ability, Frank. It's the triggers I'm worried about. If he's overly concerned about making the team, and it's making him nervous, it could impair any progress he's made up to now. Maybe we should tell him that's it's okay if he wants to forget about trying out."

Frank answered quickly, "No, damn it! He signed up to do it, and by God, he's going to try! Doctor H said not to coddle him. We're not going to push him either, but we have to see him through this. He dwells on everything too much. He overthinks everything until he gets himself all worked up."

Ginny was quiet for a moment and then asked, "Why do you think he feels it's so important for him to make the team?

"Frank looked surprised. "Because he wants to play football for the junior high school team."

Ginny lowered her eyes as she continued, "Do you think it has anything to do with our reaction to what happened a few years ago when he tried out for the town's sixth grade team…remember, Youth Football?" She paused and let out an exasperated breath. "I know he felt he embarrassed you in front of the other fathers, and I didn't handle it so well either because of his weight at the time."

Frank eyed Ginny, "What are you saying?"

"I'm saying that maybe he's trying to prove something to us and it's really not making the football team…to play football. His goal is to show us he can do it."

Frank shook his head again. "No, I don't think that. He left the tryout that day to change his ripped pants. I told him he'd get cut."

Ginny slapped her knees with both hands, "That's just it, Frank! They didn't cut him! You just didn't want to take him back to the tryout because of how you felt about the situation." She paused, "He's been living with that memory all this time. What do you think all the extreme work outs are about?" She paused, "It's all about that and what he perceives what we think about it."

Frank looked up and into Ginny's eyes, "So actually, it's us and our reactions that are causing his anxiety and lack of confidence over making the team."

Ginny lowered her head and nodded. "I think so, Frank."

Wednesday finally arrived and the day's classes seemed to pass faster than the usual school day. At ten minutes to 2:00 PM an announcement was made over the school's PA system. ALL NINTH GRADE BOYS INTERESTED IN TRYING OUT FOR THIS YEAR'S FOOTBALL TEAM SHOULD REPORT DIRECTLY TO THE GYMNASIUM FOR A SHORT MEETING WITH COACH MURRAY TO BE FOLLOWED BY TWO HOURS OF EXERCISE AND SKILLS ASSESSMENT ON THE FOOTBALL FIELD.

Soon the final bell rang. Joey and a few friends headed for the gymnasium to meet Coach Murray. The boys joked and teased each other in nervous excitement as they walked the long corridors that led to the gym. Everyone spoke excitedly about what it would be like to wear the school's red and white uniform, and run out onto the field in front of admiring fans. It was going to be great. People cheering, the band playing, and cheerleaders spurring them on. Joey was quiet and just walked along with the nervous bunch.

The new football candidates were directed into a far corner of the huge gymnasium by one of the assistant coaches. Mr. Daly pointed toward the gym's double doors, "Through those doors, boys. Don't dress yet. Just go on out onto the gym floor and wait for Coach Murray. He'll be out in a few minutes."

Little by little, a crowd of eager thirteen and fourteen-year-old boys began to fill the corner of the gymnasium.

Joey and a few of his friends wandered around and shared worries with other incumbents. A tall, lean, blond haired lad asked Joey, "What position are you going out for?"

"Halfback. Right or left half...as long as I'm in the backfield."

The blonde-haired boy looked Joey up and down and smirked, so his judging was obvious. "Halfback? You're gonna' get mopped up! You gotta' be about 125 pounds soaking wet."

Joey tipped his head to one side and considered the boy's size. *What's he talking about? He's only about 120 and not very muscular. Must be trying to scare me out of that position.* "I'm 135 and I'm not worried about it."

The other boy shrugged his shoulders and walked away.

The group of incumbent players had grown to about sixty souls before Murray walked in. Unbeknownst to the group of boys, there were only 35 slots available. Suddenly, the shrill sound of a whistle cut the air. Coach Eric Murray walked through the double doors. "Everyone on the bleachers! Let's go...and listen up. If you talk while I'm talking, you're gone."

Everyone hurried over to the bleachers and jockeyed for a seat close to the bottom level. Murray waited until everyone was settled and continued, "I'm Coach Murray and that is how you will refer to me during tryouts and if you make this ballclub. I want you to show Assistant Coach Daly your permission slips and get to the locker room to change into your gym shorts and sneakers as fast as you can. Be out by the track in ten minutes. I'm going to kick your asses with calisthenics followed by laps and sprints. Any late comers are cut. Go!

The bleachers emptied quickly accompanied by a lot of pounding feet from people jumping to the floor and scuffling along the bleacher seats.

Joey rushed into the locker room after dropping off his permission slip to Coach Daly and frantically searched for an empty locker. He looked up at the clock on the wall. He had eight minutes left. Everyone pushed and shoved as they dressed. Joey was one of the last to finish dressing and slammed his locker shut as he broke into a run for the track.

Murray waited at the side of the track holding his stopwatch. He was a big man of six foot, four inches and looked to be about 275 pounds. He had the broadest shoulders Joey had ever seen. Joey was overwhelmed. *This is serious*, Joey thought. *It's really happening.*

Most of the team was already assembled and Murray eyed his stopwatch as he glanced at the last few candidates racing for the track. Joey reached the track and wandered over to the rest of the team. A few more seconds passed, and the rest of the late arrivals showed. Murray pushed the button on his stopwatch. "Time!" He turned and faced the latecomers. "Stop where you are and turn around, boys. You're late...and your cut. Go home."

Joey got a sinking feeling in the pit of his stomach. *Man! This guy is tough! How am I ever going to make it through this tryout?*

Murray turned around and looked at the remaining candidates. "Everyone on the field and line up on the twenty-yard line. I want five rows of ten people, every five yards." The coach worked the boys lightly just to loosen them up. After about ten minutes he blew his whistle. "Alright, let's go! Everyone line up on the track across from the fifty-yard line. I want one lap around the track. You have two minutes. If anyone comes in after that, you will all have to do it again."

The boys lined up in a pack and Murray pushed his stopwatch again. The group of worried players took off in a confused bunch. Murray yelled out the passing time continually, "Thirty seconds...lets go! You're not even halfway yet."

As the group of candidates rounded the first turn, the pack began to separate. Some of the candidates began to slow and fall away from the pack and a few began to pull away. The majority of runners stayed in a loose bunch in the middle section.

Joey was at the front of the pack with the leaders, and pulling away. He crossed the finish line at sixty-nine seconds and trotted to a stop. As he bent over with his hands on his knees to catch his breath, he heard Murray shout into the warm September air. "Ten people over two minutes. Everyone back on the starting line. Do it again."

One of the heavier players complained, "Hey Coach. We just crossed the line. Can we have a short break?"

"No breaks! Whoever doesn't start on my mark is cut."

Joey could feel himself transitioning into his workout mode. He began to relax and fell into step with Murray's requests. One by one, lap after lap, the group of incumbents began to dwindle.

Finally, Murray put his stopwatch away. "Okay, get on the field and meet Coach Daly on the goal line. I'll be on the fifty-yard line. We're going to do 50-yard sprints. I'll be timing you. Anyone over ten seconds should go home to his mother. Anyone looking for a backfield position should be under seven seconds."

Time after time, Murray tortured the boys by sending them back to the goal line. "Trot back to that goal line! If you walk, you are cut." The next group of runners stepped up to the goal line and Murray held his stop watch in the air. "I'm not seeing the times I want. Let's go, ladies! Push it! I don't care if you throw your lunches up. I want some speed here!"

It became obvious, the group of candidates were tiring. "Okay, gentlemen. Take a knee for a couple of minutes. We have calisthenics next.

One of the candidates asked, "Coach, can we have some water? It's pretty hot out here."

Murray spun around fast to face the boy. "No water! If you can't handle it…leave."

Murray blew his whistle and twirled his right arm in the air. "Just like at the beginning of this nightmare, line up on the twenty-yard line. I want five rows of ten people five yards apart." The coach began with several repetitions of jumping jacks, followed immediately by sit ups, and pushups. There were squat thrusts and footfire. The whole process began all over again as the boys worked in the hot September sun.

Murray led the boys through each exercise by audibly counting out the repetitions and using his cadence. "If you can't keep up you can leave, gentlemen. You gotta' want this." Coach Daly walked through the ranks and made sure everyone performed their exercise correctly. If anyone cheated, he was brought over to the sidelines and given more to do.

The calisthenics were brutal. It was a hot afternoon and by now everyone was soaked in sweat. Joey began to second guess himself, *This is pretty tough...and it's getting worse. If ninth grade tryouts are this bad, how am I going to handle high school tryouts next year. I don't know. Gotta' get thru this first.*

Murray walked among the tortured boys as they sweated through their calisthenics, "Anyone who thinks they can't continue may stand up and head for the showers. There is no shame in that. Just be honest with yourself." One by one, people began to stand and walk off the field.

Through the entire session, Joey remained focused and intent. His nervousness had long since dissipated, and like a machine, the boy awaited the next command. Finally, it was over. Murray stopped the calisthenics and had a quiet conversation with Daly. "How many did we lose so far? I have to get it down to thirty-five people."

Daly looked at his player list. "Ten have left the field, Coach. You cut five of them for being late."

"Okay, that's enough for today. Let's wrap it up."

Murray turned to the tired bunch of athletes. "Okay, gentlemen. You're done for the day. Good job...and thank you for sticking it out. You may walk to the showers now. Please meet here on the track tomorrow...same time, for a do-over. We have two more days of this hell before I can make a decision. Go home and get some rest." With that, the two coaches walked slowly back to the school talking quietly to one another. That quiet discussion is what bothered the boys most.

Joey showered and changed into his street clothes. The plan was for him to meet his father in the parking lot outside the gym. He leaned against the brick building and began to think about the tryout and how it had taken everything he had. What about those other guys? They just seemed to give up after they realized Murray wasn't going to let up. The ones that made it through the day were hanging on by a thread. Their coordination was off, some were limping, and all of them were moving very slow. Would they come back? He also realized that his nervousness had subsided once he began participating in the tryout's activities. After he saw what he could do compared to everyone else, a new level of confidence took over. The anxiety disappeared with the nervousness as if he needed to compare himself against the other candidates. From that point, he just responded to the coach's requests. Joey never considered having an episode or an embarrassing moment once he realized he could handle the situation.

Suddenly a new fear entered his mind. He remembered that he saw Coach Daly write his name down when he arrived late to the track. What was that about? Daly also stood next to him during the pushup part of calisthenics and criticized him for not going low enough, and as a matter of fact, kept coming back to his place on the field during the calisthenics, and told him to push harder…'dig deep' as he called it. Did they think he wasn't putting out? And, he always followed up his comments by writing something in that notepad he carried around. Joey finally let those new concerns go. He was too tired to care at this point. He satisfied himself with the fact that he had done his best.

Frank's white station wagon came around the corner

and pulled up to the curb Joey stood on. Frank smiled as Joey flopped into the car. "So how did it go, hotshot?"

Joey shook his head from side to side. "It was tough, Dad. It's gonna' be the same thing tomorrow. Ten guys quit and five of them were cut before they even got to the track."

Frank nodded his head and began to drive away. Knowing the triggers for Joey's episodes, Frank sneakily asked, "What about you? Were you nervous?"

Joey nodded. "Yeah, I was nervous until we actually started running and doing sprints. Then it went away."

"Did you feel like quitting or giving up?"

"Nah. I was surprised at how hard it was, but I never thought about giving up. I just thought that if it was this hard for ninth grade football, it was going to be murder next year in high school."

A smile appeared on Frank's normally serious face. "Good boy, Joe. Just remember, you can take whatever they have to dish out."

Frank pulled into their driveway and Joey followed his dad into the house. Ginny was at her usual spot between the sink and the stove. She turned and smiled. "Hey, Joe! How were the tryouts? You look exhausted."

Joey walked through the kitchen to put his gym bag away and empty its contents. "It was pretty tough. Probably more than it had to be, but I think they're just trying to get rid of the guys who aren't so serious about playing. They only have so many places on the team."

"Well, supper is ready. Get washed up and come eat."

After Joey left the room, Ginny turned to Frank, "How do you think it went? He seems tired but not upset."

Frank sat down to the table. "Well, I asked him if he had been nervous and he said he was until they began the running and exercises. He probably compared himself to everyone else and realized he had nothing to worry about. He didn't say anything about missing starts or any delayed responses, or getting embarrassed, so it seems as if it went well."

Ginny smiled, "Well, I want to ask him some pointed questions at dinner."

Frank shrugged his shoulders as he picked up the evening paper.

Soon, the entire Hall family had come into the kitchen and seated themselves for supper. The big news remained on the subject of football tryouts. Joey offered some information and answered a few questions from his older brother, Brian.

Ginny waited for an appropriate opening in the conversation and asked, "Joey, how many guys showed up for tryouts?"

"About sixty-five. Some of them just looked like they weren't serious, but I know the coach only has thirty-five openings."

Ginny grimaced, "So, that's why it was so tough. He wanted to cut people to get to a specific number, and also cut the people he felt weren't serious without really giving them a chance."

Joey didn't look up from his dinner. "I guess. The way he did it was pretty nasty. It was like, 'one wrong move and you're done.' Joey paused a moment and added, "and the way he spoke to those guys was pretty mean."

Ginny pressed he boy, "How did that make you feel, when you saw some of your friends getting treated like that?"

Joey looked up, and not at anything in particular, and answered his mother. "It was ugly, Mom. Those guys didn't deserve it. I mean, he said he'd cut anyone who talked while he was talking and then he cut a few guys that were late to the track…just a few seconds behind me." Then Joey turned and looked right at Ginny. "During those killer sprints there were guys kneeling down and ready to cry, begging the coach to give them a rest." Joey paused again and added. "I guess I felt bad for those guys, but I didn't like to see them whining like that. I mean, we were all in the same boat. On the other hand, those coaches didn't have to be so tough. It was hot and they wouldn't give us water."

Ginny leaned forward across the table. "Do you feel like you want to continue? You don't have to ya' know."

Joey turned toward her and quickly responded. "He's just weeding guys out, Mom. The coach can only keep thirty-five guys. When it was at its worst, I got a little pissed and just dug deeper into myself…looking for some kind of extra strength. I tried to put the pain out of my head and focused on the trees at the end of the field and the sun setting to my right. It was hot, but the sunset was beautiful." He stopped talking and his face became serious, "I wasn't going to let them tell me to leave the field…and yes, I have to continue. There are two more days of the same kind of thing before they let us know who is on the final roster."

Ginny and Frank looked at each other and smiled weakly. The boy was determined and focused on a specific goal. They knew Joey had persevered through a high stress situation that lasted for two hours and hadn't reported anything even remotely related to his episodes.

It was hard to watch their son go through such a physically demanding experience coupled with the emotional behaviors of others on the field, including the coaches, all tied to the stress of being accepted based on his personal attributes. They realized getting cut from the team might be devastating for the boy, but if he made the team, it could prove extremely positive. For now, the parents satisfied themselves with the fact that he was coping with the situation and so far, had not experienced any episodes.

CHAPTER 30

The end of the week had arrived and the Halls were sitting down to supper. Friday nights were always special because the pressure of classes were gone for a couple of days and there would be no tortuous football practices for two days. Ginny was first to begin the mealtime discussion. "Joey, I received a phone call from Doctor H this morning. He's read into your discovery about not having an episode when you're alone and has compiled that into your medical history log." She paused before bringing up the next item, "The doctor is anxious to see how you've made out through the pressure of football tryouts and asked for us to come see him. Because this is an informational meeting for their practice, it would be a free visit for us. He'd like to see you tomorrow."

Joey dropped his shoulders and chin to indicate his feeling of inconvenience. "C'mon, Mom! Tomorrow is Saturday and I'll have to use up part of the day going all the way up to the hospital and back, not to mention the hour-long visit."

Everyone at the table remained quiet and continued with their dinner. Frank looked up from his meal and said,

"Hey buster, this isn't about you! This is for the good of others who may be going through the exact same thing as you. You're getting better, so can't you be a little more gracious and give up some of that precious time off for the good of others?"

Once again, Joey had been guilted into doing something he didn't want to do. He looked over at his dad and then down to his plate of food. He nodded his head. "Yeah, I guess. When do we have to be there?"

Ginny smiled matter-of-factly, "Nine o'clock. We have to leave here at 8:15, so be ready."

Saturday mornings were usually sacred to Joey. It was the only time he could decompress and just do whatever he wanted. There were no time constraints, no classes, and nowhere to be in particular. As the boy got older, time off from the regular schedule became more important as his responsibilities increased and his free time lessened.

Joey sat in the front seat of his mother's car as they drove to the hospital. He was bored already and sat slumped against the side of the car. Ginny glanced over at him and smiled. "How are you feeling this morning, Joe? Still feeling sore from the week's tryouts?"

"A little, but I'm almost through it. Some of those guys were still in pretty bad shape last night after we finally finished up."

Ginny's expression became serious, "How many guys were cut? I think you said they started with sixty-five candidates."

"They cut thirty guys because they only have spots for thirty-five players. There were some sad faces in the locker room last night…and some really pissed off guys too." He paused and looked over at his mother. "What do you think Doctor H is going to ask me about?"

"Ginny spoke as she drove. "Well, as I said last night, he wants to discuss what he's found about your episodes and what it may have to do with being around other people, and he also wants to make a change to your medication. He seemed very positive about the whole thing."

Well, I hope he takes me off those Diamox pills. Dad said they're a diuretic and that's why I have to go to the bathroom all the time."

Ginny nodded her head and said, "Yes, they are that, but that's also why you need to drink a lot of water…all day long, to keep from getting dehydrated."

Twenty minutes flew by and soon they were at the hospital sitting in Doctor H's office. Since it was a private visit, and on a Saturday, there were no other patients in the waiting room. Doctor H met them at his office door and welcomed them in.

Once they were all seated, the doctor flipped his notebook closed and looked at Joey. "Well, it's always a treat to see you, Joe. I want to hear about everything since we last met. Tell me, how did football tryouts go?"

Joey smirked and raised his eyebrows. "It was a tough week. Tougher than it had to be, because they only had a certain number of openings…but I made the team."

Doctor H raised his arms in the air as if jubilant. "Of course, you did! I had no doubts about that." He paused and leaned forward across the desk, "How did you feel about all that stress and tension, the coaches shouting to go faster… all of that stuff?"

Joey shrugged, "It went away after we started on the first day. I knew I was at least as good as anyone else and probably in better shape than most of them. After that, the nervousness went away. It was not knowing from day to day what might be different that bothered me."

The doctor flipped open his notebook and wrote some notes in Joey's medical history, then looked back at the boy. "Do you think you had any seizures?" Joey gave the doctor an ugly glance and Horowitz noticed it. He continued, "Uh…I mean episodes that entire time, either on the field, during school, or at night when you were at home?"

Joey shook his head. "I know I didn't have any during the tryout sessions. I was too focused on getting through the day. Had a couple during school through the week when I was talking to other kids between classes, but at night I was so tired, I usually fell asleep after I finished my homework."

Doctor H looked at Ginny. "Fatigue, especially extreme fatigue, is one of the triggers for this disorder…and it didn't seem to happen. That's a good sign."

The doctor looked back over to Joey, "You know…you can still have these episodes when you're sleeping but you'd never know it."

Joey looked concerned, "When I'm sleeping? I didn't realize that."

Doctor H saw the boy's surprise. "It's not a concern, Joe. It's just part of the disorder. Your brain is always working, even when you're asleep." He held up some of Joey's EEG tests, "You've been having these EEG tests since you were in fifth grade, and they all show it. We are not concerned about that at all. It's the frequency and duration of those episodes that we watch…and yours has always been the same, meaning that we can control this easily with the right medication. We just need to figure that specific combination out…and I think we're getting pretty close."

Joey immediately responded, "Can you take me off the Diamox? It makes me want to go the bathroom all the time. Sometimes in the middle of a test at school. What if it happens during a football game?"

Doctor H smiled understandingly at the boy. "Can't do it just yet, Joe. We have to have another EEG before I can make that decision. The combination of medicines I have you on now seems to be working, but we have to refine it a bit." He looked at Ginny, "I want to increase the Zarontin by one pill a day and drop the Diamox to two a day." Then he looked back at Joey, "That might help your situation a little."

Ginny became serious again. "What are some of the side effects of these medicines doctor?"

"As you know, the Diamox is a diuretic and increases the frequency of urination. The Zarontin is kind of a mood drug. It can cause depression and anxiety, insomnia, mood swings like irritability and insomnia, but based on Joe's age and active life style, these side effects will probably never surface. If they do, call me right away." He paused and added, "The only thing I'm just a little concerned with is his balance. Zarontin can induce dizziness and that coupled with football could be a problem."

Ginny cocked her head to one side, "Frankly, I'm a little concerned. The effects from Zarontin seem kind of harsh.

Now, you've mentioned dizziness to the list. I have to admit the side effects worry me."

Doctor H smiled. "They shouldn't. These are what the side effects...could be, but not necessarily...will be. As I said, he's a healthy, active young man, and probably won't see any of those except the increased urge to urinate. We'll monitor his blood levels every six months and make changes if need be, but for now, it's the combination of those two drugs in specific doses that are the controlling factors." He paused and concluded with, "And of course, combined with exercise, competition, and a good mental outlook, everything should be fine."

Ginny turned her head to look at her son and smiled weakly. "What do you think, Joey?"

"I'm good with all of it, Mom. I don't like taking pills as part of my day, but if I have to, I will." Joey shrugged and added, "None of that stuff is gonna' happen to me anyway."

Ginny nodded at Joey as if she understood and turned back to the doctor. "Okay then, we'll try the new dosages."

Doctor H wrote the prescriptions down and handed them to Ginny. "He'll be fine Mrs. Hall. You're making the right decision."

CHAPTER 31

Doctor Howard Baldwin sat at his desk and went over the practice's *Patient Listing and Recent Appointments* book. Eventually, he noticed the entry for last Saturday's appointment with Ben Horowitz and Joey Hall. *"Humph! I see Ben is now entertaining patients in secret on the weekends. I wonder if that is part of his plan to keep Joey Hall's information from me and Petrillo.* Baldwin flipped the patient book closed and stared out his office window. *I'm convinced that guy is hoarding information. He won't allow me or Petrillo to look at the child's medical history…and we're his partners. 'Patient confidential,' he says. What a bunch of crap! There are seminars and opportunities for papers and medical books on this disorder, and Horowitz keeps it all locked up…for himself.*

The frustrated neurosurgeon rose from his desk and paced the floor. *This is such a rare case and Ben is holding us back on its research and any opportunities it can offer, not to mention our opportunity for professional success and acknowledgement in the medical community.* Baldwin continued to pace the floor and decided to speak to Horowitz. *I think another discussion about professional disclosure is warranted.* The annoyed doctor went back to his desk and wrote himself a memo to meet with Ben Horowitz tomorrow. Baldwin stood up and nodded his head, *and that'll just be me and Horowitz this time. We'll leave Petrillo out of this for now.*

The next morning, Dr. Howard Baldwin sat at his desk sipping coffee as he waited for Dr Horowitz to arrive. He impatiently glanced at his watch. It was approaching 7:30 AM. *Where is that guy? He's usually here by now.*

As if on cue, he heard the waiting room door open and some shuffling of papers, followed by footfalls to Horowitz's office. Baldwin smiled, *Finally, the old codger is here. I'll give him a minute to get settled and then go in there and make my demands.*

Just then, there was a knock at his own office door followed by its slow opening. Ben Horowitz poked his head into Baldwin's office and smiled. "Good morning, Howard. I brought you and Petrillo some coffee."

Startled at Ben's intrusion of his quiet time, Howard put on a face and replied, "Oh! Well...thank you, Doctor. Come on in and have a seat. I have been meaning to speak with you before the rush of patients arrive."

Ben Horowitz smiled and walked in carrying two coffees with him and sat down. He passed Howard's cup to him, "Black, with one sugar just as you like it."

"Thanks, Ben. And, what do I owe this nicety to?"

Ben shrugged, "Nothing. I just felt you and Petrillo have been a little distant lately, and I thought I would just make a little gesture. No big deal."

Howard picked up his coffee cup and nodded at Ben before taking a sip. "Well, since we're both here, and alone, let me ask about your patient Joey Hall."

Ben Horowitz cocked his head to one side, "Come on,

Howard. We've been all through this. I explained to you and Petrillo that I promised the Halls that if they agreed to my keeping a medical log and living history on their son, it would be discrete and confidential. I do not intend to compromise their trust and it is my sincere hope that you and Doctor Petrillo can understand my position."

Howard nodded back at Ben as he took another sip of his coffee. "Yes, yes. Petrillo and I understand, but we feel as if you're keeping valuable information all to yourself when you could be sharing it with your partners."

"Howard, neither you or Petrillo has a case even remotely close to Joey Hall's. I've told you before, that if that were the case, I would gladly share with you what I know about it, but not as it pertains specifically to my patient."

Baldwin raised his right hand in the air. "That's what I'm alluding to! We need to know how the triggers effect a certain type of individual, and if it's different in every case. We need to know Joey Hall and its effects on his personality type before we can generalize any outcomes."

Ben pursed his lips and sat back in his chair while he took another sip of his coffee. The older neurologist simply sat there without answering Baldwin for an uncomfortably long time. It was obvious he was considering Baldwin's accusations and demands. At the same time, Horowitz felt disappointed with his partner's assumptions. Baldwin's words instilled a sense of guilt that his compiled research on the disorder may be compromising its cure.

Finally, Ben looked up from his coffee and into Baldwin's eyes. "I'm sorry, Howard. It's my intention to keep patient confidentiality under any circumstance, and when the time is right, I will make my research public knowledge…with the patient and his parent's consent. That is my final answer to this conversation."

Ben began to rise from his chair and Baldwin leaned across the desk while throwing his coffee cup into the waste basket. "Ben! Before you leave and close the door to this conversation…to all concerned…consider this! You are already past retirement age…by at least two years." The younger doctor paused for effect, "If something happens to you, or you simply just retire, I will access those files on Joey Hall and just assume ownership, as if they were mine. As your partner in practice, that is my legal right, so I will eventually have those files and all that research, to use as I see fit, once you are gone."

Ben stood from his chair and solemnly eyed his distraught colleague. "All that is true, Howard. I however, still have the patient's best interest in mind and will stay on as head of this practice, for as long as I am physically and mentally capable. When I feel it is time for me to leave, I will make the decision as to how my patient load will be divided." Ben Horowitz turned to leave and turned back to face Baldwin. "Unfortunately, because of the attitude and aggressive behavior you have displayed regarding this case, in the past and…just now, you will not be one of my choices for Joey Hall's case." Ben Horowitz turned and quietly left Baldwin's office.

"Can we force him out? He is, after all…two years beyond retirement age."

Doctors Baldwin and Petrillo sat in a downtown restaurant safe from prying ears, discussing their situation regarding Doctor Horowitz.

Baldwin shook his head, "No, no. He's too valuable to the science of neurology. The medical board will want to keep him around as a consultant or to teach. If Doctor Goldbloom ever got the impression that we were trying to force out Horowitz, there would most assuredly be hell to pay. Remember, Goldbloom is the Resident Chief of Neurosurgery, not to mention his affiliation with Hoagland, Chief of Neurology for the Northeast region."

The two doctors remained silent for a few minutes as they stared into their drinks. Each considered ways to get access to Joey Hall's medical history, but everything pointed to legal expenses, or illegal practices which could end their careers rather abruptly.

Petrillo clicked his glass with his forefinger. "What if we began speaking to him in a condescending manner when in private...and especially among our colleagues, as if we were covering for him in his advancing age. Let the listeners get the impression that his own partners are questioning his credibility as a neurosurgeon."

Baldwin looked up from his drink and nodded his head. "That may be a start! He's got an excellent reputation, so we'll have to be careful as to how we go about it." A wicked smile crossed Baldwin's face as he continued, "We should try to attack his credibility, not only among hospital staff... but in front of his patients."

Petrillo nodded and added, "Well, I've looked at his attendance, and until recently, his medical history shows very few and far between absences. It appears that in the past year, he's been out with different medical problems... markedly more than in past years. We might be able to use that information to our advantage too."

"Okay, let's go with that. We'll start painting a picture of the good doctor that will make him appear as if he's in declining health, both mentally and physically. Once the patient community gets wind of that, rumors and speculations will do the rest of the work for us."

Petrillo nodded back at Baldwin and added, "Not to mention the medical community. They'll begin to ignore him and his position when his credibility is in question."

CHAPTER 32

As the first scheduled football game for Tobacco Valley Junior High School approached, the new team just finished their warm up lap around the track and stood in the pouring rain waiting for the coach to start the practice. The players meandered around the football field near their assigned warm up area. The rain was a soaking one and seemed to come down harder, as they awaited Coach Murray. Cold rain dripped from their helmets into the gap between their practice jerseys and their necks. Water found its way under their shoulder pads and travelled down their backs and chests, and their feet had been soaked halfway through their quarter mile run around the track. A darkening sky with a chill in the air made the conditions all the more uncomfortable.

Finally, someone shouted, "Hey, the coaches are coming out!"

Everyone turned toward the school's team entrance and watched as coaches Murray and Daly approached the football field clad in hooded rain coats and holding umbrellas. The players formed their usual formation near the goal line for calisthenics and tightened up their rows and columns.

The coaches walked across the track and to the front of the assembled team where Murray addressed the waiting players. "Good afternoon, gentlemen. I see that you've completed your warm up run around the track and that you're wet. This is football, gentlemen. Get used to it. You'll be playing in much worse conditions than this as we get closer to Thanksgiving, so get tough. I don't want to hear that your cold or wet. Deal with it or leave the team. I don't need any pansies out here."

Murray surveyed the wet boys standing in front of him. Everyone remained quiet awaiting his instructions. "Okay, let's start with our cals. Jumping jacks, on my count…begin." Murray counted the repetitions audibly then shouted, "Pushups! Get down in that water and give me ten good ones!" The entire team dropped to the saturated ground and waited in the ready position. Again, Murray counted out the reps while the team performed the exercise. "On your backs! Fifteen sit-ups…begin." When their sit-ups were complete, the coach shouted as he walked among the saturated players, "Get up…jumping jacks! Let's go! I'm doing you a favor. The more you move, the more you'll warm up."

The coach repeated the entire routine two more times. On their third set of pushups, Murray held the boys in push up position with arms extended for an extended period of time. "Hold it right there, boys. Tough it out! Think through the pain and discomfort."

Joey held himself in push up position and watched the water dripping from his helmet. His entire uniform was soaked through and stuck to his body. He looked down at his extended arms and noticed his hands were completely submerged under the puddling rain water. *"Why am I doing this?* He thought. *This isn't going to make us better football payers. Everyone else I know is home and dry, and watching television.*

Then Murray's voice cut through the wet air, "Begin! I want to see you go all the way down…chins touching the field." The boys lowered themselves into the wet grass and puddles.

Joey continued to consider his circumstance and asked himself again, *Why am I doing this? After all I've gone through to get here, and this is part of the glory?* Then it hit him. *My dad! I'm doing this for my dad. I have to show him I can do this, especially after what happened in Youth football…and I know he's so proud I made this team.*

It seemed as if everything made sense once he realized why he was tolerating this abuse. Joey dug deep within himself and finished the assigned exercise. His discomfort seemed to fade away as he listened to Murray's instructions. "I want the backfield at the other goal line with me for sprints. Defense and everyone on the line, meet Coach Daly at the fifty-yard line for the sled drill." He paused and sarcastically said, "Maybe the mud will help you push it to the other side of the field."

Everyone trotted off to their assigned areas and continued with the practice. The sky began to get darker, so Murray motioned Daly over for a quick discussion. "Let's get through these drills as quickly as possible. Have them push that sled across the field a couple of times only. I want to get them scrimmaging while introducing some of the new plays before it begins to thunder and lightning."

Daly looked up at the grey sky and nodded back at the head coach. "Okay, Coach. Give me twenty minutes."

Murray nodded as he turned back to his backfield players. "Okay guys, forty-yard sprints, then we'll do some passing practice."

After the sprints, Murray placed the team's two quarterbacks on the thirty-yard line facing the goal line. Then he split the number of halfbacks and fullbacks into two lines, each to the designated quarterback on their side of the field. Murray stood on the goal line facing his players, "I'm going to shout out a pass pattern and I expect you to run it. Your quarterback will pass the ball to you. Once you get the ball, turn upfield and run it over the goal line. If you catch the ball and drop it, I want you to dive for it and curl yourself around it, as if it's a loose fumble."

Joey waited in line for his turn to run a specific pattern the coach requested. He became nervous as past memories of missing the "GO" command ran through his mind due to the occurrence of an episode. The boy focused on what was happening in front of him and promised himself that would never happen again.

Time after time, Joey watched the halfbacks run the requested patterns and drop the wet football. He felt sorry for the unfortunate player that dropped a caught pass as he dove for the loose ball, throwing up a huge splash in some cases, as he struggled to get possession of it. Finally, it was Joey's turn. Murray broke the monotony and drudgery, "Hey, it's Mr. Hall's turn! Let's see what Mr. Hotshot can do." He nodded at the quarterback, "Matt, Number 2, Slant Left."

Joey hated to be singled out and immediately became

nervous. It was still early in the season and Joey wanted to make an impression. He got into his ready position and heard Murray shout, "Hut 1!" Joey ran two yards out and then slanted his angle upfield toward the sideline while looking over his right shoulder. The ball seemed to be a little ahead of him, so Joey had to leap for it, only getting a few finger tips on the pigskin. The ball deflected off his fingers and splashed into the mud and water, tumbling into the end zone. Joey followed, landing on his stomach, and slid over the goal line.

Joey stood from the puddle, picked up the ball, and ran it back to Murray. The coach slapped the ball out of Joey's hands, "I told you to curl yourself around that loose ball, Hall…like it's a fumble! No good!"

Joey was not in the mood for such harshness. He stood in front of the coach and watched the ball tumble back over to the goal line and looked back at Murray, "You said to do that if we caught it, Coach. I only got the tips of my fingers on it."

"What are you a wise guy?"

Joey looked into the coaches' eyes stoically. "No…I'm not. I just did what you asked."

"Hall go get that ball and jump on it…and you better curl around it, like it's your best girlfriend!"

Joey trotted over to the ball and dove into the wet grass as the ball floated in a shallow puddle. He grabbed it with one hand and drew into his gut, then rolled over, jumped to his feet, and trotted back to Murray.

Murray eyed the saturated player from head to toe and smiled. He accepted the ball from Joey and said, "Good job, son. Now, go get back in line and hold onto it next time."

Another twenty minutes passed, and Murray assembled the team by the goal line again. "Okay, I want the following players to line up in position." One by one, the coach called eleven players by name to their playing positions. The last call was, "Joe Hall – Fullback."

Joey ran to his position and stared at the ground. *Fullback? I was trying for halfback. Ah, I guess it doesn't matter now.*

Coach Daly called out his defensive team and had them do the same.

Murray walked around the offense and defense and adjusted their positions and where they should be standing. "This is the first team. The starters...until they screw up or disappoint me. The rest of you guys will fill in for them when they're tired or hurt...and when I call for Second Team," he pointed at the players that remained standing, "you're the people I'm asking for."

He looked back at the first team and announced, "Consider yourselves lucky to be having your first scrimmage in the mud."

Murray pointed out the 'holes' the backs were assigned to run through when they carried the ball and made them walk through three offensive running plays. The boys ran the plays over and over with full contact with the defense, until the entire team began to show signs of fatigue and waning interest.

"Okay, boys that's it...take a knee! You're done for the day." The coach looked over the wet and tired team of ninth graders. Their usually white practice uniforms were caked with mud. "This is our ball club, gentlemen. Always do your best no matter what, and never give up. That's all

I want." The coach paused and finished with, "Now, go get a hot shower, and get some rest. Tomorrow will be better."

The nightmare was over. The boys were too tired and uncomfortable to run to the showers. No one spoke. Everyone just focused on getting to the building where it would be warm and dry. Joey thought hard about the wet and rainy practice as he trudged to the player's entrance, *Hmm, Murray's excuse for today was 'this is football. This is how it's going to be. Like it or leave the team.' I guess I have to accept that.* Then he reasoned with the situation, *There will be good times that'll make up for days like this. At least I did it and didn't give up.*

Never once did Joey consider whether or not he had an episode. He had focused on getting through a demanding practice session. His greatest fear was about missing a cue command to begin a drill, or miss something he had been asked to do. He vowed that never again would he be left standing alone at the start of anything.

That night, the Hall family sat at the kitchen table as Ginny served the evening meal. As usual, Frank began to ask the kids how their day went. He began with Joey. "I'm guessing they postponed practice today. What a downpour!"

Joey glanced at his dad and frowned. "No, Coach held practice."

"Please tell me they didn't make you guys practice in that downpour. How could they expect you guys to do anything except get wet?"

Joey cocked his head to one side. "Murray told us just

before cals, 'this is football and if anyone doesn't like it, they can leave the team.''

Frank put his fork down and looked over at Ginny by the stove. Ginny raised her eyebrows and shook her head from side to side, then she mouthed the words, *'We'll talk later.'*

Frank turned his attention back to Joey. "It had to be miserable out there! There was wind and a steady down pour. Did you actually practice any football?"

"Yeah…toward the end. We practiced pass patterns and had to dive for the ball if we dropped it. Then he set up the first team and made us run some backfield plays with full contact against the Defense. I think he was just trying to see if we were tough enough." Joey paused and looked at his dad. "They have me at the fullback position."

Frank picked his fork up. "Really? That's great, Joe.

Joey saw that Frank was annoyed and quickly added, "There is a fullback play called forty-four. It's a handoff from the quarterback to me, the four back, and I'm supposed to carry the ball through the 4 hole…you know, right off the offensive tackle."

Frank shook his head with a frown, "But, I don't like the idea of running you guys in the rain and mud like that. He's treating you guys like a herd of cattle."

Ginny gave Frank the high sign with a quick hand gesture, and he began to backoff. Frank tried to be positive, "Well, you made first team and you're going to be a ball carrier…congratulations!" He paused and then finished with, "I hope he doesn't do that to you guys again. It was probably just a test to see who would stay under those conditions." The upset father remained quiet for the rest of the meal and just listened to the rest of the family as they described their day.

After the rest of the family had retired to their bedrooms for homework, Ginny and Frank sat at their usual place in front of the fireplace and discussed Joey's practice in the rain. Ginny looked up from her knitting and gave Frank the opening he was looking for. "I know you want to discuss the rainy practice, but let's keep it a quiet one."

Frank leaned forward from his chair. "It's not what you think, Ginny. As dangerous as that is for increasing the possibility of injuries, I was mostly concerned about what was going on in Joey's head. This is something he's not used to. And then, to be forced to practice in the rain and mud, could have triggered an episode."

Ginny put her knitting down for a moment. "And, what if it did, Frank? We decided to let him do this, and Doctor H is behind it one hundred percent. Joey is as tough or tougher than any of those other kids, so I think we have to just let it go. He didn't complain about it all…he didn't even bring it up until you asked him about it. And even then, he tried to put a positive spin on it by telling you he made fullback on the first team." She paused a moment and looked into Frank's eyes, "Remember, we are not supposed to protect him from what every other kid is going to be experiencing. Just let it go."

Frank sat back in his chair and nodded his head. "You're right, you're right. I guess I came on a little strong. But the idea of…"

Ginny cut him off, "Let it go, Frank."

CHAPTER 33

⸻⟨✧⟩⸻

Joey's days consisted of school, football, and family. The woods were always there and he still hiked through them whenever he got the chance. The extreme running he'd practiced in the past was put aside temporarily, as he was getting enough of that at football practice. The woods continued to be a place of silence and solitude…a place where judgement and prejudice didn't exist. School became more of a social event. He looked forward to seeing his friends that now began to segregate into different social groups or 'clicks,' as they were referred to. There were the Greasers, Gearheads, Geeks, Hippies and the Band People to name a few. Unfortunately, the clicks promoted judgement and prejudice, and increased social pressures between members of the different groups. Joey accepted everyone for what they were, but naturally fell into the group referred to as 'the Jocks.' There was enough competition among his own group, that one continually sought a break from that pressure, so he looked to other groups at times, like 'the Band People,' who were musicians and naturally very unassuming and laid back. But no matter what he experienced at school or practice, Joey knew he had the luxury of going home to a family that understood him, not to say that judgement or competition didn't exist there, but it was understood that you still belonged, no matter what you said or did, because it was…a family.

The day had been dragging. Joey looked at the clock. Phys Ed class was over and he had fifteen minutes to get changed, get across the school, and up to the second floor for Algebra class. He tied his shoes quicky and stuffed his gym clothes into his locker. *Oh, man, I'm gonna' be late to Mr. George's class again. I hate the way he looks at me when that happens…like he's so disappointed. If he only knew it's one of my favorite classes, maybe he wouldn't be so tough on me.* Slamming his locker shut, he turned and raced out of the locker room and down the hall. The clock was ticking. Joey raced up the three flights of stairs to the math and English department and watched forlornly, as the door to his math class slowly closed. *Damn it! Here we go again.*

Joey stopped to catch his breath and slowly opened the classroom door. Everyone was seated and Mr. George was already standing in front of the class calling attendance. He turned to the door as Joey walked in. "Well, I'm glad you could find the time to join us, Mr. Hall!" Mr. George was animated in his statement and sat on the edge of his desk as he waited until Joey found his seat. Then the guilt trip began. "What's your excuse this time, Hotshot?" He nodded to the people that sat around Joey, who were also football players…the first team quarterback and two halfbacks. "Your pals seemed to have been able to get here on time."

Joey gave his team mates a quick glance, then looked back to Mr. George. "Sorry, my last class is Phys Ed, so I needed time to change and come all the way across the school to get here. It's just a bad schedule."

Joey heard quarterback, Craig Stiller murmur, "Bad excuse. Don't explain. You'll just make it worse."

George put his attendance sheet down and looked at the floor nodding his head. "I see. So, it's the school's fault for not considering your personal requirements."

Joey began to say something, but George cut him off. "When is football practice tonight?"

Joey looked curiously at the teacher. "Uh, well we have to be on the field and suited up by 2:30."

George nodded his head at Joey and said, "Well you're going to be right here with me at that time. Do what you have to do...tell your coach...whatever, but you're going to be right here. Just you and me...practicing quadratic equations." George glared at the boy for an awkwardly long time. When Joey said nothing, he added, "I'm sure Coach Murray will agree that your studies, especially algebra, is more important to your future than football."

Joey frowned but continued to lock eyes with Mr. George. *Murray is gonna' be pissed and then he'll probably give me laps or bench me. Shit!*

When Joey said nothing, George brought his attention back to the rest of the class. "Okay, everyone turn to page 63. We're going to start with quadratic equations today."

Joey's seatmate Craig, leaned toward Joey. "Murray is going to kick your ass."

Algebra teacher and math department head, John George, sat on the desk in front of Joey's assigned seat and looked down at him. "What are your plans for the future, Joey?"

Joey sheepishly looked up at the teacher and shrugged his shoulders. George pressed the boy. "I know you must have a direction and I know you're not planning on being a professional football player. Go ahead...tell me."

Reluctantly, Joey offered one of his best kept secrets. "I've always dreamed about going to either the Naval Academy or the Coast Guard Academy. I like the military and I want to be on a ship."

George sat up straight and folded his arms across his chest. "Well, now that's quite an aspiration! You're going to need good grades for that, and if it's one of those academies you want, that means you want to be an officer...on a ship, I take it."

Joey nodded and shrugged his shoulders. "I guess."

George leaned forward into Joey's face. "Well, you're not going to get there by coming into algebra class late with your homework half done. Aside from the requirement of good math grades, punctuality is one of the most important stipulations at the academies."

Joey bowed his head and listened without answering. George went on. "You're bright enough Joe, but to get to Annapolis...or the Coast Guard Academy, you're going to need to excel in many areas...not just sports. You're going to have to be organized and punctual...to start with, and right now you're late for football practice too."

Joey nodded his head. "I know. Coach Murray is pretty mad at me right now. He kind of said the same thing to me."

George smiled, "Okay, I'm glad we had this talk. Get your act together. Be on time from now on, and do your homework. No more unfinished assignments." He paused and waited for a response. Joey made none so George said, "Now, that I know where you're headed, I'm going to be watching you a little closer than the other students. If I think football, or sports in general, is getting in the way of your studies I will step in and talk to your parents."

George got the boy's attention with that. "That won't be necessary, Mr. George. I'll shape up."

George sat back on the desk and flipped his hand in the air. "Okay, finish that last homework problem and get out of here. Coach Murray is probably going to make you run laps for being late to practice."

The teacher walked back to his desk smiling. *That boy is a rare one and I'm going to do what I can to see he gets to where he needs to be.*

That evening, as Joey explained the reason for his late arrival to football practice, Frank glanced at Ginny with raised eyebrows. Getting only a frown back from Ginny, Frank looked back to Joey. "Well, I guess we could get you into some trade school if you can't keep up your grades, but if this behavior keeps up, you're going to have to quit the damn football."

Joey quickly looked up from his dinner and gave his father a serious look. "I'm not doing bad, Dad. I have a C average. It's just that Mr. George thinks I can do better, and he thinks football is affecting my performance."

Frank started to say something, but Joey sat up straight and cut him off. "I'm not quitting football!" I'll do better in algebra. I'm just beginning to get the hang of it. Just give me a chance."

Frank was shocked at the boy's sudden outburst. He stared at Joey for a moment and nodded his head. "Okay, Joe. Make sure you do."

CHAPTER 34

The new football team had its first game of the year and lost. There were more casualties from the game than Coach Murray was comfortable with. At the next practice, he brought the boys through their calisthenics and warm up drills, and discretely watched boys for reactions from the game of two days ago. Since it was tradition to have the day following a game off, it was the first chance the coach had to observe the team for any out of the ordinary behavior. He saw none and called the first team to line up on the field. The boys stood waiting for the coach's instructions as he walked silently through the backfield and along the offensive line, making slight comments to the players. Finally, Murray walked to an area outside of the assembled team and addressed the boys. "Okay guys, listen up. You got beat up pretty bad Wednesday afternoon. Sixty-eight to nothing is pretty bad, and we walked away from that game with thirty percent of our team on the injured list, but you should know that there was a terrible mix-up. It wasn't your fault…none of you personally, or as a team." Murray paused a moment and took a deep breath before continuing. "It was a miscommunication between the coaches of both teams. They sent their varsity squad to play us instead of their ninth-grade junior varsity. I should have realized it when I saw the physical size of their players. We were lucky to get out of that game alive."

Murray scanned the players that stood before him and the rest of the team that waited by the side lines. Their jerseys were ripped, and in some cases, missing from the shoulder pads to the waist, and extremely dirty. Their new white helmets showed red paint scratches and scrapings from the other team's red colored helmets. Murray quietly nodded his head and looked at the entire team. "But none of you quit or refused to go back out on the field...and here you all stand ready to get back to it, two days later... the first practice after the game. I'm proud of you all! You stuck it out and even though they were all physically bigger than us, they outnumbered us by at least twice the amount of players." Murray started to walk around the first team nodding his head. "I owe all of you an apology for letting you play those guys. It's my fault and I promise it'll never happen again." The coach stopped walking and pointed at his disheveled team, "But now, you know you have it within you to play against a larger, older team of athletes and still come out ready to play." Murray paused as he scanned the entire team again and then continued, "Okay, that's enough of that. It's over." He looked back over to the first team...Five of the regular eleven were on the injured list. "Second Team ends, guards and tackles get on the field and get ready to scrimmage!" Then he looked back to the rest of the players, "Coach Daly, scrimmage the second team between plays with the first...substitute where necessary."

The practice scrimmage continued for the next thirty

minutes. The players, still sore from their experience of two days ago, moved rather slowly, and ball execution in the backfield was sloppy. The quarterback, Craig Stiller tried to toss a lateral to Joey on an end around sweep several times, only to throw it ahead, above, or behind him. Murray was emphatic, "Do it again." Finally, on a repeat play, the ball came right to Joey. He clamped onto it, placed it under his outside arm, away from the oncoming defensive players, and turned the corner upfield to run for the touchdown. Everyone had finally come together as a team and executed the play perfectly.

Murray blew his whistle and walked over to the first team. "Boys, that was perfect!" Then he slapped Joey on the helmet as he returned to the huddle with the ball. "Guys, some of you guys are going to turn out to be great football players." He paused for effect and turned to Joey, "And, Joey here is going to be one of them. Nice run, Joe. Let's see some more of that."

Joey beamed as his teammates patted his shoulders and helmet, and was taken aback at the same time. The famous football coach had singled him out amongst the entire team and complimented him! The boy suddenly felt a huge surge of confidence and satisfaction. *Somebody finally acknowledged me for what I can do!* Joey was elated and felt a personal triumph he'd never experienced before. Suddenly, he was more focused and relaxed than he'd ever been before. He wanted to do more and show everyone, that he had a special place on this team. It was a special moment.

During that happy moment, Joey happened to look toward the sideline and saw that Mr. George from algebra class stood watching the practice, discreetly positioned back and away from the other spectators, as if he didn't want to be recognized. When he saw that Joey realized he was there, the teacher smiled and left the area.

From that moment on the football field, Joey grew into a different person and a better athlete. His confidence level soared and it seemed as if very little of his conscious focus ever touched on his special disorder again. The frequency of those episodes decreased dramatically and his mental outlook about everything became increasingly more positive.

Off the field, his teachers began to realize the difference in Joey's studies, especially in math and english. The following week, Joey struggled to get to algebra class. He skipped the required shower after Phys Ed and ran down the corridors and up the stairs to the school's second floor. Mr. George noticed as he entered the classroom before the bell rang. It had been a week since their after-class discussion and Joey hadn't been late since. George picked up the quizzes from last week and addressed the class. "These are last week's quizzes on quadratic equations." The frustrated teacher scanned the class, "Were any of you listening when we went through this material last week? I can't believe what I saw here." The teacher flipped through the quizzes. "Ah, here's one where someone actually listened…and obviously understood what I was saying." He looked up from the pile of papers, and at the class. "Joey Hall. Well done! See what can happen when you get to class on time?"

Joey smiled back at the teacher but with a reddened face before he looked back down at his desk. Being singled out, especially for doing better than his peers was always uncomfortable for the boy. Joey just prayed for the moment to be over. Luckily, George saw Joey's embarrassment and decided not to push the point.

Finally, the bell rang, and it was time to change classes. Joey was relieved and began to relax. He was on his way to English class where he always felt comfortable and loved the teacher's personality. He knew he was going to a safe place, a friendly place…a place he considered a sanctuary among some of the other more structured and demanding classes

Joey settled into his seat in English class, which was in the last row and at the far corner of the room, near the windows. Mr. Lamont stood at the door to greet everyone as they passed into his class. Once everyone was seated, Lamont…a portly little man with a serious face, closed the classroom door and stood before his students. "I'd like to discuss sentence structure and the use of dialogue that we discussed last week, and if we have enough time, we'll go over the compositions you handed in on Friday." The teacher pursed his lips and looked over the top of his glasses at the class. "I have corrected them, but it looks like we're going to have spend more time in this subject area." He paused and looked over to Joey sitting at the far end of the room. "Mr. Hall, please see me after class. I'd like to have a word with you before you move on to the next class."

Joey once again reddened up and nodded back at the teacher. *Man, what could I have done now?*

The bell for changing classes finally rang and everyone rose from their seats and began filing out. Joey, being the farthest from the door, was obviously last in the exiting line of students. *Maybe he forgot about wanting to talk to me. I'll just keep following the line out. If he says anything...I'll tell him I forgot.*

Joey was almost at the door, when suddenly there was an abrupt, "Mr. Hall! Please close the door and come back to my desk."

Ah, crap. He remembered. Joey acknowledged the english teacher, closed the classroom's only door, and walked back to Mr. Lamont's desk.

Lamont shuffled through a small pile of papers and put them back on his desk. "Mr. Hall, thank you for obliging me. I read your composition and I feel you have a knack for this sort of thing."

Joey was embarrassed. He knew the English teacher was a published author and considered him a celebrity. He wondered how the man could even consider his ninth-grade composition worthy of such a compliment.

"Uh, well thank you Mr. Lamont. I just did it the way you told us to."

Lamont stood from his desk and clasped his hands as they hung down in front of him. "Joe, I am on the board at Boston College. If you allow me to select all of your classes from now until you graduate...and promise you will become an english major, I will get you into that college after graduation from high school."

Joey didn't know what to say, but realized he needed to say something. He thought quickly and remembered the United States had just landed a man on the moon. "Thanks, Mr. Lamont but I'm going to be an astronaut."

Lamont pursed his lips and frowned. "Yes...well, if you change your mind, let me know." The teacher turned back to his desk and waved his hand in the air. "That's all, Mr. Hall. You may leave now."

Joey's ninth grade year continued with mild upsets in school and at home, but his overall lifestyle seemed to be settling out. He was maturing. His interests began to broaden and the need to be accurate and specific... about everything, intensified. That may have been part of a natural process driven by his performance in school and sports, or as a natural progression in his maturation process, or a combination of both. Whatever it was, the entire scenario was developing as Dr. Horowitz had promised years before.

Joey's self-confidence seemed to have peaked by spring of that year and the frequency of episodes and embarrassing incidents had subsided. He had a reputation as a scholar and athlete allowing him flexibility where some incidents could be ignored, excused, or assumed to what he had just been involved in.

It was now the spring season, and time for the junior high school's track and field season to begin. Unlike football, there were no "cuts" in trying out for the track team. There were plenty of uniforms and a larger team meant more opportunities for the team to accumulate points during a competition.

Once again, Joey's best friends and coach prodded him about going out for the team. Unbeknownst to most other people, Joey had already planned on going out for the team, just as his older brother, Brian had. Even though Joey had his own interests, he always seemed to try and follow in Brian's footsteps. Maybe he chose that path because he knew it was a safe choice, as he had already seen his brother go through it, and knew what he might experience. It may have also been, that after all, he looked up to Brian and wanted to emulate that same aura of competence and success.

It was common knowledge Joey had been a successful hardball pitcher in his earlier years and had proved that competence, but he also had another learned talent that most children his age didn't possess. His father had introduced him to a track event known as the shot put at the age of eight. Through the years, Joey and Brian spent countless hours in the backyard, under Frank's direction, using form and style, in lieu of brute strength to see how far they could throw the metal ball. 'Throwing the shot' became accepted as kind of an activity shared by Frank with his two boys...and sometimes with daughter Cheryl. Not for competition, but as something that was fun and different.

It didn't require much of a decision on Joey's end. He had spent several years on the baseball mound and decided he would go out for track instead of baseball. In his mind, he was tired of being the center of attention in front of cheering, admiring fans, and sometimes shouting, angry audiences from the opposing team. It was time for a more singular and personal approach to winning and contributing to a team effort.

CHAPTER 35

⸺⸺⸺⸺⸺ ∽ ⸺⸺⸺⸺⸺

Spring had arrived in Tobacco Valley and Joey was excited, as it always showed itself as a new beginning... for everything. The dark, wet, and cold winter had left the scene and the new bright and warm spring weather moved in. The buds on the trees began to blossom and the days got longer. It was such a positive time of year.

Joey was leaving the locker room for his first track practice when Coach Murray walked up to him and announced what events the boy would be involved with. "Hey, Joe! I've already decided what your running events are going to be. I'm going to have you in the 100 and 220-yard sprints, and the half mile relay." The coach smiled and looked out to the waiting track and spoke as if he was thinking out loud. "That ought to pull in at least fifteen points every meet from you alone."

Joey stopped walking and looked Murray in the eyes. "I'm not gonna' run, Coach."

Murray's mouth dropped. "What do you mean, you're not gonna' run? I've already scoped out the other teams' best runners and you're a guaranteed win at every meet with that speed of yours."

Joey shrugged his shoulders, "It's not what I want to do. Track is a personal event for each contestant, and I want to be a field athlete. I want to throw the shot put and discus... and maybe the javelin."

Murray threw his hands up with his palms facing upward, as if he couldn't understand the boy. "You're wasting all that natural speed on...field events? You're not even big enough to be throwing that twelve-pound shot to be competitive amongst some of the better shotputters."

"Coach, my dad showed me how to throw the shot when I was about eight years old. I like doing it and I've been doing it ever since. I want to see how I compare with everyone else."

Murray turned and began walking toward the track, shaking his head. "You're not big enough, Joe. Some of these guys are monsters. You've got to have a lot of weight behind you to get that shot into the air. You'd do better as a sprinter."

Joey followed the coach and added. "Maybe so Coach, but I have the style down. Style is everything in the field events."

Murray and Joey walked in silence a little longer and then went their separate ways. Murray went out to the track and the incumbent runners, and Joey continued on to join the field athletes at the far end of the track.

The coach was right. The shot-putters were huge but most of that was intimidation. Assistant Coach Ford saw Joey approaching and nodded his head. "Hi, Joe. The sprinters are on the track by the fifty-yard line."

"I'm with the field guys, Coach. I'd like to throw the shot and discus."

Ford looked up from his clipboard and looked at Joey standing between two large shot-putters, both taller than him and outweighing him by at least fifty pounds. "Oh, does Coach Murray know that?"

"Yes, he does. He's not good with it, but I told him I just want to be a field guy."

Ford lowered his clipboard so that it hung by his right hip. "Okay, fall in behind Mark and Bill, and we'll give you a chance. If you're not within a foot of their throws, I'm gonna' send you back to Murray."

Joey nodded his head in agreement and stood awaiting his turn. Joey's body style was what human anatomy defines as a mesomorph. He was slim but muscular, not overly tall, and well proportioned. He watched as the two giants ahead of him stood and heaved the circular metal ball into the air. He thought, *Hmmn, no style. All they have is to just stand and throw. I got this!*

At last, it was Joey's turn. The boy was excited to show the doubters what he could do. Coach Ford handed Joey the twelve-pound metal ball. "Okay, kid. Let's see what you got."

Other spectators had rushed over to see what Joey, a former hard ball pitcher on the baseball team, was doing in the shot put circle. Someone sarcastically added, "You can't pitch that like one of your fastballs, Joe...you have to...put it." There were chuckles and laughter to follow, but Joey just afforded those guys a quick look and walked into the shot put circle. He began to concentrate as everyone watched. *They think I can't do this, but I have to block them out. Come on...concentrate.* He began to focus on his backward slide across the circle, the position of his back, how he held the shot in his three fingers…and suddenly someone shouted, "Well, we're waiting!"

Joey had just experienced an episode as he prepared to throw the shot. Coach Ford noticed the delayed hesitation and walked into the circle. He rested one hand on Joey's shoulder and reached for the shot, with his other. "You don't have to do this, son. Just go back with the sprinters."

Joey realized he had overthought the situation and let the onlookers get to him. He stood up and lowered the shot put to his waist holding it with both hands. "Oh! No thanks, Coach. I was just concentrating."

Ford stepped out of the circle. "Okay, when you're ready, Joe." The coach looked at the twenty onlookers and nodded his head. "Let's have it quiet please."

Joey returned to his crouch facing the back of the circle. He took in a few breaths and shuffled backwards across the circle, spun around, and launched the shot put into the air at about a forty-five-degree angle. The shot sailed over the field and landed with a thump about five feet ahead of the closest throw.

Joey landed on his right leg, bounced on it a few times, and walked out the rear of the circle. Ford's mouth dropped open, "Where did you learn to throw like that, Joe? I've never seen a ninth grader even use that style before."

Joey shrugged. "My dad showed me. I've been doing it a while." Purposely, Joey went and stood between the two largest shot-putters to give everyone a message that it's not all about size. The two boys looked down at Joey and he returned their looks with a large grin. It was at that moment, he decided that this would be his special event and he would make it his rule to stand next to the largest shot-putters before every competition, just to make that point.

That night at dinner, Joey considered telling his parents about having had an episode at track practice. He figured there was nothing to worry about since it was anything but an impact sport and the extra seconds it took for him to come back to reality were excused as overconcentration which comes naturally in a sport like track and field. Joey dawdled with his food and waited for his siblings to leave the table. Just as his dad was finishing his coffee, Joey decided to make his move. "Hey Dad, I threw the shot at track practice today. Murray wanted me to go out for the sprinting team, but I told him I'd rather throw."

Frank looked up quickly and put his coffee cup down. "Oh, I'm sorry Joe. I forgot to ask about that. Are there more tryouts? How do you think you did?"

"There aren't any tryouts. Everyone makes the team. You just have to keep coming to practices and participate in the scheduled track meets. If you skip practices or meets, then you'll get cut."

Frank leaned forward, "So, how far did you throw the shot?"

"Well, it was my first throw in a while, but they measured it at thirty-five feet. It was about five feet further than the rest of the guy's throws."

Frank nodded his head. "That's a pretty good throw for the beginning of the season, Joe."

Joey looked sheepish, "Yeah, but everyone was sort of needling me because they know me as a baseball player or a sprinter. Even the coach told me he didn't think I was big enough."

At that, Frank smiled and sat back in his chair. "Oh, really? And what did he say when you overthrew the big guys?"

"He was kind of shocked that I knew how to throw like that." Joey paused and lowered his head a little. "I had a small problem before I threw it though." Joey paused for a moment and Frank's face suddenly became serious. Joey continued, "I got a little nervous because I felt I had to prove I could do it and when I was down in my ready to throw position, I had a little episode."

Frank remained stoic. "Did anyone notice?"

"Yeah, someone shouted something like, 'Well, we're waiting,' and the coach tried to take the shot from me, but I just said that I had been concentrating."

Frank sat back in his chair again. "Well, don't worry about it, Joe. It probably did look as if you were just concentrating on the throw…and I bet everyone forgot all about that after they saw how far you threw."

Joey pursed his lips and nodded his head. "Yeah, I guess."

Inside Frank felt bad for his son. He hated the fact that Joey may have to go through life making quick excuses when an episode presented itself. As he looked into Joey's eyes, he tried to hide his disappointment that the boy had another episode, especially while performing in front of a group of people.

Joey recognized his dad's expression as being happy about the choice he'd made and also that he'd thrown farther than even the two biggest guys on the field team. Suddenly, all his concerns vanished. Joey smiled, "Tomorrow, I'm gonna' relax and work on my spin. I'll throw it even farther. Probably start throwing the discus too."

Frank forced a tight smile, "That a boy, Joe! You're going to be great."

That night as Frank and Ginny lay in bed, Frank brought Ginny up to speed on Joey's incident in the shot put circle that afternoon. "I'm glad he felt like he wanted to tell me about it, but I don't think it was bothering him. It was more like something he thought I should know."

Ginny stared into the darkness as she listened to Frank. She was quiet for a moment and said, "I agree. He realizes the frequency of those episodes have decreased and I think he realizes we still worry, so he felt obligated to tell us something happened. Not to worry us, but to keep us informed." She thought a little more and added, "If you think about it, the situation included the typical scenario like being the center of attention...which makes him uncomfortable, accompanied by all the regular triggers with an added feeling that he had to prove himself." She paused and continued after considering what she had just told her husband, "I'm glad he did that. I'm glad he chose such an individual sport like track, and I'm happy with how you handled it, Frank."

For the first time in a long time, the parents were coming to grips with Joey's situation. They were becoming more comfortable with the disorder and how Joey was beginning to instinctively handle it.

CHAPTER 36

The track season finished with Joey's performance as the top-rated shot-putter in the region. The boy reveled in his position among other track athletes, but never spoke about it. If people questioned his success, he would admit to it, but offhandedly gave the credit to his father. His status in school had climbed to the popular level and he was respected by students as well as teachers. Joey enjoyed the so-called, celebrity status among his peer group. Whether it was something he needed or just something that made him feel accomplished, the boy's entire life had changed. His studies were above average and his spirits soared every day to the point where he looked forward to going to school.

Track season ended with Joey's team finishing with an undefeated record. He had taken every first place for the shot put, in every track meet, except one that he wasn't allowed to participate in. He had defended himself in a fist fight with another ninth-grade boy who had challenged his character in front of the entire cafeteria one lunch time. It may have been due to a jealous classmate that looked to tarnish the boy's student status or just general adolescent behavior, but the incident resulted in his exclusion from his first track meet and suspension from school for three days. The school's Good Citizenship award was also taken from him, as it turned out to be bad timing and how the school's position would appear.

Joey shrugged it off and spent the three suspension days writing a short story about his experience as a football player. Ginny and Frank supported the boy's position and encouraged Joey to consider it...an unplanned vacation. When the school called Ginny to remind her what Joey had missed out on, she explained that she understood but supported Joey's reasons for defending himself. She added that she thought it was unfortunate that a model student, as her son, would be stripped of an award for one unfortunate incident.

It was June and ninth grade came to an end. It had been a wonderful year. A year of new and exciting experiences that began to mold the boy's idea of which direction he would take in his future years.

At dinner on the last night of the school year, Frank came home and made an announcement to the family. "We're finally going to go on vacation. Mom and I have made plans to take you guys to Cape Cod for a couple of weeks. We're going to be right on the water, where you can fish and swim, fly kites...whatever you want." He looked at Joey, "There will plenty of boats for you to see...fishing boats, sail boats...all kinds."

Joey was excited. He thought, *Right on the water! Boats and ships!* His English teacher, Mr. Lamont had left him with a parting gift. It was a fat paperback book about an incident that had happened in World War II aboard a United States naval destroyer…. *I'll take that book Mr. Lamont gave me to read too. This is gonna' be great.* Joey wouldn't come to realize for years that the next few months would be the basis on which he would mold his career.

The date had been set. The Hall family would leave for vacation in two weeks and stay on the shores of Cape Cod Bay, or as New Englanders commonly referred to it, The Cape. Joey was excited, but worried about leaving his pet beagle Hunter, alone for two weeks. In Joey's mind, the anxiety over the dog was almost not worth leaving for vacation. He repeatedly asked his parents if there might be some way to bring Hunter with the family.

His father's answer was always the same. "They don't allow dogs at the motel, Joe. We'll put her in a nice kennel for a couple of weeks. People do it all the time. She'll be fine."

Joey didn't feel comfortable with the kennel idea. He wondered what Hunter would be thinking after they dropped her off in a strange place. *She's gonna' think we're leaving her. When she sees us walk out that kennel door, she's going to think we gave her up.*

The anxiety was almost too much for Joey to handle. The thought about leaving Hunter began to occupy most of his daily thoughts. It began to affect his behavior and mood to the point that it became noticeable to those around him, especially his parents. Ginny pulled Frank aside one night and discussed the situation in private. "Frank, Joey is really obsessing over leaving Hunter for vacation. That's all he thinks about lately. He's had more episodes in the last two weeks than he's had in the last six months." She forlornly dropped her gaze to the floor. "He's not the happy kid we knew this past year. Maybe we should forego the trip to the Cape and just stay home…. just do day trips."

A serious look crossed Frank's face. "Hell no! The boy has got to deal with reality. You said it yourself…don't coddle him. He's going to have to face uncomfortable circumstances throughout his life and this one is minor. It'll be good for him to see that leaving Hunter is hard to live with, but when he sees Hunter is fine after vacation, he'll realize that everything turned out okay."

Ginny pressed Frank, "But, I'd hate to see him lose any ground he's gained over the past few years. He's become a new kid…and right now he's agonizing over the whole thing."

Frank stood up from his chair. "We have other kids, Gin. What about them?" Frank stood and waited for an answer from his wife. He nodded his head, "It'll be fine. You'll see. We'll drop Hunter off at the kennel on Friday and I'll let Joey have as long a goodbye as he wants. Guaranteed…. once we start heading out to the Cape, his focus will change…as well as his mood."

The day finally came when it was time to bring Hunter to the kennel. His father shouted into the house. "I'm bringing Hunter to the kennel now. Whoever wants to come, has to get in the car now. We're leaving for The Cape as soon as we get back."

Joey and his sister Cheryl, climbed into the back of the station wagon with Hunter and took the terrible ride out to Hunter's temporary home. The kennel's owner was waiting for them and put her own leash on the dog, which

Joey didn't care for. She looked at the Halls and smiled, "C'mon. I'll show you where Hunter is going to spend the next two weeks."

Frank, Cheryl, and Joey followed the kennel owner down a wooded path to a long wood structure divided into separate gated bays. To Joey, they resembled covered stalls. The ceilings were low and the only access for light and air was from the gated opening at the front of the bay. Joey hated the place. He looked at his dad to see his reaction, but Frank seemed very matter of fact about the place.

When they arrived at Hunter's bay, the attendant couldn't get Hunter to enter, so she looked at the Halls and told them it would be better if they left. Joey wouldn't have it, but Frank insisted it would be easier for everyone. Reluctantly, Joey and Cheryl turned to leave as Hunter strained at the attendant's leash, barking and trying to pull free. Joey stopped to look back at Hunter and saw the terrified dog panicking. "Dad, she doesn't understand. Let me go back there for a minute. I'll just talk to her for a minute."

Frank turned Joey around. "Keep walking, Joe. Don't turn around, don't look at her. You're only going to make it harder."

Joey was devastated. What must his faithful hound be thinking? He was sure she thought they deserted her. That last image of his panicked dog remained in his memory for years to come.

CHAPTER 37

The first few hours driving out to the Cape were torture for Joey. No one spoke about Hunter or what her kennel looked like, and no one was happy or comfortable with what they had left Hunter to. Joey slumped against the car's back seat and watched the world go by without seeing anything. He worried about his beloved beagle…his best friend. He felt that surely, she must think he betrayed her trust. Joey was getting anxious. He didn't want to be in this car or going… anywhere. He should be going back to get Hunter to bring her home. Everything began to bother him. He was in a foul mood.

"Hey, Joe!" Frank had noticed Joey's silence and realized where it could be heading. "There's going to be a lot of interesting things to see on the way to the Cape. I bet you're looking forward to seeing the ocean and all the different kinds of boats."

"Yeah, maybe, Dad. Right now, I'm just worried about Hunter."

A smile crossed Frank's face. "Are you still thinking about the dog?" He paused and when Joey didn't answer he added, "C'mon. Do you think I'd leave Hunter where anything could happen to her? She's important to me too, ya' know. Did you ever consider that?"

Joey looked away from the window and at the back of his father's head. He felt as if his dad hadn't considered how anyone else felt. "Well, she's my dog, Dad…and she's with me the most. I just don't know what she thinks about us leaving her in a strange place."

"And you're never going to know that. You're going to have to trust me and your mom, and just get on with it. I'm not going to let you ruin this vacation because of the dog. Now, that's the last I want to hear about it."

The rest of the family just listened to the conversation, but remained silent. Joey began to offer one last comment. "But I keep seeing her face…" Joey had stopped talking because he began to experience an episode.

Frank was listening and assumed what might be happening to the boy. About three seconds passed and Joey hadn't finished his sentence. Frank raised his voice to get the boy's attention and shouted into the back seat, "Joe!" There was no answer. Ginny knew what was happening and put her hand on Frank's, as it rested on the front seat arm rest.

Frank felt Ginny's hand but continued, "Joe, you're having another daydream!"

Joey snapped out of it and remembered what he was going to say. "I just keep seeing the look on her face when we walked away from her at the kennel."

Ginny began to squeeze Frank's hand hard and turned her head, so he could see she was looking at him.

Frank got the message and replied to Joey, "Okay, Joe,

I'll turn the car around right now and we'll go back to the kennel, so you can check on her."

For a moment, Joey felt like he really wanted that to happen. He thought, *That would be so great...but we're already two hours into this drive, and then we'd have to turn around again...and Dad is still not going to let her come with us. I'll have to go through leaving her all over again.* He reluctantly answered his father, "Uh, no. I'll get through this. I just have to get used to the idea that she'll understand."

Ginny relaxed her grip on Frank's hand and smiled warmly at her husband.

Another hour of driving passed. The car remained silent except for some desultory talk between the parents. Finally, they passed over the Buzzard's Bay bridge and Frank pointed out a point of interest. "Hey guys! Look below the bridge. On the left, you'll see a big World War Two battle ship docked down there."

Everyone tried to get a look at the big ship, but as soon as Joey saw it with its banners, and the American flag waving from the ship's top mast, and her huge guns facing fore and aft, he was transformed. It was so impressive and stately looking. "Wow! Look at that ...a real battleship... that was in the war! Can we go down there and look at it?"

Frank's plan had worked. He knew they'd be passing the historical site and waited to surprise Joey with it. He smiled and replied, "We can, Joe. It's now a floating museum and we'll be able to go aboard and tour it, but not until our return trip home. I promise it'll be one of our stops on the way."

Joey sat back in his seat and felt different about everything. *I'm gonna' get to tour a real battle ship.* His obsession with Hunter and the kennel evaporated as he reached into his back pack and pulled out the book Mr. Lamont had given him. He stared at it for a moment and read the title, *The Caine Mutiny*. He thought, *This is about a destroyer-minesweeper, but it's still about naval ship of war. I'll start reading this to get ready for the battleship tour.*

The boy's entire personality had gone back to normal. Joey was back.

The next couple of weeks passed without incident. The family played pass football on the beach or sometimes just had a game of catch with the baseball. They swam in the waters of Cape Cod Bay, went for long walks along the shore, and visited several wharves that were populated by fishing vessels and sailing ships of all sizes. Joey was in his glory. He read his book when he laid on the beach, in the car or in the motel. Usually, in the morning, he took out his binoculars and watched several large ships as they traversed the northern part of the bay. It was turning out to be a great vacation.

The evening strolls along the beach at low tide were special. It was his favorite time of the day, and the tide was out. It was a sense of freedom, heightened by a light breeze that blew through his hair and over his body. When he looked out over the bay, the setting sun in the far west set the mood with its colorful display of yellow, orange and red. Joey decided he could live by the ocean. This is where he wanted to be.

Finally, it was time to pack the car and make the trip

back home to Tobacco Valley. Before he left, Joey asked to go back to the beach and get one more look at Cape Cod Bay. He walked to the rear of the motel and up to the shoreline. Gazing out into the bay one more time, he savored the feeling of the clean, fresh salt air as it encircled his being. He closed his eyes and felt the warmth of the sun on his face, and thought about the peaceful vacation he had just experienced. There were no episodes, no family strife, no schedules to keep, and no responsibilities. It was a wonderful way to live.

Joey opened his eyes and looked back out over the water again, taking in a deep breath of cool ocean air. *This is where I want to be,* he thought. *This is the life I want.*

Suddenly, his concentration was interrupted, "It's not over yet, Joe." Frank stood behind his son as he watched him enjoy the morning sun. "We'll be back. Maybe not to this same place...but we'll come back to the Cape."

Joey turned to face his dad. "Yeah, I know, Dad. It was great. I just hate to leave."

Frank smiled and walked up next to his son. "Well, just remember. We still have a stop to make at the Battleship Massachusetts in Fall River on the way back...and maybe we'll stop at the Coast Guard Academy too. I know you've been reading up on that place. I think that kind of life may suit you."

Joey turned to face his dad. "I can't wait to get on the battleship." Joey paused a moment, then added, "I'd really like to visit the Coast Guard Academy, Dad. I think I might want to try and get in there."

"Well, let's look it over first. I think their training ship,

Eagle is there right now. Maybe they'll let you have a tour on that too."

The two started to leave the beach and as they walked, Frank reminded Joey, "We'll go home first, unpack the car, and then go pick up Hunter. She's probably anxious to see you."

Joey stopped in his tracks, "Can't we pick her up on the way home?"

Frank kept walking to the car. "Joe, just get in the car please. Home first, then Hunter."

The tour of the Battleship Massachusetts was more than what Joey could have imagined. When they arrived at the ship's wharf, Frank bought the tickets and waved to the boys. "Go ahead. Go through the whole thing. Have a ball."

Brian and Joey started up by the ship's bridge and worked their way down into the bowels of the ship where the engine room was. They inspected everything more than once. "Let's go back to the bridge, Brian. I want to stand where the captain stood and see what he saw."

Brian rolled his eyes, "C'mon, Joe. We've been there twice already. I want to go back to the main deck and climb through her big guns."

Joey nodded, "Okay you go to the guns and I'll be on the bridge." The boys split up and Joey was in his element. He couldn't get enough of the ship or any information about her past. He tried to imagine what it might have been like to sit in the captain's chair and command a ship of this size. Little did he know, that he'd be back someday, but in a different capacity.

The afternoon spent climbing around and through the battleship was something that Joey would never forget, but as soon as he left the ship's wharf and met up with the family, he looked at his dad and said, "How long will it be before we get to the Coast Guard Academy?"

Ginny and Frank looked at each other forlornly, but realized it had been a promise. Frank gazed up into the sky, "It's about an hour from here, Joe."

Ginny and Frank were okay with the extra stops before continuing home because they realized that Joey was at that point in his life where transitioning into different life choices were at the forefront of his mind. They'd head for the academy next as long as the rest of the family wasn't complaining.

Joey watched the passing scenery through the car's window. He was already excited by what he'd seen on the battleship and couldn't stop talking about it. Now, he anxiously awaited his visit to the Coast Guard Academy and a tour of their training ship, Eagle.

Soon the academy grounds appeared outside the car's right-side window. "Hey, Joe. Look down and to the right of the bridge. That's the academy."

Joey pressed his face up against the window. There was a huge tall ship, with bare masts, white with a red stripe on the side of her port bow, and docked at the academy's wharf. "Is that the Eagle, Dad?"

Frank had already seen the ship, but let Joey make the discovery on his own. He smiled, "That's it, Joe. It's called a three-masted barque, and it's almost 300 feet long. We'll be down there soon, so just sit back and enjoy the view. We'll see about visiting the place once we get through the main gate."

Frank and Ginny shared a quick glance and smiled warmly at one another as Frank continued to drive. They had noticed a huge change in Joey's behavior since the beginning of the trip. Once he had been distracted by something that was at the core of his interest, the whole idea of leaving his beloved dog, Hunter behind became secondary. His anxiety had vanished and so had his episodes. The idea of his dog was not diminished, but allowed by the boy, to be put in an appropriate place in his young mind until he could do something about it. Joey's interest in boats and ships, the sea, and the military occupied the thoughts at the forefront of his conscious mind, and allowed him to re-direct thoughts or ideas. The vacation had turned out to be a positive endeavor. Now, the trick was in controlling the excitement of the moment.

The academy was beautiful, nestled alongside the Thames River in New London, Connecticut. The family walked through the grounds and finally down to the training ship, Eagle. She sat quietly in the river, moored to her wharf. Tourists could be seen on her deck while a few sailors stood by. This time the whole family wanted to go aboard.

It was such an inspiring site and experience to walk the decks of such a famous ship. Joey was in awe...more so than he was on the Battleship Massachusetts. Once the family had their fill, a tour of the academy grounds followed until the heat of the day took its toll. Ginny was first to complain. "Okay, this has been great, but it's getting hotter and I'm getting tired. Cheryl is pretty uncomfortable too, so we're done. I suggest we all get something to drink and head for home."

Joey was sad to see his visit come to an end, but had a feeling about this place. It was a feeling like it was somewhere he was supposed to be. He promised himself that he'd return.

CHAPTER 38

The ride home seemed longer than it had to be. Joey's thoughts turned to getting the car unpacked as quickly as possible so they could pick up Hunter from the kennel. Frank noticed Joey's hurried efforts. "Joe, slow down. We'll be on our way to get Hunter shortly. You're just making the anticipation worse by rushing around so much."

"I know Dad, but the waiting is awful. It's been two weeks."

Frank stopped what he was doing and made the boy sit down. "Look, one hour, two hours, or even a whole day isn't going to make a difference at this point. Dogs don't think like that. In Hunter's case, she just knows she hasn't seen you for a while. However long it takes us to get back up in the hills to Hunter's kennel doesn't matter. You're going to see her today...sometime."

Frank paused a moment to let that sink in. "You have to start thinking like this. As you get older, you'll see that you're not going to be able to do things how and when you want to, or when it feels right for you. That's just life... and if you let that bother you, you'll be uncomfortable and irritated most of your adult life." He paused again, "You need to start thinking this way for your own good."

Joey was quiet for a moment and said, "Okay, Dad. I'll start trying that. It doesn't sound easy, but I'll try."

An hour later, Joey and his sister Cheryl, rode back up into the hills with Frank to bring Hunter home. Finally, the turn into the kennel's gravel drive appeared on the right. The children were excited and guessed at Hunter's reaction when she saw them. They jumped out of the car and watched their father pay the attendant.

The anticipation mounted in the children as they approached Hunter's pen. Joey experienced an episode on the way, but no one noticed since he was just following the others as they approached the kennel area.

"Okay, she's right inside." The attendant bent down and looked under the pen's roof. "Hunter...come on out girl."

There was no movement from inside the pen. It was hot with only one opening and smelled stuffy. The attendant called again, "Hunter, your family is here. Come on girl."

Frank kept his eye on the kennel's opening and in a serious tone said, "Joe, go on in and get her." Frank gently pushed the attendant aside with the back of his left forearm so Joey could pass. Dutifully and in a crouch, the boy ambled into the dark, low roofed pen. The sight he saw would stay with him for the rest of his life. Hunter sat in a corner looking frightened and shivered badly. She appeared as if she couldn't move.

Joey's heart sank. He quickly crawled over to her and gathered her up in his arms. "Hunter! Are you okay girl? What's the matter? It's me...Joey!"

The dog showed no reaction except to exude fright.

Frank watched the whole scenario and turned to the attendant. "What happened here? What's wrong with the dog?"

"Uh, I don't know sir. It's probably just a reaction to seeing you guys again." He went on. "She's been fine, but hasn't been eating much, which is normal when their routine is broken."

In a crouch, Joey lifted the dog off the pen's dirt floor and carried her out of the pen. "She's scared to death, Dad." The other dogs from nearby pens barked and growled continuously.

Frank looked Hunter over and glared back at the attendant. After a moment, Frank turned back toward the children, "Okay, let's get her home where she can relax."

On the way home, Joey held Hunter on his lap and stroked her back while speaking in a low, soothing tone. She fell asleep several times during the thirty-minute trip, but woke back up with a start each time. The dog had been traumatized. Whether it was the kennel environment that the dog couldn't tolerate, the kind of care she received, or more specific to the dog...her reaction to being left in a foreign place for the first time, Joey couldn't be sure. He only knew that something had transformed his dog.

Joey compared her behavior to his own when he was in a stressful situation and had no resources to counter with. The boy realized that even though she was an animal, the surroundings any living creature is subjected to for an extended period of time can have a definite influence on that individual's behavior. Living conditions, a difference in routine, and daily attention were only a few of the ideas that ran through the thirteen-year-old's mind. Living in a hostile environment and lack of friendly interaction were at the fore-front of Joey's reasons for Hunter's behavior, but that would be something he'd never be able to prove. However, he was sure of one thing. He'd never forgive his father for what Hunter had been forced to endure.

That night after dinner, as the family settled into their normal routine, Frank sat with Joey on their patio. "How's Hunter doing?"

Joey sat across from his dad and whittled on a piece of wood. "She's finally sleeping without waking up every ten minutes."

Frank nodded his head, "I'm sorry she went through that experience, Joe. Something obviously upset her to make her act like this. But you have to know, I wouldn't have brought her there if I thought this kind of thing would happen. I thought I was doing the best for her under the circumstances."

Joey kept whittling and didn't look up, "Yeah, well it wasn't the best thing, Dad. She's probably changed forever."

Frank realized the boy was upset and picked his words carefully. "How are you doing with all this?"

Joey stopped whittling and finally looked into his father's face. "It was a great vacation, Dad…but it wasn't worth what happened to Hunter. She'll probably never be the same again."

Frank saw that he had the boy's attention and leaned forward. "Joe, I am just as upset about Hunter as you, but I can't undo what's been done. If I could prove she had been mistreated or abused, I'd go after that kennel and make sure they got their license to house animals revoked, along with a fine for maltreatment. But I can't prove anything…

there are no marks on her and we weren't there to witness anything." He paused a moment and continued. "Joe, I want you to remember this terrible thing, but I want to remind you that bad things are going to happen in life. Things like this are unforeseen and sometimes unpreventable. If you let them interfere with future events or the attention you need to give the current events, you will be living a nightmare. You're getting older and should be able to find a way to deal with some of those circumstances without allowing them to affect what might be happening to you or those around you…or the progress of some future event."

Joey seemed as if he was considering what his father had just dropped on him and looked concerned. Frank continued, "Someday you'll be responsible for more than just yourself. You'll probably have a family with children, and more dogs, a house, and a job." Frank paused and considered Joey's interest in boats and ships, "You might even be in command of a large ship someday. You'd really have to prioritize problems then." Frank was silent for a few moments. When Joey looked at him again, he knew he had struck a nerve. "You have to be able to put disappointment, and in some cases, tragedy in its place. Consider it for what it is and then put it aside until you can attend to what is happening around you at the present time. I'm not saying to forget about it…just don't let it stifle you for what you need to be doing now."

Joey looked back at his dad and nodded his head. "I get it, Dad. You know, I was so excited about ships, the Navy, and the Coast Guard until I got home to Hunter. It all went away for a little while, but now I know where I want to go with all this."

Frank smiled, "And where is that, Joe?"

I want to go to the Coast Guard Academy and someday be the captain of a Coast Guard ship. I want to be in the service of others…and I want to be able to make a difference in people's lives."

Frank sat back in his chair and smiled broadly. "You have it in you, Joe. You have all of what that might take, and I'll help you get there, but it's going to take a lot of work… and studying.

"I know, Dad. I'm gonna' do it."

CHAPTER 39

·· ⟨⟩ ··

September arrived, and the Halls were preparing for the upcoming school year. Joey was entering his 10th grade of school, commonly referred to as his sophomore year. The boy had grown to almost six feet tall and weighed 180 pounds. His workouts were more extreme than ever and the high school's coaches had been calling him to come tour the new high school and made offers to take him to professional football games in the region.

After the last call from the area's football coach, Frank and Ginny sat down to talk one night, when Joey was out with friends. Their concern was that although Joey's disorder had diminished dramatically, he still experienced episodes and the condition's triggers could still instigate an episode if the scenario was intense enough. The parents sat outside alone on the patio. They wore serious faces, but not worried ones. Ginny was concerned about the new higher intensity football program. "Frank, I'm worried about Joey's step up to the more demanding level of high school sports. It's more intense, more physically demanding, and includes more pressure. The competition is greater at this level with much more interaction from the coaches on the players private lives and Joey is beginning to get letters from colleges. I'm not sure I want him playing at this level…and if he does, do we tell the coaches about his disorder?"

Frank sat in his chair and leaned in toward his wife. "He's taking sports more seriously than ever and keeps saying it is one of the ways for him to get into the Coast Guard Academy." Frank paused a moment and looked up from the patio floor into her face, "He's getting very good…at everything, including his interest in his studies. He's focusing on those things because of what he wants to be some day. We're going to have to watch the situation carefully…and watch him for any kind of signs that indicate he may be overextending his efforts. As for telling the coaches, I feel that if they knew about his problem, they could harm his progress and any future with the Coast Guard. It's my feeling they just don't understand enough about the disorder and how it will someday disappear."

Ginny listened to Frank while nodding her head in a way that wasn't in agreement, but that she understood Frank's thinking. "You realize that playing at this level can put in him in greater danger physically as well as mentally, knowing he may never get into the academy anyway."

Frank nodded his head. "I realize that Ginny, but everything in life is a gamble, and this is a positive one. Joey's efforts are with the idea of bettering himself and following his dreams. If he doesn't try, it'll never happen." Frank paused a moment and added, "Don't mention this to Joey, but if the Coast Guard's administration…or powers-to-be, found out about his medical history, Joey would probably…never be a consideration for the academy."

Ginny sat back in her chair shaking her head. "Well,

he has an appointment with Doctor Horowitz next month. We'll get his take on the matter and see what he thinks."

Frank raised his eyebrows. "We've depended on that man so heavily over the years. If anything ever happens to him, we'll be sunk. He's getting on in age and was pretty old when we first met him so many years ago."

Ginny pursed her lips, "I know. I've thought about that too. Well, he still has an appointment with us in October and if anything ever did happen, we still have that medical log and living history, he's been keeping on Joey all these years. That is our property and we could request those files to give another neurologist to pick up where Horowitz left off."

Doctors Baldwin and Petrillo sat in a dark and quiet corner of a favorite restaurant specifically chosen for confidentiality, and miles from the hospital. Baldwin leaned forward across the table and spoke in a hushed tone. "I have checked Horowitz's patient schedule. It looks like he's going to see Joey Hall this month for his annual appointment and well-being check. It is next Saturday at 11:00 AM. I'm going to be there with the excuse that I need to look over some patient files and when I see the Halls come in, I'll nonchalantly walk out into the waiting room to get a book and strike up a conversation. I'll ask about the boy and mention something about his progress with Horowitz that may make them question the doctor's credibility."

Petrillo pursed his lips and nodded favorably. "What are you going to say?"

Baldwin continued, "When the parents respond, I'll start talking about Horowitz…while wearing a sad face, and allude to some questionable and worrisome observations from the staff. I'll be sure to mention the doctor's behavior is of course only rumor, but how unfortunate it must be for a doctor of his caliber to have to shoulder those accusations, especially at this point in his career."

Petrillo pursed his lips and narrowed his eyes. "Sounds like a good plan, but I would keep it light for now and just vaguely suggest any questionable possibilities regarding Horowitz's memory and behavior."

Baldwin nodded in agreement. "We'll have to be very careful as to how we approach this. We'll start small with insinuations and let it snowball. Once the general public gets hold of it, we'll have little left to do, but let's put on a sad face for Horowitz and pretend we're sorry for him."

Petrillo added. "I agree. But I also want to start getting into Horowitz's head."

Baldwin looked confused, "What do you mean?"

"We should start condescending to him. Everything he does or doesn't do. We'll treat him as if he's elderly and anything that he forgets to say or do is okay, because he's been doing it…for so long. We'll fabricate things that he said he was going to do but must have forgotten, and then we'll start to get him to second guess himself." Petrillo sat back in his chair. "When his patient load begins to dwindle and the staff no longer takes him seriously, he'll begin to feel inadequate as a doctor and hopefully retires."

Baldwin smiled and gently bumped his fist on the table. "You got it! Even the best doctor can be made to look as if he were the worst."

CHAPTER 40

Spring tryouts for the new high school's football team had been rigorous, but everyone knew they were only a prelude of what the fall would bring in just a few months.

The August tryouts were extremely demanding. Expectations of the new high school coach for new players were high and the physical demands were above what Joey had anticipated. The workouts in the heat of August were tortuous. Once again, there were only a limited number of available positions on the new team and there were twice the number of candidates.

Ginny had been correct as to the high school's higher expectations of the players regarding physical and emotional limitations. Frank and Ginny worried through the next two weeks about Joey's progress and how it could be influenced by the new demands, but as Frank pointed out, Joey had not complained once. His daily appearance revealed an expected level of fatigue and lameness as to the boy's physical reaction of what he was experiencing, but the parents watched his daily emotional balance to a closer degree.

Joey didn't display anything different from what he'd shown in the past few years except a higher level of fatigue and maybe more exasperation caused by the higher demands imposed by the coaches.

Finally, the trial period was over, and the new team prepared for the school's first football game. The team was below average, with regard to the size of a high school football player, but that point was one that was intentionally ignored. The boys would need to make up for that in play execution and speed.

Game day for Joey's first year in the new high school finally arrived. It was an away game in a different state. Many of the players' parents and fellow classmates took the opportunity as a reason to get away for the day and travel to see the new team play.

The game was set up in northern Massachusetts and well out of Tobacco Valley's competition circuit. Coach Newton's plan was an attempt to get his team accepted into a higher level of play, and today would be their debut. If all went well, Johnsville Public High School's Huskys would enter into a new division with better competition and higher ranked schools.

Frank left Joey off outside the school's athletic area. "Okay, Joe. Good luck and have a good game. We'll be following the player bus up to the game."

"Thanks, Dad. See ya' later."

Joey entered the varsity team's locker room where Coach Newton patiently awaited his players' arrival. Finally, all forty players sat in front of the new coach. Newton was a mid-sized man, bald and looked to be in good physical condition for a middle-aged man of thirty-five. The only thing Joey knew about him was that he was strict, by the book, and dedicated to the sport of football.

Newton stopped pacing and glanced over at his assistant coach, Garvey. "Is everyone here?"

Garvey nodded to indicate everyone scheduled for the away game was present.

"Alright guys, I want everyone to enjoy the ride. It's about a two-hour trip and I want you guys rested and ready to go when we get there. Relax, go through your playbooks, talk quietly, but no loud or raucous behavior. He looked around the room, "Does everyone understand?"

Everyone knew the coach's temper and remained quiet. "Okay, let me tell you the importance of this game. If we win, we will be accepted into the new Valley Wheel Conference. That will mean an entirely different game schedule against better schools than this town has ever played before. If we lose, we'll be right back where we started…and I don't want to be there anymore. We're better than that…we've been better than that for a few years now. So, play your best, do your jobs, and give me one hundred and ten percent."

Newton paused and looked around the room. "I mean it, gentlemen. I won't accept anything less. Anyone out there that I think is dogging it or not playing the way I trained them, will be sidelined. I won't tolerate missed passes, missed blocks, interceptions, or fumbles." He turned to the defensive team huddled in the back of the locker room, "There better not be any offsides calls or mis-tackles either. You make two mistakes, and you may lose your position to someone that wants it more than you do." The coach looked around the room again. "I can't be more sincere, gentlemen. If you lose this game for me, there will be hell to pay. Next week's practices will be a nightmare, so get it together and make me proud. Play like we've shown you and we will win."

Newton turned to walk out of the room and suddenly stopped. He turned to the three sophomores that had been recently recruited onto the varsity team and pointed at them since they were sitting together. "Fulton, Trotsky, and Hall. I'll be watching you guys closely. If you show the slightest hesitation or fear...you are gone. I'll send you right to the bus and you can stay there until after the game." Then Newton walked up to Joey and grabbed his jersey just below the neck line. "You're a halfback, son. Get me some touchdowns or I'll have to put an upperclassman in your position. Nobody's position is guaranteed on this team... especially not a sophomore's."

Joey remained as stoic as he could. He felt as if the team was being admonished for something they hadn't done yet. "I'll do my best, Coach."

Newton nodded at the boy. "Yes, you will!" Newton walked past Garvey and without looking at the man mumbled, "Get them on the bus."

The Huskys ran out to the football field and began their warm ups, followed by the backs and receivers setting up near the goal line for pass practice. The linemen and defensive players went to another area nearby, followed by their own coaches to practice their starts off the line.

Finally, the coaches called the entire team back to their designated side of the field. The battle was about to begin.

Joey was nervous. The coach had seen him drop two passes just a few minutes ago and was worried about his playing status. As if on cue, Newton walked up to Joey and grabbed him by his facemask. "Okay Hall. Here's the deal. I think you're nervous. You dropped two beautiful passes out there during warm ups, so you're on the bench for now. I'm going to put Bobby Jones in there for a while. If he does well, I'll keep him there, so just have a seat on the bench. I'll call for you if I need you."

Joey was devastated. He went back to the bench and sat down. *My whole family is coming all the way up here to see me play and Newton benches me before the game even starts.*

The band began to play the Star-Spangled Banner and Newton shouted, "Everyone up and on the sideline! Stand straight and take your helmets off!"

Immediately following the national anthem, the coin toss followed, and the Husky offense took their place on the field. The other right halfback, Bobby Jones, an upperclassman, took Joey's place on the field. Joey wondered what his father was thinking. That was supposed to be him out there. What Joey didn't know, was that his family had got lost and weren't at the game yet.

The first quarter played on, and the opposing team was ahead seven to nothing. The Huskys were getting pushed around on the playing field and suddenly there was a player down. It was the other right halfback, Bobby Jones. Joey heard Newton's drill sergeant voice, "Hall! Joey Hall!"

Joey jumped up from the bench and ran over to Newton. "I'm here coach." Once again, Newton grabbed

Joey by his helmet's facemask. "You're going out there for Bobby. We think it's his arm. I'm calling one of your special plays…929 sweep. You get that ball and take it in! We're on our own 42-yard line, so you better turn on that speed of yours, and get it out of our backyard."

Joey knew the play immediately, *929…pitch out sweep to the left sideline.*

Joey ran out to his team's huddle and leaned in to where the quarterback knelt. "What do you have, Joe?"

"929 sweep. On two."

The quarterback repeated the play to the huddle. "Okay guys, you heard him, 929 sweep, on two…and give him some good blocking."

The quarterback stood over the offensive line and called the signals. "Hut one, hut two."

Joey sprang from his set position in the backfield and ran left toward the sideline. The quarterback turned and tossed the ball to Joey. He snagged it from the air and began to run at half speed as he looked for approaching defenders. The offensive line seemed to pull to the left and literally created a human corridor along the side of the field. Joey extended his strides and was at a full run along the field's sideline. His heart was racing, and his breathing was fast and shallow. The crowd was screaming and Joey could see the yellow goal posts getting closer. It seemed like an eternity. He was running smooth and fast with the football tucked under his left arm. He could hear heavy breathing just behind him. *That's gotta' be the defensive safety,* he thought. *He's gotta' be close.* Then Joey saw the five-yard line just in front of him, followed by a grunt from behind and a severe tug at the back of his jersey. At that speed, the tug was just enough to throw off his balance, and Joey landed in the grass just a few yards from the goal line.

The opposing team's tackler...the defensive safety, put out his hand and helped Joey to his feet. "Nice run, buddy. You almost beat me."

Joey thanked the boy as he jogged back to the huddle and knew what had happened. The excitement of making the first touchdown of his high school career coupled with the nervousness of pleasing his coach had instigated an episode. Doctor Horowitz had always reminded him that it wouldn't stop him from doing whatever he was doing, and in most cases, would allow him to continue the motor skills in progress, but not with the same focus or intensity he had before. Joey realized it had caused him to slow his running just enough to allow the defensive safety to grab his jersey.

Another player came into the huddle with another play, but before he gave it, tapped Joey on the shoulder. "Hey Joe, Coach wants you back on the sideline. Says you probably need to catch your breath after that long run."

Joey turned and ran over to Newton on the sideline. Newton looked at the boy with no expression. "Looks like you ran out of gas out there. Guess we need to do more wind sprints next week. Get back on the bench for now. John Miller is going to take over for you."

Joey felt embarrassed and defeated. He sat on the bench and watched the game unfold before him. His team failed to carry the ball over the goal line, and they had to punt to get the ball back up field again. Newton turned around and glared at Joey. "That's your fault, Hall. You better hope we don't lose by a touch down!

The exhilaration of just having executed a tremendous

play had been completely erased, and the boy's self-confidence destroyed by one negative comment from the coach…the person one was supposed to impress.

The injuries began to add up. The Huskys were taking a beating. One of the players had been tackled on a run up the middle, and wasn't able to get up. As the other players got off the prone figure, substitute halfback John Miller remained on the ground. Once again, Newton turned back to the bench. "Hall! Joey Hall!"

Joey ran up to the sideline and stood awaiting the coach's demands. "Get out there for John. He won't be back in the game, so you're it! You're going to go off tackle. Call the veer buck-right play." Newton grabbed Joey by the facemask again and leaned into the boy's face. "Break for the sideline as soon as you can, and get over that goal line… and don't trip this time!"

Joey felt an added sense of pressure now. The team was losing and there were no other right halfbacks to back him up. It was only him for the rest of the game. He felt nervous as he ran out to the huddle and gave the play.

The quarterback looked into Joey's eyes. "That's you, Joe. Off tackle and veer to the right. Don't screw it up."

Joey felt a sense of distrust by his fellow team mates now. He knew he hadn't done anything wrong. It was all because of how Newton had handled the tackle from his long run. His sense of inadequacy was replaced by a surge of adrenaline that coursed through the boy's body. "I know. I got it. Just get the ball to me."

The quarterback called a quick signal and handed the ball off to Joey. He took the ball through the line and off tackle. He twisted and turned to break several tackles and saw the sideline out of the corner of his eye. Joey stood up and turned on the speed. One defensive player dove at Joey's feet, but he easily vaulted the attack as if it was a fallen log in the woods back home. Joey was finally clear and turned up field, but once again was knocked out of bounds on the twenty-yard line by the same defensive safety that had taken him down earlier.

The defensive safety stood over him and offered his hand. The two boys' eyes met as Joey stood up. The defensive safety smirked, "Hey, I'm just doing my job, man. Good run though." With that, he turned and ran back to his own huddle.

Play after play, Newton sent Joey's plays out to the huddle. The team was losing badly, so Newton went for broke and chose a risky play. A new player brought the play in, "Coach wants 122 bootleg pass." He turned to Joey and said, "He told me to tell you to pass it to the furthest receiver downfield, no matter what the coverage is."

The play looked as if it was just a pitchout to Joey in the backfield for a sweep attempt. The plan required two offensive guards to pull from their position on the line, and run to a place in front of Joey to block any defenders. The action required Joey to run out toward the side line while catching the toss and pass the ball to a receiver downfield. It was a longshot, and the play had a zero-success rate, but it was Newton's last-ditch effort to keep from getting shut out.

The quarterback looked into Joey's eyes. "Are you up for this, Joe? You've been getting pretty beat up out here."

Joey nodded. "I'm okay. Just give me a good toss so I

can get out to the flat and have a little time to set up before I throw."

The quarterback nodded and looked back at the rest of the huddle. "Okay guys, 122 bootleg pass…on two." He looked at the two guards. "Keep those linebackers off Joey as long as you can. We need this pass to get to the receivers or it'll be a shutout game."

Once again, the quarterback called the signals and pitched Joey the ball as he ran through the backfield. The guards pulled, but didn't get there fast enough. Joey set up for the throw and suddenly everything went black. Joey lay motionless under a pile of defenders.

Newton saw the mass tackle. "Oh, Shit!" He glanced over to Assistant Coach, Garvey. "Get ready to send out the medical team."

One by one, the players got off the pile and went back to their huddle. Joey remained on his back, not moving. Garvey looked at Newton, "I'll send in the medics."

Newton grabbed his arm, "Wait! Give him another second. We have time for two more plays. We can still pull it off."

Joey began to stir and struggled to his feet. He shook off the pain and walked into the opposing team's huddle. The opposing team's defensive captain saw Joey enter his huddle and looked concerned, "What are you doing, man? Are you okay?"

Everything became clear now. Joey had an episode after the tackle and was now in the opposing team's huddle. There was no hiding his mistake. Joey was dressed in a white game jersey and white pants, while the opposing players were in red jerseys and red pants. Then he heard

Newton's shouts. "Hall, get out of there! Hall! No fighting! Get back to your huddle!"

Realizing that everyone thought Joey was about to start a fight because of the hard hit and piling on, Joey thought fast. Everyone in the huddle looked concerned for him. The facial expressions of these so-called tough guys, revealed kindness and concern for him. Joey quickly patted the players' backs that stood on each side of him before he ran back to his own huddle. "Good tackle you guys. Good tackle."

To everyone else, it appeared a normal reaction to a stunning tackle. Joey's own team mates thought he had been giving the other players trouble about the hard hit… and the audience on the sidelines never knew the difference. Joey's quick thinking had worked.

Finally, the game was over. The score was 38 to nothing. Newton stood silently on the field's sideline with his head down and his hands on his hips.

Garvey murmured, "Coach, the boys are coming off the field. Do you want to talk to them here or on the bus?"

Newton raised his right arm with his thumb in the hitchhiker position. "Get them on the bus…Now!

Coach Newton boarded the bus full of exhausted and sore players. He stood and panned the interior that consisted of forlorn and disappointed faces. The bus was quiet. Finally, Newton nodded his head and began speaking in a low tone. "Well boys, our chances of getting into the Valley Wheel Conference are gone. A 38 to nothing loss ensures we aren't even a consideration for that level of play." The coach paused a moment for effect and continued. "What in hell were you guys thinking out there?" The tone of Newton's voice began to rise, "Your play execution was awful! There were missed passes, fumbles, missed tackles… what happened to the team I thought I knew?" He shook his head and looked down at the floor, "I guess it's back to fundamentals. You guys had no business being on the field with the kind of players you just went against."

Newton looked around the bus and into each boy's face. Most of the players looked down and not at the coach.

Finally, Newton noticed Joey sitting in an aisle seat about mid-bus. "And then there is you, Joey Hall. Because of you, we missed a touchdown and were shutout! Why? Because you ran out of gas five yards from the goal line. Are you that out of shape that you allowed the defensive safety to catch you after leading him for fifty-three yards down the sideline?" Newton nodded his head at Joey. "That means to me that if Joey Hall couldn't outrun that safety for only another five yards, the rest of you must be out of shape too. So, here's the deal. You can look forward to two weeks of wind sprints and track work…in full gear, rain or shine. Anyone that misses a practice is cut."

There was a comment from the back of the bus. "Thanks a lot, Joe."

The coach looked around the bus one more time and shook his head. "There won't be any talking on this bus… by any of you, all the way home! I don't want to hear you or look at your faces. I'm disgusted!"

The coach turned and sat down next to Garvey. "Okay, driver take us home."

That night when Joey came home for dinner, the family was waiting. Frank was the first to speak, "Hey, Joe! We got lost and missed the first quarter of the game, but I heard you had a long fifty-three-yard run. Wow!"

Joey shrugged, "Yeah, but it didn't help. We still got shutout." The boy turned to go in the other room. "Thanks for going to the game, but I don't want to talk about it right now." He turned and went upstairs to his room.

Joey laid on his bed and stared at the ceiling. *I don't get Newton. He puts me at starting halfback, then benches me before the game even starts because I dropped a couple of passes in practice, then puts me back in because the substitute halfback is an upperclassman, only to put me back in when the substitute gets hurt.* Joey became more upset the more he thought about it. *He never said nice run, and blames me for the way the game went.*

Joey felt bad about having had an episode during his long run. He wondered if that was going to be the story of his life...of almost doing something great, only to be compromised at the last moment because he allowed his emotions to trigger an episode. He decided at that moment, that nothing...no one, no situation, no threat, not anything, would ever get him worked up again where it could influence his performance in anything he said or did. Of course, he realized there would probably be isolated instances he'd have to work on, but he resolved to dig up the courage within himself to quell his fears, nervousness, feelings, or excitement.

Joey considered the tools he might be able to use to accomplish his control over his emotions. His usual workouts and focus on schoolwork helped, but he had to remind himself that if he got too focused in those areas, they too could lead to worry. Deep breathing exercises, meditation, and reading helped. How could he not get worked up over something he deeply cared about, or its outcome?

Hmmm, the outcome, he thought. Joey began to think about the advice Dr Horowitz gave him. *Why am I worrying about what could happen before I even start anything? If I can convince myself that I've done everything I can, and consider the event or problem for what it is, instead of making it more that it really is, I should be fine. I used that during football tryouts when things got extremely hard. It kind of gave me a safe place to go when things around me seemed beyond reach or were unreasonable.*

Joey began to feel better immediately and knew what he had to do. He resolved to keep this advice in the forefront of his mind until it was a natural way to think. He smiled and got up from the bed. He had a plan and would make it work.

CHAPTER 41

The football season passed without further incident. Coach Newton had his revenge on the Huskys for a few weeks, but soon the unhappy coach realized he had almost as many players on the injured list as he did that were able to play. Reluctantly, the coach brought the practices back to regular workout status. As for Joey, his new plan had been working and life was good on and off the field.

The football season had finally come to an end and winter sports were now on the boy's mind. The new high school had a pool and there was talk about the first swim team in the little country town. Joey was excited, but welcomed the wait to practice patience until it was confirmed that there would be tryouts for the town's first swim team.

Frank sat at the dinner table one evening after dinner and asked, "Hey Joe! Are you going to try out for the new swim team at your school? It sounds as if it's right up your ally."

"Yeah, I'm gonna' go for it, Dad. They're going to have a meeting for all those interested, tomorrow night after school. I'll need Mom to pick me up afterward."

Ginny turned from her usual place at the sink. "That's fine. Just give me a call on one of the school phones when you're ready to leave."

Joey smiled, "Okay. That will be easy since this school even has public pay phones in the main lobby. I'll call as soon as it's over."

The following day after school, Joey sat in one of the school's open lecture rooms off one of the main hallways and waited for the meeting to begin. Across the hall, a student committee of some sort had just ended. Joey sat and watched as boys and girls poured out of the classroom. Presently, a pretty sophomore girl came through the door and saw Joey sitting alone. She smiled, and turned back toward the classroom to say goodbye to the people she'd just been with, and then came across the hallway.

Joey remained slouched in his chair. *What a beautiful girl! I think she's one of the school's cheerleaders...seen her at some of the football games.* He tried not to stare, but now he noticed she was crossing the hallway and coming straight toward him. *Uh oh, she's coming over here! Aw, jeez. I don't even know her name.*

Too late. She stopped right in front of him. "Hi, aren't you one of the football players?"

Joey sat up straight. "Yeah, I was, but the season is over now. I'm Joey Hall. I'm waiting to go to the swim team meeting in about thirty minutes."

She smiled, "Oh, you're a swimmer too! My name is Charlie. I was one of the cheerleaders. Right now, I'm running a committee for the prom in May."

Joey noticed everything about her, including her bright blue eyes. She had long black hair, a nice figure, and beautiful teeth. He didn't know what else to say, but he wished she would stay longer. She smiled again when Joey said nothing. "Well, it's nice to meet you. I have to go. My ride is waiting."

Joey was still without words. She turned back toward him as she walked away. "I'll see you around school. I think we're in the same class."

He smiled back and gave her a quick wave of his hand. Joey watched as she walked away. He had taken note of everything. The light green dress she wore with a sort of bib arrangement between the shoulder straps, the way she looked at him, and the tone of her voice. He was enamored with her. *I know who she is, but I think she's out of my league. But she did come across the hallway to meet me.*

Joey's concentration was interrupted by the school's public address system, "ALL BOYS INTERESTED IN THE SWIM TEAM TRYOUTS PLEASE REPORT TO THE GYM. THE MEETING FOR ALL INCUMBENT SWIMMERS BEGINS IN FIFTEEN MINUTES."

Joey snapped out of his shock and quick conversation with his new friend, Charlie. *Better get down there. I'm about as far away from the gym as I could be.*

The swim team meeting began just as the first meeting with the football team did. The coach stood in front of the bleachers looking at a clipboard ignoring everyone that walked in. He was a tall man and had the slim, muscular build of a swimmer. A whistle and stop watch dangled from around his neck, and he wore a baseball cap that said Husky Swimming. The coach looked to be around thirty-five years old and seemed to be of the serious type.

Eventually the coach looked at his watch and instructed

one of the boys to close the gym doors. "Good afternoon, gentlemen. I'm Coach Langley. It appears we have a larger turnout than I need for the team, so there will be tryouts. I only need about thirty people and we have about twice that in the bleachers." He stopped and paused as he perused the students. "You guys do realize that this is one of the hardest endurance sports you could be trying out for...right?" He paused again and watched the boys' faces. "There will be long distance racers, sprinters, and divers. We'll spend a few days with everyone trying everything, and then I'll put you where I think you can best help the team." He looked at the team again. "If you're not good with that you may leave now. I need hardworking, dedicated athletes...not afraid to be pushed beyond their limits."

No one in the bleachers moved or said a word. Langley perused his audience of fifteen and sixteen-year-olds. *I'll probably get half of these guys back for tomorrow's tryouts.* No one moved, so the coach dismissed the meeting. "Okay, then. I want everyone at the pool in your swim suits, tomorrow afternoon, ready to swim hard.

That night after dinner, Joey sat in his room and thought about the new coach and what he had said to the team. It seemed as if all the coaches had the same opening speech for a new complement of prospective athletes. It was always about hard work and punishment, and if you didn't like it...there was the door. Joey remembered that he had never even told his parents about what football coach Newton had said after the first game of the season. That terrible moment on the bus when he admonished him in front of the entire team. If his father had known about that incident, it was guaranteed his dad would have forced him to quit football, so he just let it go. But, what was this coaching behavior about? He considered his new resolution about refusing to allow anyone's behavior or threatening words cause him any kind of anxiety again, especially where it might cloud his thinking or affect his performance. *This guy is just another bag of wind looking to scare the weaker athletes away, so he doesn't have to work as hard to dwindle the number of incumbent athletes from the team roster. I'm not going to worry about him or what he says he can do to us during try outs. I'm an above average swimmer and if they lose me…for whatever reason, they will be the losers.*

The next afternoon, about half of the people that had showed up for the swim team meeting yesterday, showed up for the first tryout. Coach Langley came out of his poolside office and blew his whistle. "Okay, line up at the shallow end of the pool behind the starting blocks in columns of four people. The first guy on the block will dive in when I blow the whistle. I want you to swim down the lane and back as fast as you can. When that man touches the wall, the next guy dives in, and so forth. Just keep going through the lines like that until I tell you to stop. Anyone that can't make two laps of the pool during his turn is cut." The coach smiled and smiled at the nervous swimmers, "So that means that if you guys perform as I want, you should each be sprinting down the pool and back every forty seconds. It's the beginning of the season, so twenty seconds each way…max. By mid-season you'll be doing that race in less than thirty seconds."

One by one, swimmers were dropping out of the requested laps. Some began to run for the lavatory to vomit their lunch. Langley kept up the pace for twenty minutes before he called an end to the torture. The boys were all in the pool leaning against the wall in the shallow end trying to catch their breath. Joey saw the smug look on Langley's face and decided to throw it back it on him. "Hey, we want more, Coach. We're just getting warmed up."

The swimmers in Joey's general area looked at him in horror and his best friend Jim Fulton leaned into his ear. "Are you crazy? He's kicking our ass. We don't want any more of this shit."

Joey smiled back and said, "It's all a mind game, Jim. He's lost five guys already. He won't go there."

The coach looked down into the pool at the breathless swimmers. "You like that, Mr. Hall? How about I give you guys a few more then?"

Joey nodded his head as he looked into the worried faces of the exhausted swimmers around him and nodded his head. "Yeah, okay...whatever. We're already wet."

Langley squinted his eyes at Joey, "Yes well, unfortunately we have other events I need to get to. We'll have time for more of those sprints another day." The coach stiffened and walked to the other end of the pool. He smiled viciously at the tired swimmers, "Take a breather and then we'll do some slow distance laps to loosen up."

Fulton murmured to Joey, "You're lucky he didn't push that, Joe. The guys would have made you pay...big time."

Joey smiled at his friend, "Your welcome."

That evening Frank asked Joey about practice. "Well, Joe. How was your first swim team practice?"

Joey was quick to answer. "It was okay Dad. Coach tried to weed out the weaker swimmers. You know...the usual weed 'em out routine, so they can cut the team down, but it wasn't anything I couldn't handle." Joey took a drink of water and brightened up. "I met this girl yesterday before the team meeting. She was just finishing up a meeting of her own and we started talking. She was one of the cheerleaders during football season and she recognized me."

Frank and Ginny exchanged a serious glance. Frank nodded his head and raised his eyebrows. Ginny smiled warmly at her son and asked, "That's nice, Joe. What's her name?"

Joey swallowed a forkful of spaghetti and replied, "Charlie."

Once again, the parents exchanged confused looks. This behavior was totally unlike the son they knew. Normally, he would go on and on about the day's tryouts or practice, in such detail someone would have to find a way to change the subject. But this time, Joey changed the subject to a new girl he met in the hallway.

Ginny came over to the table and sat down. "So, what is she like, Joe?" What does she look like?"

"She's very pretty with black hair and blue eyes. She's a little shorter than I am and has a nice figure." He paused a moment and added. "Well, of course she's got a great figure...she's a cheerleader. She does all those gymnastics and jumping around at all the games and parades, so she's probably in pretty good shape."

Ginny began to press Joey, "So, you just met her?"

"Yeah, I've seen her around school, and at the

football, and basketball games, but I never thought she'd recognize me."

Ginny patted Joey's left arm, "There's probably a lot of other girls that recognize you, Joe. Give yourself some credit."

"Well, I kind of like this one, Mom. When she talks to me, it's like there is nothing else around. She gets my full attention with just a few words."

Ginny smiled, gave Frank a quick glance, and began to clear the table of dishes. "That's nice, Joe. I hope we get to meet her someday."

Joey just nodded at his mother. "Maybe you will."

The weeks flew by. Swim practices were extremely hard, and Joey had been excelling in sprint races and was anchor man on the final relay of the meet, usually scheduled as one of the final races. Because of his talent and dedication to the team…and demonstrated leadership, Joey was appointed Swim Team Captain. The position was appointed by the coach and Joey felt comfortable, only because everyone agreed with the choice.

It was finally time for the meet against Johnsville's rival school and it appeared as if it was going to be a close meet. The coaches always had a pretty good idea of which team had the advantage just by comparing their swimmer's times with the competition.

Swim Coach Tom Langley sat in the school cafeteria with a pencil and paper scratching out swimmers and assigning them to races they'd never swam before. Coach

Newton was Langley's office mate and asked him one lunch time, "It looks like you're working real hard on that meet's strategy, Tom. It must be going to be a close one this time."

Langley, looked up from his scribbling and nodded his head. "Yeah, it's going to come down between two races… the 50 and the 100-yard freestyle."

Newton asked, "Who's your fastest swimmer for those two races?"

Langley's face was back in his paperwork. "Joey Hall for us, and Jack Hardy for them. They're within a second of each other."

Newton slapped the table as he stood to leave. "I'd put my money on Hall. I had him in football. He's got heart and the stamina to go with it. I don't think he'll let you down. I don't know much about the other school's…Hardy, except that he's a good athlete."

Langley only nodded his head as he continued to stare at his race sheets. He penciled in Joey's name for center lane in both races.

Finally, the day of the rival swim meet arrived. Joey had begun to walk Charlie to all of her classes, and a new relationship had begun to blossom. Charlie had also taken on a new responsibility as Swim Team Manager. She listened to Joey worry over the upcoming meet and finally felt it was time to let Joey know what she had overheard from some of the athletic coaches a week ago. "Joey, I heard the meet is going to come down between two races. It's going to be you against Monson's, Jack Hardy. You guys are in lanes three and four that night…center pool. It's supposed to be quite a spectacle. Have they spoken to you about that yet?"

Joey stopped walking and looked at Charlie. "Lanes three and four are reserved for swimmers with the best times." He paused as he considered the responsibility. "It's gotta' be the 50 and the 100-yard freestyle, and I didn't think I was even close to Hardy's time. He's a well-known swimmer in the region."

Charlie hugged her books close to her chest and began to walk with a smile on her face. "Yup, center lanes. Everybody is going to see how good you are."

Joey walked alongside of Charlie silently and remembered his promise to himself to not allow rumors affect him emotionally or otherwise.

Charlie noticed Joey's silence. "Why so quiet? Does that bother you?"

"Nah, I just don't understand why they haven't told me about how important those two races are going to be."

Charlie smiled and turned toward him. They had arrived at her classroom. "They probably didn't want you to get too worked up over it. Those are two of your best races, and they probably figured you realized you'd be swimming them anyway, so why put any pressure on you." She reached up and kissed him lightly on the cheek. "You're going to be great…Captain." Charlie turned and walked into the classroom leaving Joey alone in the hallway.

The bell rang, shocking the boy out of his thoughts. *I can do this*, he thought and walked to his own class.

Meet day had arrived and Joey led his team of swimmers out into the pool area. The spectators were seated in the stands to the right of the pool entrance. Spectators from Johnsville, clapped and cheered as their team walked single file into the pool area. As his team watched and waited for their own race to come up, Joey tried to push away the thought of how close the meet was going to be. Team advantage made several turnovers and finally, the short 50-yard sprint was called. The swimmers took their places on the starting blocks with Jack Hardy and Joey Hall, side by side at center pool, in lanes three and four. Lanes one and two and five and six were occupied by swimmers with slower times.

Joey was nervous. He stood in lane three awaiting the official to announce the swimmers, and the ready command. Suddenly, he heard Hardy's heavy breathing from the block next to him. Hardy was audibly hyperventilating…an intimidation tactic to unnerve your opponent. Joey knew what his opponent was doing and tried to ignore it. Finally, the swimmers were given the 'get set' command followed by an extra-long pause before the starter's pistol was fired. Joey paid too much attention to Hardy's breathing and suddenly sprang off the starting block in anticipation of the actual start. All the other swimmers remained on their starting blocks except Hardy. Joey's false start had induced him to leave the block, and he dove into the water right after Joey.

There was silence in the pool area. Both swimmers swam back to the pool edge and climbed back up on their starting blocks. There was an awkward silence as the official walked up between the two swimmers with a microphone and announced, "Lanes three and four have illegally false started. They are allowed one more start. Another false start from either swimmer will result in disqualification from the race."

Joey could hear the dripping water landing on the quiet pool surface as it fell from his and Hardy's bodies. It was embarrassing and felt as if it was an audible reminder to everyone within earshot of his failed start. He had in, effect, thrown off Hardy's timing with his early start.

The official commanded ready positions and once again gave the 'set' command. A longer pause was instituted by the official. No one moved. Silence engulfed the pool area. When the gun finally went off, Joey Hall and Jack Hardy were last off the starting blocks, in an effort to avoid a false start. The 50-yard sprint is short and fast, requiring only an average time of twenty-four to twenty-six seconds to complete. A mistake on the start or at the one flip turn at the opposite wall, can mean the race. A swimmer from lane two placed first. Joey and Jack tied for second place. The swimmers crawled out of the pool and Joey and Jack faced one another with a cordial handshake, as they peered into each other's eyes, knowing they had both intimidated one another, but in different ways.

The swimmers went back to their seats at each end of the pool and waited for the 100-yard freestyle. The race required four laps of the twenty-five yard pool with three flip turns. The race was a lung burner, as it was an all-out sprint but long enough to be considered a mid-distance race.

Once again, swimmers were called to their starting blocks with Joey and Jack at blocks three and four. This time there were only two contestants. Joey in lane three and Jack in lane four. The usual start sequence commenced, and the official kept the two swimmers in the start position for an unreasonably long time before firing his starting pistol.

Finally, the gun went off and the swimmers were in the pool swimming the meet's most important race. Every time Joey turned his head to breathe, he could hear the crowd's shouts and whistles. It was loud and the race was close. Underwater, Joey could see Jack's hands as they entered the water. He was right next to him. The first wall appeared and both boys executed their flip turns, as if in unison. Joey came out of the turn and then there was nothing…no memory of the last few seconds. He was still swimming, but when he realized what had just happened, he had slowed enough to allow Jack a slight lead. The excitement and anxiety were overwhelming. Joey knew he and Jack were approaching the next wall…or was this the final lap? Joey panicked, *Damn it! I must have had an episode! What lap is this? If I still have another fifty yards to go and sprint it, I'll use up all my energy on this lap and he'll win for sure.* Joey thought quickly. Seconds were passing and Jack was ahead. *I can see his arms in the water. I'll just stay with him and pace my speed with his.*

Joey was relieved to see that as they approached the wall, Jack prepared for his flip turn, so Joey knew they still had fifty yards to go, and two more turns. Joey completed his turn one body length behind Jack and began to catch him as they went into the last fifty yards. The crowd was shouting encouragement and clapped for both boys. Once again, Jack and Joey went into the final turn together and sprinted for the final wall.

The boys touched the wall simultaneously and tied.

The timers' stop watches revealed the same times for the two boys so first place points were shared by each team.

As a result, the Huskys won the meet by a narrow margin gained by their dive team. The race had not played out as everyone expected or surmised. Unforeseen circumstances played a large role in the outcome of the meet resting on the performance of others. Once again, Joey had learned about anticipated pressures and responsibilities placed on him that really shouldn't have been there to begin with.

After the meet, Joey sat thoughtfully in front of his team locker considering how he had let the excitement of competition compromise his performance. *I let it happen again. Damn it! Why do I let these what-ifs bother me so much? The meet was won by the dive team anyway. It really didn't come down to me and Jack.* He shook his head from side to side. *I really have to stop taking what other people say or insinuate so literally. It's cost me a touch down in football and now a swim race. I guess I have to do some meditation before the meet…deep thinking to consider the reality of what is about to happen…not what might happen.* He smiled to himself, *At least I had the presence of mind to figure it out and pace myself with Jack's speed. I could have beat that kid.*

CHAPTER 42

⁓

"So, tell me more about this young lady in your life," Doctor Horowitz, looked back down at his notes and back to Joey, "Let me see…Charlie?

Joey sat in front of his doctor at another of his biannual visits in the same chair he had sat in since grammar school. He shrugged his shoulders and smiled sheepishly. "We met in the hallway one afternoon while I was waiting to sign up for the swim team." Joey paused and then smiled broadly. "She's one of the school's cheerleaders and performs at all the school's sports games with her cheerleading squad. She said she recognized me as one of the football players and then we began to talk. She's very pretty, and easy to talk to." Joey smirked, "Actually, she did most of the talking. I just didn't know what to say. She kind of took me by surprise. A few days later, I started walking her to her classes and now we're kind of dating."

Horowitz listened to every word Joey said and watched his face as he spoke. "Why did you feel like she took you by surprise?" The doctor paused as he turned away and coughed.

Joey tilted his head to the side as he considered the

question. "Well, she's a popular girl, very pretty," Joey paused a moment and then said, "and I guess I just felt she was out of my league."

Horowitz nodded his head, "I see. So, you thought you weren't good enough for this girl?"

"No, I didn't feel that I wasn't good enough. I felt she was at a higher level than I was. She's involved in all these school activities, very pretty, everyone knows her...and all I do is go to practice after school and go home to my dog and the woods behind my house. I'm not a partier, so I'm alone most of the time except for when I'm with my team. The rest of the time, I'm doing homework or just too tired to go out."

Horowitz smiled and looked Joey in the eyes, "So, it appears she knows what you're all about and she approached you. She knew you are one of the school's athletes and a nice guy." Horowitz sat back in his chair and took his glasses off. "Joe, you have to start giving yourself some credit. You're a popular athlete, a good student, and a nice guy. What I see is that you lack a lot of confidence and that is why you shy away from some of these social groups." The doctor continued, "In this case...Charlie...who you could have gotten to know a long time ago." Horowitz felt good that he was able to tie Joey's basic behavioral characteristics to his escalated emotional level without mentioning the boy's neurologic condition. Suddenly, Doctor Horowitz turned away from Joey and began coughing again.

Joey remained silent and waited for the doctor's coughing fit to end. Horowitz continued when Joey didn't comment. "You need to take a step forward when you feel inferior to someone...or something, and go for it. Forget about what the outcome might be and just do it. Sometimes you might fail, but other times you may surprise yourself. None of it will hurt you." Horowitz paused as he looked for Joey's reaction to his words. "Look how you challenged the school sports programs and those tough coaches and their punishing workouts…and you persevered every time. Your one of the good ones, Joe. Please put the past behind you and take advantage of the gifts you've been given. You are on your way and there is nothing to hold you back…except your own insecurities."

Joey's mother sat quietly and listened to the conversation. She wasn't quite sure what she could offer at this point but knew this was probably the time Doctor Horowitz had spoken of early in the boy's treatment. She remembered the doctor saying, *when Joey gets into high school and finds a girl that he thinks he's in love with, there will be a marked improvement in his condition.* Ginny smiled to herself; *I think this is it. I guess we'll just wait and see how this all plays out. I just hope he doesn't get too infatuated with anyone yet. He's still got college and maybe one of the academies ahead of him.*

Doctor Horowitz turned to Ginny. "Well, Mrs. Hall, you've been kind of quiet. What is your position on all of this?"

Ginny smiled, "I'm very happy for Joey. I just hope he's able to keep things in perspective…like his studies, sports, and his future plans."

Horowitz nodded and turned back to Joey. "Okay, Joe. You heard that, and I agree with your mom." He looked back down at his notes and then back to Joey. "I see you are considering an option to apply to the United States

Coast Guard Academy." He waited for a response from Joey before continuing.

Joey smiled and nodded. "Yes, I am. My dad isn't sure about how my past with this…condition, is going to affect my chances though."

The doctor's face became very serious. "Joe! There is that insecurity again! Is this something you really want to go for?" Horowitz began coughing again and put a handkerchief up to his mouth.

Joey nodded that it was, but said nothing, surprised at the doctor's sudden change of behavior.

Horowitz leaned forward across his desk, "Then you have to try for it…harder than you have tried for anything before! You can't listen to what people say…they don't know. You have to push forward through all that crap. If you have any negative thoughts…bury them with positive ones. Do everything in your power that you think will get you to the academy. No what-ifs…and don't worry about how your choice is going to affect anyone else!"

Finally, the meeting with Doctor Horowitz came to an end and Ginny stood in the hallway with him considering some final thoughts. Doctor Baldwin observed the exchange from his open office door and came out to interrupt the conversation. "Excuse me for interrupting," and smiled at Ginny. He looked back at Horowitz, "Are you feeling okay, Doctor? If you need to leave early again, I can cover for you. I have some open time in my schedule."

Doctor Horowitz was taken aback, and his face began to redden. "Uh, oh no. I'll be fine. Thank you, Doctor Baldwin."

Doctor Baldwin smiled as if he didn't believe him and

quickly turned away. "Well, whenever you need any help, just let me or Doctor Petrillo know."

Ginny became concerned and addressed Horowitz, "Is everything okay? I noticed the coughing fits you experienced when you were speaking to Joey."

Horowitz explained, "I'm sorry. Doctor Baldwin should not have offered that. I've had some health problems over the last year, and the staff has been asking if I should consider retirement."

"Oh, I'm so sorry to hear this! Is that something you are considering?"

Horowitz, reddened again. "My health has been declining, but I would advise all of my patients and what direction they should take, well before I make any decisions. Please don't worry, Mrs. Hall. I have Joey's best interests in mind."

Ginny smiled weakly at the doctor and shook his hand. "Feel better, Doctor…and thank you for everything you've done for us and Joey." She turned away and left his office.

Horowitz waited for Ginny to leave and went straight to Baldwin's office. He closed the door and stood before the seated, Doctor Baldwin. "What, may I ask, did you think you were doing, Doctor…especially in front of a patient's mother?"

Doctor Baldwin looked up from his desk and acted as if he was surprised at Horowitz's accusation. "Excuse me, Ben. I'm not sure what you're talking about."

"That baloney in the hallway with Mrs. Hall. You acted as if I was in dire need for extra help because of my health. That is not something to be discussed in front of patients or their parents. Now, she's probably concerned about where she's going to get the care for her son that I have been providing all these years."

Baldwin remained seated and shook his head from side to side. "I don't know why you would take that as an assault against your competence, Ben. I heard you coughing from my office through your entire session with the Halls, and took the opportunity to see if I could be of help." Baldwin paused before he continued. A sheepish smile crossed his face, "You must admit you haven't been in the best of health the last few months and your memory seems too have been a bit off."

Horowitz straightened and stood rigid as he listened to the accusations from Baldwin. "My memory? My memory is fine!" He cocked his head and eyed Baldwin curiously. "What is all this about?"

Baldwin stood from his chair and walked around his desk. He reached out and patted Horowitz's shoulder. "Hey, it's okay, Ben. We're all going to get there someday, but in the meantime, just know your friends here in the practice will cover for you. We've got your back. Don't worry." Baldwin smiled in a patronizing manner and patted Horowitz again as he brushed past him and left the office.

Doctor Ben Horowitz stood in Doctor Baldwin's office alone, confused and mildly upset. *What is going on here? I feel fine except for that blasted cough. They're questioning my memory? Where is that coming from?*

CHAPTER 43

On the way home from his appointment with Doctor Horowitz, the car was quiet. Ginny seemed as if she was in deep thought with an unusually serious look on her face. Finally, Joey broke the silence. "Hey, Mom. Do you think Doctor H is going to be okay? I don't ever remember him coughing like that. He looks a lot thinner now too."

"Well, we talked about it outside his office while you were in the foyer looking at magazines. One of the practice's doctors came out and said something about it, but Doctor H seemed to minimalize it." She paused a moment and added, "It's his retiring from medicine that worries me. We've put all our trust in the one doctor that finally knew something about...your condition, and if he retires, we'll have to start all over again."

Joey turned toward his mother, "He's going to retire?"

Ginny shook her head, "Not right away...he told me that. But you know, Joe...everyone gets on in life and there comes a time when everyone has to consider what is right for them to do...with regard to themselves and for everyone and everything they may have an influence on.

The sixteen-year old boy turned away and watched the scenery that passed outside the car.

Ginny anticipated Joey's concern. "I don't think it's something we have to be concerned about yet. It's just the way Doctor Baldwin looked and the way he spoke to Doctor H. He made me feel like maybe we should start thinking about finding a new doctor."

Joey quickly turned back to his mother, "I don't want a new doctor, Mom. Everything is going great with Doctor H and I want to stay with him. He knows me and everything I'm about."

"Oh, don't worry about that. Of course, we're staying with Doctor H. The way you've been improving you may not have to see him for too much longer. Your main concern right now is to focus on school, the upcoming Track Season, and just having fun. Dad and I will worry about the rest."

Spring was in the air and track season for the new high school was on the horizon. Once again, Joey found himself showing up for tryouts and practice. The usual laps around the track, and the same calisthenics, but now there was a different responsibility. The pressure to be better was greater on each athlete in this individualized sport. Rather than a coach standing over the entire team, a track athlete had to have an inner coach to push himself to hone his particular events. Joey especially liked that about track season. It was more like in his earlier years when he ran through the woods and swam in his pool with no one telling him what he should do next. There was no pressure for performing in front of a superior, like a coach. No fear of doing something incorrectly and maybe risk getting removed from the next competition's line up. There was more freedom and concentration on self-improvement than the other team sports were designed for. Joey was equally a competent baseball player, but the boy had enough regimentation during the football and swimming seasons for one year.

The season also appealed to Joey. It was springtime. A time for a fresh start. The sun was brighter, the air was fresher, and the positivity of buds blossoming and new green grass growing made life in general a happier experience. Joey loved to see the progression of flora and fauna as the season progressed. There was more to look forward to each day. The track athletes all had tans before anyone else because they were outside running distance miles along the town's treed roads or around the school's track. Event practices were naturally outside as well.

As the season warmed and the buds bloomed, everything was right in his life and Joey began to break local records, including his own, in the shotput and discus. His relationship with Charlie was flourishing and Joey had fallen in love. The couple attended their junior prom in late spring, and Joey's episodes had dwindled to an occasional occurrence, but with shortened durations. His awareness during an episode was more conscious on his end, and any embarrassing incidents were only a memory now.

Joey had begun working with his guidance counselor on the long process for application to the United States Coast Guard Academy, which bothered Charlie. The girl was also in love, and each partner understood they were still young and had at least two years ahead of them before they had to face any real decisions.

Soon, another track season had had come to an end and Joey was maturing nicely. Charlie attended all of Joey's home meets and offered support where she could. However, the thought of Joey moving toward a career in the Coast Guard meant that he'd be leaving her soon for at least several extended periods of time and the thought began to damper her excitement about the relationship. One Friday night in late spring, as they walked the neighborhood surrounding the girl's home, Charlie thought she'd try to discuss some of her worries about where the relationship might be going. It was a warm late spring evening, the sun was setting, and there was the tiniest bit of breeze in the air. Joey was tired from practice and seemed quiet. Charlie figured Joey might be thinking the same way, so she decided to address her concerns about where the relationship was going. "Joey, have you heard anything about the next step in the academy application process?"

"Joey gave Charlie a quick glance and looked back down to the sidewalk. "Nah, it's still early. I still have to get letters of recommendation from coaches and teachers, a transcript of all my grades since freshman year, and a documented list of all my accomplishments…and I still have to take my SATs and get a decent score. My guidance counselor, Mr. Gordon is working on all that…with some of my input of course."

Charlie was quiet for a moment and pursed her lips before speaking. "Why do they need all that? Can't they just look at your high school transcript and talk to your coaches and teachers? This seems like so much work...and you're still not guaranteed entrance into the academy."

Joey stopped walking, but continued to hold Charlie's hand. "What's all this about, Charlie? We knew this was going to be a long, hard road, but the academy is the prize at the end." He stopped for a moment as he searched Charlie's face for some sign of understanding.

"It's going to be your prize, Joey...not mine! We haven't talked about how all of this is going to affect our future together. I've been thinking a lot about this and it's all about you and where you're going. What about me? What happens to me when you get accepted for the academy, and go off to your first year? They already told you there won't be any chance of coming home until the following summer."

Joey seemed surprised, "We kind of talked about this, Charlie. There will be a Parents Weekend in the fall, and you can come with my mom and dad to visit me. Then, I'll come home on leave in the spring for a couple of weeks."

Charlie answered sarcastically, "Oh, wow! I get a weekend and maybe a couple of weeks the following summer...if they don't assign you to that training cruise for the summer."

Joey let go of Charlie's hand. "Well...what do you want, Charlie? You're right. We haven't talked much about this part."

"I thought maybe you could get a job at the place where my dad works...as an apprentice...after graduation, and go to school at night. Then we could get married."

Joey's head jerked back in surprise. "I'm not getting married until after the academy or college. You're going way too far into the future, Charlie. We've got things to do first, then we can get married. And, I'm not going to work in your father's shop. I'm going to be the captain of a Coast Guard rescue ship."

For the first time since Joey had known her, Charlie got angry and let it show. Her face turned red, and she glared at Joey as she had never done before. "Oh…is that right? That's your plan?"

Joey stood blankly staring at his special Charlie. The whole conversation had taken him by surprise, and he was at a loss for words. Joey said nothing.

Charlie waited for what felt like an eternity before continuing. Then she raised one hand in the air as if to say, 'I give up,' and said, "I think it's time we took a break." Charlie turned away from Joey, snapped her long black hair to the right and behind, and strutted away.

Joey watched her walk away and couldn't believe what was happening. It all came about so fast. She walked faster and faster and Joey called after her, "Charlie, don't leave. We have to talk about this."

Charlie ignored the boy and walked faster. She never turned back.

The summer of Joey's junior year had arrived, and more trips to Cape Cod had been planned for family vacations. Life was moving along without Charlie and Joey needed to distract his conscious thoughts from those about Charlie. He chose a book to read that he'd already read two years before. It was Herman Wouk's, The Caine Mutiny, written in 1958. Although, the story involved a warship and not a rescue/law enforcement vessel, which Joey would have preferred, the story was about life aboard a ship at sea, details of operation, and unforeseen circumstances that satisfied the boy's intrigue. It was the story he needed to carry him through the summer and feed his interests about life at sea...and deal with the pain he was feeling about Charlie's absence.

One summer night, after dinner, Ginny stared out the front door and watched Joey. It was a repeat of the past several weeks. He just sat on the front steps and eventually went for a walk. Frank came up to her asked what was wrong. She nodded to the glassed front door, "Look at him. He's miserable. He hasn't even gone for a run or a workout. I think it's all about Charlie." Ginny paused and brought her hands to her mouth. I hope his break up with Charlie doesn't affect his progress with his condition. Remember what Dr. Horowitz said about him meeting a girl he thinks he's in love with and how that was going to make a huge difference...with everything? Well, Charlie has definitely helped him improve, and I hope this break up doesn't cause him to lose anything he's gained."

Frank saw the back of Joey through the glass door and nodded his head. "I'll go talk to him and see if I can lighten things up."

Frank purposely came around the front of the house and approached Joey from the side, as if he hadn't been watching him. "Hey Joe! Aren't you going to go for a run tonight or maybe do a little work with the weights?"

Joey's head was down as he stared at nothing but the

sidewalk. "I don't know, Dad…maybe. Really haven't been in the mood lately."

Frank sat down next to his son. "Got Charlie on your mind…don't you?"

Joey nodded his head but said nothing.

Frank continued after a moment. "You know, Joe. Charlie's choice to leave may be for the best."

That comment got Joey's attention. He turned his head up to the side with a surprised look. "I thought you liked her, Dad."

"I do like her, Joe…but you guys were kind of rushing things. You've got the Coast Guard academy in your future, not to mention all the preparation for that. There's still your senior year in high school…and then all the sports. The academy's liaison officers said you'd have to play football for them as part of the deal." Frank paused and added, "You don't even know if she's the one you're going to end up with, so you can't let her leaving affect your progress… in any of that."

"Hey, Dad! We don't know about the academy yet… and I don't even know if I want that anymore. I don't even know if I want college. I might just sign up for the Coast Guard as a regular sailor. I'll see if I like it. If I do, maybe I'll just make a career of it."

Frank's temper flared, "In a pig's ass! You're not joining the Coast Guard or the Navy as a regular sailor. I won't sign for you. You're going to go to college. We'll find some college somewhere that'll take you." He paused and said, "You're going to let your whole future and everything you've worked for go down the tubes…because of some girl?"

Joey began to get angry, "Some girl, Dad? Really? This is my life and I'll decide about the academy or regular college…or joining the Coast Guard."

Frank stood up from the porch steps. "Okay, buster! Let me tell you what I really think." Frank stood rigid and a stern look crossed his face. "Once the government gets a look at your medical history from Dr. Horowitz, your career in the academy or on a ship…especially one that is responsible for saving lives at sea, is finished. Do you think they're going to let you be in charge of a crew or a ship, or people's lives with that background?"

Frank knew immediately he had let his temper get the best of him and had said all the wrong things. His face showed remorse and flushed with embarrassment at the same time. He stared into his son's eyes for a long moment hoping Joey would forget what he had just said.

Joey stood from the porch steps and nodded his head. He walked across the lawn and away from his father. Frank was silent and watched him go. *I've done everything I could for that kid. I can't let him ruin his future now.*

CHAPTER 44

The summer was uneventful. The vacation to the Cape was not what it had been in the past. It seemed hollow and unexciting. The only place Joey felt comfortable was when the family visited some fishing ports. The atmosphere of the harbor and the presence of his favorite things, like boats and ships, were what he needed to put his life in perspective. Only here, in this maritime setting, could he let his mind wander and consider the future. Eventually, someone would feel as if he was getting too thoughtful or serious, and say something to break his concentration, and the fantasy was over. The boy would come back to reality, to his family, and to his present state of loneliness enhanced by a great emptiness in his soul.

Joey hadn't spoken of Charlie since that night on the porch steps with his father. Everyone in the family looked for an appropriate time to bring up her name in some way that might get Joey to smile or say something about what was troubling him. Joey remained silent on that score and kept his emotions to himself.

Inside the boy was hurt. He knew he had only considered himself and what he needed to do for his future, but what bothered him the most was that he had let that overshadow what the love of his life also needed. He felt so responsible that he began to look for negative feelings about the academy and his future. He let letters from the academy's application committee pile up unopened, and inwardly knew he was letting everything fall apart. He needed to see Charlie.

Frank approached Ginny one evening after they had returned from vacation. "Have you noticed any difference in Joey's progress regarding, you know…his problem?"

Ginny was aware of the conversation between Joey and Frank that early summer evening two months ago and answered coldly. "You mean his progress with how to deal with the Charlie situation?"

Frank flushed, "Okay, I know I handled the whole thing wrong…and said the wrong things about Charlie, and the academy. I'm talking about his episodes. Have you seen him have any?"

Ginny raised her eyebrows as if she were thinking of the answer and replied, "No, Frank. I haven't seen anything except sadness and boredom. He needs to find it in himself to call Charlie and get things straightened out…even if they don't get back together." Frank started to say something but Ginny cut him off, "Even if they don't get back together, he needs to talk to her…for his own good. Then maybe he can get back on track with his life." She turned toward Frank, pointed at him, and said, "This time, stay out of it."

One night a few weeks before the end of summer, Ginny walked up to Joey as he leaned over the edge of his pool. "Thinking about going for a swim?"

"Nah. I'm not in the mood, Mom. The water is getting colder now."

She leaned on the pool rail next to him and smiled. "All these excuses you have for not doing the things you love to do…don't fool me. This is all about Charlie. You need to call her or just go over to see her, and straighten things out. I guarantee, whatever the outcome, you'll feel altogether different."

Joey stared into the pool's water. "I don't know, Mom. I wouldn't know what to say at this point. It's been too long."

Ginny patted his forearm, "Did you ever think she might be going through the same thing as you?" Joey quickly turned toward his mother with a look of surprise. Ginny continued, "Of course you didn't. You were thinking of yourself again. She's probably been waiting for your call all summer."

"But, Mom, she said…"

Ginny pushed herself away from the pool's railing and said, "Do it! Call her…soon." Ginny walked away smiling to herself.

Joey looked back to the stillness of the pool's water. *I did it again. Feeling bad for myself instead of thinking about how Charlie felt. Now, I've wasted a couple of months…summer months…that we looked forward to all year, and wasted all that time.*

Joey stared into the water for a long time, not really thinking about anything in particular. Then he slapped the top of the pool's railing and murmured, "I'm going to walk over to Charlie's house and see if she'll talk to me. I don't know where it'll go, but I'm tired of thinking about this all the time."

Ginny watched her son from the kitchen window. She knew he was thinking about what she had told him to do. *C'mon, Joe. Do it. Just go over to see her.*

Suddenly she saw Joey slap the pool's railing, turn and walk toward the house. *I think he's going to do it.* A weak smile crossed Ginny's face. Maybe an end to the boy's drudgery was finally at an end.

Joey began walking to Charlie's house. It would be a mile's travel, but the boy felt he needed the time to consider what he might say or how he would say it. He wasn't sure about what he was doing, but he just kept walking. There were too many scenarios to consider. Maybe she'd just tell him to go away...or what if she had started seeing someone else? He stopped walking with that thought. If she was seeing someone else that would make him feel worse than what he was feeling now. Joey considered the worst scenario and began walking again. *If that's the case, it'll be over and done, and I'll just have to move on. There won't be any other choice.*

Joey had been so deep in thought he didn't realize how far he'd travelled and found he was just around the corner from Charlie's house. He stopped and took a deep breath, walked across the street, and up the driveway. Suddenly, the kitchen door opened and Charlie came out of the door with a basket of laundry and saw Joey. She put the basket down and placed her hands on her hips. "What are you doing here? I thought we broke up."

Joey stopped where he was. "Uh…hi, Charlie. I thought we were just taking a break." He said to himself, *she looks mad. Maybe this wasn't a good idea.*

With her hands still on her hips, she glared at Joey for a few moments longer before saying anything. "That's what it started out as, and then you didn't call me all summer!

Joey was sweating. "I came to talk to you…about this. I know it's all my fault and I didn't handle any of it right. I'm sorry."

Charlie walked up to Joey in the middle of the driveway. "What made you walk over here…or suddenly decide that you wanted to talk to me?"

Joey had his head down. "I thought a lot about what you said and why you wanted to take a break. I finally realized I was too absorbed in what I was going through and not that you might be going through some of the same things." He paused and looked up at her with a sheepish look. "It took me a while, Charlie. This whole thing is all I thought about…all summer."

"Yeah, well it ruined my summer as well. Did you expect me to just wait around until you decided it was time to talk?"

Joey felt their conversation was getting worse the more they talked. "I don't know, Charlie. I really don't. The academy application process and what that might bring, you leaving me…everything was a lot for me to consider."

Her hands were back on her hips. "Well, what did you do all summer?"

"Not much. I went on vacation with my family, but I

haven't worked out or seen any of my friends. Been alone a lot."

She walked a little closer to him and spoke a little softer. "How is the academy process going?"

Joey shrugged his shoulders, "I don't know. I haven't responded to any of their letters for interviews and testing dates. I might just let all that go. I told my dad I might just join the Coast Guard and enter as a regular sailor after graduation."

Charlie looked at Joey and cocked her head to one side. "Really! After a lifetime of preparation with all of that in mind? How could you do that to yourself?"

Joey shrugged his shoulders again and looked back down at the driveway. "The Coast Guard was going to be my life. It was what I wanted to do…and I wanted you to be there with me." He paused, "If all of that caused me to forget about you and what you needed…where it caused us to break up, then it wouldn't be the life I dreamed of anyway, so I'll just do something else."

Charlie folded her arms across her chest. "It sounds like you've done some serious thinking." She paused and squinted at Joey. "I don't want to be the reason to ruin your Coast Guard career. I just wanted you to consider your priorities. I see that I was mixed up in that somehow, but I think we can talk now." She reached out and took Joey by the hand, "C'mon, let's go sit under the carport. We have a lot to talk about."

CHAPTER 45

Joey's senior year of high school was only a week away. Ginny walked along their neighborhood's sidewalk to clear her head. There were so many new things entering into the family's lives. Brian was applying for colleges all over the United States and Cheryl was approaching dating age. She smiled to herself as she thought about her conversation with Joey about Charlie and that he should go talk to her. *I guess he still considers my advice as worthwhile. Whether they continue to stay together is one thing, but he needs her now... and personally, I think they are well suited for each other. She's the kind of girl that will wait for him until he graduates from the academy or until he gets settled after college and lands a good job. At least we know his disorder has improved to the point where his emotional level is no longer a trigger. The break up between him and Charlie only caused a temporary depression and hurt feelings, which is normal for a boy of his age.*

When Ginny finished her walk, she found Joey standing by the mailbox reading his mail. "Hi Joe, I see you got some mail. More academy stuff?"

"Yeah...one of them is, but this one is for my appointment for my driver's license test. Do you think Dad will be okay with this?"

Ginny put her hand on the boy's shoulder. "Of course! He was right there when we asked Doctor H about the possibility of getting your driver's license, and whether we were risking any safety concerns. He heard the doctor say you had pretty much outgrown the condition, and if it did happen while you were driving, it would have about the same effect on your driving as if you had just sneezed." Ginny paused and added, "He'll probably want to talk with you about it anyway...just to enforce the importance of the increased responsibility, but he's good with it, Joe. Go for it."

Joey put the envelope in his pocket and smiled at his mother. "I've got to show this to Charlie! She's really sick of having to walk everywhere or having to double date all the time."

Ginny smiled but said nothing. She realized that the couple knew having a driver's license at their age was a valuable opportunity, but not a priority. Ginny looked over Joey's shoulder as he opened the second letter. "Well, what does it say, Joe?"

The letter was from the United States Coast Guard Admissions Office. "They are asking me for an oral interview in New London, Connecticut and depending on how that goes, there will be a congressional study of my background. If I'm still a consideration, the tests, both physical and mental aptitude, begin."

Ginny stepped back from Joey's shoulder and looked him in the face. "Okay, Joe. We have to see Doctor H and tell him about all this. A congressional study means they're going to want to know everything about you...so we have to get Doctor H's feedback on your medical history file."

Joey looked at his mother with a defeated expression. "Why, Mom? Dad already told me. It's pretty much done and over."

Ginny gave Joey a stern look. "Joe, if you get into the academy and then graduate, you'll be a Coast Guard officer...probably on a ship of some sort. That means a lot of responsibility under some probably dangerous situations. The people that will be considering your eligibility have to know these things about their candidates." She paused and took a deep breath before continuing. "I know you're pretty much over the condition...and it was a childhood affliction, but God forbid, if something ever did happen and your past was brought up, it could bring a whole different twist to the outcome."

Joey threw the envelope on the driveway and sarcastically added. "Oh, okay. So, we should probably tell them every injury I had in football, and every time I got the flu...and probably about Charlie too."

Ginny faced Joey stoically and met his eyes. "That is correct, Joe. This is a big thing with even bigger consequences." She stared into his eyes for a long time without saying anything. Then she patted his shoulders and turned away from him. As she walked into the house she said, "Dinner is in twenty minutes."

Ginny and Joey Hall sat in front of an aging Doctor Horowitz. The neurosurgeon appeared thinner than Joey remembered, his hair was completely grey, and he seemed to be hunched over as he sat at his desk. His usually pale face, now revealed several wrinkles and his fingers trembled when he held his pen to write notes.

It started as every meeting did with Doctor H. Joey and his mother sat quietly in front of the good doctor while he perused Joey's medical log and wrote notes for the impending discussion. Finally, the doctor looked up and gave Joey and his mother a weak smile. "Well, it's good to see the both of you again." He glanced at Ginny and asked, "How is your husband? I haven't seen him in some time now."

Ginny reddened and smiled, "Oh, it's Saturday and as usual, he's working. He said to say hello."

Doctor H smiled and looked back at Joey. "I see you've had quite a year young man." The doctor flipped through his notes while he audibly listed the new events in Joey's life. "Let's see…another successful football season, Swim team Captain, and two local records in spring track." The doctor paused a moment and looked up at Joey, "I see you broke up with your girlfriend, Charlie. How did that go?"

Joey fidgeted in his seat and turned red. "Well, we're back together again after a long summer of not seeing each other. It was pretty depressing, but after I thought about it, I realized it was probably all my fault." Joey continued with that thought and explained about the academy's requirements and their future expectations.

Doctor Horowitz kept his focus on the boy waiting for any fallout Joey may have wanted to add based on that experience. The doctor wrote down some notes in Joey's log and looked up at him smiling. When Joey said nothing, he continued, "Well, good for you. It looks like you survived that ordeal without any major setbacks." He stared at Joey silently giving him more time to discuss the break-up. When Joey didn't offer anything, Doctor Horowitz rubbed his chin and continued, "My next question is about how you feel about the academy entrance requirements. It's going be a grueling process and probably be spread over the better part of a year. Do you think you're up for something like that?"

Joey's face became serious. "Yes, I'm ready for it. The whole thing almost caused me to lose Charlie, but I learned from it. I know it's going to be tough…just like any team tryout or any midterm exam, but I'm ready."

Doctor Horowitz took off his glasses and placed them on the table. "Joe, it's going to be a hundred times harder than any team tryout, and the entrance exams will be worse than any exam you've ever studied for. The big difference now is that you'll be competing with the best of the best, and there are only so many openings available." The doctor paused and put his glasses back on and tended to a coughing fit. When he recovered, he said, "If you really want this, Joe…I mean if you feel it in your bones that this is something you want to do…you have to go after this harder than anything you've challenged before. You cannot let the pressures of physical extremes or mental exhaustion be a deterrent. Just like in sports when you made yourself embrace the torture of what you were experiencing…you must do that here, but at a higher level."

Ginny had been waiting for this opportunity and intervened. "Doctor, we've seen Joey challenge obstacles that we didn't even want him to consider…and he succeeded. His father and I worry that although he may succeed in whatever testing they put him through, his past may be exposed for the wrong reasons and that may cause him to fail."

Doctor Horowitz sat back in his chair. "I assume you're talking about the medical history that I have kept on him all these years?"

Ginny nodded her head and Joey looked concerned.

"At this point, the disorder is pretty much a thing of the past. Joey has overcome every obstacle that has been placed in his path, and nothing that happens in the future, whether it's something he's involved in or something that was caused by him, can be traced back to a disorder that he experienced as a child. His EEGs have all been normal for the past year, and the number and frequency of his episodes are almost non-existent at this point...with continuing progress. I see no reason to pass any of this personal information on to the academy or any government agency, because of the disorder's rarity and also because the wrong person could get ahold of it and make the wrong decision regarding Joey's future based merely on the general ignorance about it."

Joey's facial expression showed that he immediately began to relax and sat back in his chair. Ginny also felt a sigh of relief and smiled. The doctor noticed the change in the two and offered, "Everyone is born with something... or develops something, somewhere along their life's path. No one is perfect...ever." He looked back to Joey, "It's all in how you handle the situation. You have had the courage to challenge everything you have ever wanted to do or accomplish...despite what your parents thought you should do. And, that is an admirable thing. You talked it over with them...and me, and then figured out what you would need to do and how you'd consider the harder parts of it. And you persevered. This is no different, Joe."

The doctor looked back to Ginny, "You and Frank have been wonderful with him and supported not only his interests, but my advice as well…putting aside your own fears. That is also admirable for you as parents."

The doctor sat back in his chair and nodded at Joey. "You're going to get into that academy and you're going to be an officer in the United States Coast Guard. They will be lucky to have a person of your grit and determination. I'm proud of you, Joe."

The doctor paused a moment, and it looked as if Ginny was about to cry. Doctor Horowitz continued. "This most likely will be our last meeting…unless something unexpected happens. I am retiring at the end of the month. Due to health concerns and a dwindling practice…I feel it's time for me to leave."

Ginny quickly asked, "What will happen to his medical history file?"

"I will speak to our Resident Chief of Neurosurgery, Doctor Goldbloom, and have all inferences to Joey removed. The file will go to our research center for the betterment of any other patients that may need the same assistance as Joey did."

Ginny smiled, "Thank you, Doctor."

Doctor Horowitz stood from his chair and shook Ginny's hand. Then he took Joey's hand and held it while he spoke to him. "Do your best, as you always have. Nothing is too hard. You have the ability to do whatever you may want to accomplish. You have the gifts inside you to make things better for everyone. Use those gifts and push hard through any obstacle that gets in your way. Don't ever give up."

Joey turned red and nodded his head.

Doctor Horowitz nodded his head as he looked the boy in the eyes. "Promise me."

Joey smiled weakly at the doctor and said, "I promise."

Doctor Horowitz released the boy's hand, nodded, and led Joey and Ginny out of the office to bid them good luck and farewell.

It was an emotional end to a long and arduous struggle.

CHAPTER 46

Senior year for Joey began with football season. The feeling was bittersweet because Joey felt that each practice, each game, every time he put his uniform on…he was one step closer to the end of his football career. It was a career he made happen. He knew he had pushed it to the absolute limit, against what his parents had wanted. He spent so much time trying to suppress the negative attitudes and suggestions from people he had looked up to…people he had trusted with his most personal secret. The worse the feeling of failure…the more he embraced the challenge to forge ahead. It was a constant mental struggle to search for **what he needed to do, to make what he wanted to happen…not what anyone else thought he should do**. In his young mind he realized he had only a limited concept of what could happen, but he believed that by finding ways to overcome those negatives, he could accomplish his goal.

Joey relied heavily on Doctor Horowitz's open mind and rational decision making. Without telling him what to do, the doctor was always matter of fact about the topic and erred more on the side of challenging any negative outcome. Joey drew strength from that and realized he would do anything within reason, as long as he felt he was within the doctor's guidelines.

Joey also respected his parents and their feelings, but had the intelligence to realize that most of their concerns came from a parental fear of what could happen to him if he wasn't careful. So, he listened to most of Ginny and Frank's fears, but filed them in a place where they wouldn't overshadow everything he wanted to do.

Now in his senior year of high school, Joey began to allow selected individuals knowledge of his secret life concerning his rare childhood disorder. He realized the effort for secrecy fostered an additional amount of stress. The constant pressure of having to think of an appropriate excuse as to what had just happened also contributed to his internal stress. The boy had enough of it and felt a new found freedom by divulging his dark secret. He also found that his admission became a part of his healing process.

The first person he divulged his disorder to was Charlie. At the risk of maybe losing her forever, he felt it was only fair she knew about what he had been through and what she could possibly be confronted with in the future. And, as he predicted, Charlie took the news very well and merely tried to understand what it was all about and how Joey had internally overcome the fears of what could have transpired in the presence of great numbers of people. Charlie understood that by challenging the disorder, Joey had put his reputation at risk. She was of course very impressed that he shared such a sensitive and personal part of his life with her and marveled at how he poked fun at himself for some of the scenarios that he had been involved in.

After listening to Joey talk about the disorder and his description of what he had gone through internally, she merely nodded her head and said, "Well, the disorder doesn't sound like such a big thing to me. It's what you went through internally to overcome the possibilities of what could have happened, that impress me. I think that was the hardest part of the problem. Keeping it a secret from everyone, especially your coaches and friends...had to be hard. Now that it's pretty much in the past, I think I'd just put the whole thing behind me and look to the future."

Joey had become a different person. He felt comfortable in who he was and felt less a need to hide anything. Consequently, he was happier and more relaxed about everything. His grades continued to improve, as did his athletic career. His senior year of swimming passed with no major highlights, triumphs or failures, but he enjoyed the sport and what it brought to him so much more. Winter gave way to spring where he rose to Captain of the track team. He cherished the responsibility more than any of the other sports because his teammates had voted him into the position. Joey felt it was a place of honor given to him by his peers and not by a coach's perception of what his skills might be. Because the Captain position was not an appointed one, Joey felt it was more of a personal obligation and excelled at the new responsibility.

When one of Joey's longtime track records was broken by an underclassman during his final high school track meet, everyone wondered how he'd take it. The audience and players from both teams were momentarily silent and waited for Joey's response. He merely walked up to the underclassman, shook his hand, and said, "Bob, I'm glad it was you who broke my record. You are a true track athlete, and I wouldn't have it any other way." Everyone smiled.

Inwardly, the loss of his longtime record was just another inner pressure lifted from his shoulders. He felt he'd had it long enough and knew that someday, a younger athlete would break it. It seemed only fitting that one of the better athletes he had mentored through the years and one he had been fond of, was the one to get the new honor.

That night at dinner, as Joey discussed how he'd been dethroned in his final track meet, Frank stopped eating and looked into the boy's eyes. "Ah, that was bound to happen sooner or later, Joe. You've got bigger things to look forward to now. You'll probably make some new records at the academy."

Joey looked up from his dinner and smirked, "I still have to get accepted, Dad. And I don't know if I'll be trying out for any of the sports teams if I do get accepted. My focus is going to be on getting through the academy, so I can be the captain of a Coast Guard ship someday."

Frank started to say something, but Ginny cut him off. "That reminds me, Joe. I got some bad news today. We received a letter from Doctor Horowitz's practice that he passed away last week. It's so unfortunate and sad after he saw you through all those turbulent years…and it's important that you realize that." Ginny paused as she got a nod from Joey and then continued. "We're going to have to go back to the hospital to get a copy of your medical history before they revise it. You may need it in the future."

Joey looked up from his dinner again. "Doctor H passed?"

Ginny came over and put her hand on his arm. "We

knew it was inevitable, Joe. He's been ill for quite some time now. I think he hung on as long as he could, to get you through." She paused and said, "I want you to remember the last thing he said to you." Ginny paused and looked at Joey. "Remember when he told you, 'it's going to be hard, but you can do it.' That was all for you, Joe. Don't ever forget it."

Joey's face was solemn. He nodded his head, "I won't forget him or his words, Mom. You can count on that."

CHAPTER 47

The next week, Ginny had made an appointment with the late Doctor Horowitz's practice to retrieve Joey's medical history and sign a document that the history could be shared among other medical professionals after Joey's name and personal information was removed. The mother and son sat patiently awaiting the new doctor in charge, and Doctor Baldwin came into the waiting room. "Well, Mrs. Hall and Joey. It seems, I'm your doctor now due to Doctor Horowitz's unfortunate passing. Please come in and we'll talk about a new plan for Joey."

Ginny and Joey looked at each other in confusion, but got up from their seats and followed Doctor Baldwin into his office. Joey made sure to glance over at Doctor H's old office. The door was open, but his name plate was missing from the door and the office was vacant of books, files, pictures, and anything else to indicate Doctor H had ever been there.

After everyone was seated in front of Baldwin's desk, he opened the meeting. "I understand you came to retrieve Joey's medical log and living history."

Ginny nodded, "That's correct Doctor. They are actually his property and may be of use in his future or when he has a family. He's awaiting acceptance papers from the Coast Guard Academy and if so, will be leaving us shortly after graduation from high school. So, he may need those records."

Doctor Baldwin sat back in his chair and smiled. "I see. But you must realize that I am his doctor right now, in light of Doctor Horowitz's passing…and I am in control of those records. Because of that, I took the liberty of looking through the history and found that I do not agree with any of the late doctor's approaches, so I am prepared to change procedures as well as prescriptions.

Ginny's face became flushed. "You should have consulted with us first, doctor! We didn't agree to your services…we don't even know you and don't want to change anything that Doctor Horowitz has instituted." She paused and said, "I think we're done here, so if you'd please give us the medical log and living history, we'll be leaving."

Dr. Baldwin realized Ginny didn't believe his story. "Well, Mrs. Hall. I'd like to give them to you, but as I said, I didn't approve of his methods…and hadn't heard from you since his passing, so I had Joey's entire history destroyed. I have only these two pages that were at the front of his file to say Joey was treated by Doctor Horowitz for a seizure disorder."

Ginny stood up from her chair. "How dare you! You had no right! We never even spoke to you about treating our son. Those records were not yours to destroy!"

Doctor Baldwin rose both hands in the air as if to calm the mother. "Please try to calm down Mrs. Hall. I am his doctor now, and I'll put an end to his disorder in due time by suggesting newer medicines and practices."

"You are not his doctor!" Ginny paused for effect, "You're fired!" How dare you tell us that you are his doctor now and that you'll be doing everything different …after we've spent almost ten years under the care of a good man."

Dr. Baldwin began to interrupt Ginny, but she continued, "You should know that Joey's disorder has all but faded away…as Dr. Horowitz predicted, so we don't need you or any doctor like you." She grabbed the two lonely papers Baldwin offered her from the desk and said, "Let's go, Joe. We're done here."

Baldwin watched the two people leave and mildly offered, "I can inform the Coast Guard of Joey's history and destroy any future he may have with them, if you decide to continue along this line."

Ginny stopped in her tracks and turned to face the neurosurgeon. "I'm afraid that would be impossible, MISTER Baldwin. You are not his doctor and no longer have any record of him. I have the last two, as you say, papers from his file. So, you have no proof he was even here or treated by anyone in this practice. If you do come up with proof, that means you've lied to us and have withheld our property and personal information."

Ginny and Joey Hall left the doctor's office and as they walked in silence, Joey quietly said, "I don't believe he destroyed that medical history, Mom. You could probably still get it from him."

A vicious smile crossed the mother's face. "Nope. We're not going there. He can't do anything with it now because if he did, he'd be incriminating himself. Don't worry. He won't be able to ruin any chances you have for the academy or for your career in the Coast Guard."

The mother and son left the hospital and drove home.

CHAPTER 48

The last days of testing for academy acceptance had passed. The physical and psychological tests had ended months ago and Joey was confident that he was still in good standing for consideration to the academy. He had no fears about Doctor Baldwin's threats. His past was over, and he felt good about moving forward to a new life at the academy. Although he realized his focus would be consumed with academy responsibilities and long stints at sea on the training ship Eagle, thoughts of Charlie would never be far from his mind. If only he could get word from the Coast Guard that he had been accepted.

Because Joey was unaware of his candidate status, he began to dwell on the outcome. Fortunately, he realized his concern had begun to dominate his thoughts and knew he'd learned that lesson a year ago, so he fought to push it to the back of his mind. Track season had come to an end and now there were high school proms, award ceremonies, school assemblies, and backyard parties to consider.

Joey just returned home from turning in all his track gear and uniforms, feeling good about being able to drive his new 1968 jalopy home from school. Ginny burst through the kitchen door of the house waving a letter in the air. "Joe! It's from the academy! We've been waiting all afternoon for you to open it."

Joey reached out the car's window and his mom handed him the letter. The address was from the United States Coast Guard Academy, Office of Admissions. Joey looked at his mother. "This is it, Mom. The final answer is in my hand."

"I know, I know. Just open it."

Joey opened the envelope and pulled out a single page letter. It began as a greeting to him and what appeared to be a standard introduction about last year's testing and his status among other candidates. Joey's heart began to sink. As his eyes moved to the final paragraph, he read, 'On behalf of the Vice President of the United States, Congressman Jonathan Murdock, and the United States Coast Guard Academy Admissions Office, it is our pleasure to offer you an appointment at the United States Coast Guard Academy in New London, Connecticut. You are expected to report as an academy cadet on 20 June 1973 between 1200 and 1400 hours.'

Joey looked out the car window, "I'm in, Mom. I made it."

Ginny leaned into the car and hugged her son. She seemed to be crying and laughing at the same time. Finally, she let go of Joey and backed out of the car window. Once she collected herself and dried her tears she looked back at her son and asked, "So, when do you have to report to the Academy? At least you'll have the summer to prepare and that'll give your father and me time to get used to your leaving."

Joey looked back down at the letter and shook his head. "No summer for me, I guess. I have to report on June 20th... one week after graduation."

Ginny's face suddenly turned red and serious. "No... no! That can't be right, Joe. There are things we need to do, people to say goodbye to. Your graduation party...," her voice trailed off as she dropped her gaze to the driveway.

A stoic look remained on Joey's face as he exited his car. He held his sobbing mother and reminded her, "I'll still be your son, Mom...no matter where I am. And for the next four years, I'll only be ninety minutes away."

Ginny stopped sobbing, "Oh! That's right!" A smile crossed her face. "I forgot that it was near our favorite beach. We can just drive down there on a Saturday or Sunday when we want to see you...right?"

Joey shook his head, "Not for at least the first year. I'll be busy. There will be a parent's weekend in the fall, but remember, I'm kind of their property now, so visitation is going to be difficult."

Ginny began to sob again. "I never realized it was going to be like...this. It sounds like we're not going to be able to see much of you in the next few years."

Joey pulled away from his mother. "According to the liaison officer, you'll be able to come to the academy to watch the cadet parades and special events. You might not be able to see me personally, but you will see me participating in some of those things...and I'll know you're there." He smiled and said, "And of course there is Christmas break with a two week leave."

Ginny stopped sobbing again while nodding her head. "Okay, okay. I get it. This is what we have now. We'll just be proud and make the most of the times that we have together."

She hugged her son and Joey thought, *Oh boy. This was hard enough. I wonder how Charlie is going to be with all this.*

That night at dinner, Joey celebrated his news with his family and planned on going over to see Charlie later in the evening. He wanted it to be just the two of them when he told her, so he could explain some of the restrictions that would be expected of him...and her.

Joey walked the mile to Charlie's house so he could think about what he was going to say and how he was going to say it to her. No matter what he thought or how he planned to say it, the news seemed inappropriate. *Oh, man! She's going to hate this whole set up. Basically, I'm asking her to put her life on hold between leaves from the academy...and if we make it through the next four years, there will always be those restricted times allowed between assignment's.* Joey shook his head as he watched the sidewalk pass beneath his feet. *I don't know...I just don't know what to do.*

Joey rounded a familiar turn and looked up to see Charlie's house across the street corner. He stopped and stared for a moment. *Okay, she's more important to me than the academy. If she doesn't want me to go...I won't go. I'll go to some college around here and we'll get married after I finish.*

Suddenly he heard Charlie's voice from across the street. "Hey, Joey! Are you waiting for a bus, or what? Come on over."

Slowly, Joey approached the house and received a big

hug from his girlfriend. "So, I see you walked. I thought you'd be taking every opportunity to drive that old junk of yours before you have to leave for the academy."

Joey managed a weak smile and nodded to some lawn chairs in the back yard. "We need to talk."

Charlie eyed Joey suspiciously. "Okay…," but otherwise kept silent.

Once they were seated, Joey gave her the news. "I got my appointment to the academy today."

Before he could say another word, Charlie was in his lap and giving him a congratulatory hug and kiss. "That's wonderful, Joe! I'm so happy for you! I knew you'd make it!" She pulled back a moment and asked, "But why so glum? This is your dream…what you've been waiting for."

Joey smiled, "Thanks, but it suddenly dawned on me… now that I'm really going…about what your life is going to be like."

Charlie got up from Joey's lap and her face became serious. "Uh, okay. I've been waiting for this day too." She paused to try and choose the right words. "I think we belong together, and I want to have a life with you some day, but I've been through this several times in my mind, and I think we should have a regular summer and see each other as much as possible. Once you leave for the academy," she paused and took a deep breath, "we should cool it for a while. We can still write and see each other when you're home, but I think if we allow the strain of a long-distance relationship, we may end up breaking up for good…and then we'll ruin any chances of a life together."

Joey sat up straight in his lawn chair. "You want to break up until I graduate from the academy?"

"Not break up...just date as time allows. And when Parents Weekend comes up, I'll come down there with your mom and dad for the weekend. If we make it through the next four years, we'll plan on a wedding after you graduate."

Joey's head dropped, "Well, first of all, we have no summer together. I have to report to the academy ten days after graduation from high school."

Charlie's right hand covered her mouth at the news. She stared at Joey before speaking. "Well, then that is what will happen for now. Anyway, you're going to be too busy to be thinking about me...and probably too tired. I've been reading all about this Coast Guard Academy stuff."

There was silence between the couple for a few minutes. Finally, Joey nodded his head and said, "If we do this, you'll probably meet someone else while I'm away."

Charlie was quick to answer, "Maybe - maybe not Joe, but we have to live our lives or we'll end up resenting each other." She leaned back in her chair. "I don't see any other way."

Joey rose from his chair and paced in front of Charlie. "Alright, I just won't go. I'll just go to one of the community colleges around here. Once I graduate, I'll get a job, and then we can think about marriage."

Charlie stood up, "Absolutely not! If you want to be with me, you have to be the guy I know...and trashing the Coast Guard dream is not you! You were made for this, Joe. You trained for this...all these years." She paused before continuing and took his hand. "You will end up resenting me in the long run if staying with me means to cancel your Coast Guard career." She turned and walked back to her chair. "You know what they say…, if it's meant to be, then it will be." She turned around to see Joey standing there with his head down. "We have to take this chance, Joe… for both of our sakes."

Joey said nothing. He nodded his head, turned and began walking toward the street.

Charlie called after him, "Call me tomorrow. We still have a few weeks together."

Joey didn't acknowledge her. He just kept walking… and never said good-bye.

CHAPTER 49

Weeks passed and Charlie hadn't heard from Joey. She tried to call him, but he was suspiciously never home. Finally, one night just a few days before their high school graduation, she walked over to his house. Unaware that it was Charlie, Joey answered the door. When he saw Charlie standing there, his heart seemed to jump into his mouth. He couldn't think of anything to say. He just stood there.

Charlie realized his surprise and after a few moments said, "Hi handsome! Come on out here and sit on the steps with me for a while."

Joey smiled and walked out the door. They sat together for a few minutes on the front porch steps without speaking for an uncomfortable minute and once again, Charlie broke the silence. "Why haven't you called me? I know you've been avoiding me and my phone calls."

Joey answered without looking from the ground in front of him. "You said you wanted to cool our relationship, but I figured waiting until I left for the academy would be too painful. It's hard enough right now."

Charlie put her hand on his thigh, "Joey, I'm not leaving you. I still want you in my life, but without restrictions.

We're young...too young to waste four years of our lives waiting for each other. I'm giving us a chance at a life together after the academy."

Joey removed her hand from his leg and stood up. He turned to walk into the house, and without looking at her said, "Bye, Charlie."

Charlie sat on the porch steps alone for a few minutes while tears slowly made their way down her cheeks. *I know I did the right thing. We'll see what happens when Parent's Weekend comes.*

Joey attended his high school graduation without the company of Charlie, but she was never far from his thoughts. He retreated into a protective part of his soul that shut out his friends and relatives...a place where no one else could go. To everyone else, he appeared to be a different person. Ginny and Frank watched for any indication of a relapse from his former condition because of the emotional impact of the break up with Charlie, the girl who unknowingly had helped to change his life. Doctor Horowitz had been right all along. Charlie had made a huge difference in Joey's maturation, especially on the emotional side, at precisely the right time in his growth process. The loss of her in his life with the increased anxieties common to an eighteen-year-old boy about to leave for college were understandable, but Joey had all of that with the increased pressure of entering a governmental law enforcement and military academy.

The extra parental attention was obvious to Joey where

it became uncomfortable for him to be around the house or in the presence of any of his family. One night at dinner, Joey waited for an opportune moment and addressed the whole family. "Look guys. I know everyone has their best intentions for me, but I am fine. I haven't had any…episodes in a long while now, nor have I felt like I was upset enough to worry that I might have one. It's true that I am fairly upset about Charlie, but our break up is her call…and because it is her call…that actually helps me." He paused a moment and went on, "I have to put that into perspective and concentrate on where I'm going and what I'll be doing in just a few days." He looked up and at everyone at the table. "So, even if I had an episode now…is that going to stop me from going to the academy?" He answered his own question as everyone remained silent and just stared at him. "No. It means that I'll just move on and not dwell on it. I'm over that…disorder. It shadowed enough of my life and good times, but I didn't let it win. I beat it and I'm going to the Coast Guard Academy so someday I can be the captain of a Coast Guard vessel that protects our coastline and people in trouble at sea." He paused again and continued. "You don't have to watch me so closely anymore. It's over."

Everyone remained silent and then glanced at one another as if they were looking for approval or some kind of common understanding. The happy laid-back Joey that everyone knew seemed to have disappeared…at least for the time being. Frank finally spoke up and wore an understanding but serious face. "Okay, Joe. We get it. None of us ever meant to make you feel uncomfortable, but I'm glad you said something. We're all behind you…every bit of the way."

Joey nodded and went back to his dinner as everyone else did. Everyone remained quiet while they digested Joey's words. Joey, their son and brother, was leaving home, and now everyone accepted it.

Life at the Hall's residence passed normally for the few days Joey had left with the family. The tension that did surface was only when they considered that final day when they'd bring Joey to the academy and watch him leave for what seemed a long time.

And when that day and time came, Joseph Daniel Hall, Coast Guard Academy cadet, said goodbye to his parents as he walked through the academy gates in New London, Connecticut.

Even as he carried his luggage past the gates to report in, he felt a terrible pain...an emptiness that he'd never experienced before, but knew he was going where he was meant to be. He stopped once and looked back at the open gate where his family was and stared for a minute. Charlie wasn't there, but her face was the only thing he saw. He picked up his one bag of belongings and entered an old and famous building called the Welcoming Center, letting the door close behind him without looking back.

EPILOGUE

Joseph Daniel Hall experienced a successful four years at the Coast Guard Academy in New London, Connecticut. Like any other cadet, Joe experienced his share of triumphs and defeats, whether it had to do with academics, physical training, seamanship, or military training. There were far too many other areas in the line of required training to be mentioned here, but Joey who became known as Joe, graduated from the academy in the upper third of his class and achieved the rank of Ensign as he crossed the exalted ceremonial stage, and received his diploma in engineering and literary arts.

Through the next few years, Charlie and Joey connected only a few times, one of them being Parent's Weekend of his first year at the academy. There were isolated instances where the couple saw each other for brief dates, usually at Charlie's prompting and planning, when Joey was home on leave between semesters. Summers were usually absorbed by the academy's required training at sea on the Coast Guard training ship Eagle or for various other specified maritime endeavors, some of which was confidential to the Coast Guard and not for public discussion.

Following academy graduation, Joey was given his first

choice for sea duty aboard a small search and rescue vessel, so he could learn not only the sea and associated weather patterns, but specific rescue and survival techniques. The assignment included the demonstration and execution of advanced boat handling skills required for his new job aboard the Ranger, a 47 foot rescue craft designated as a Motor Lifeboat (MLB).

The craft was designed as a fast response boat for use in high seas and was able to right itself if knocked over by large swells or surf. The work was demanding, dangerous, and required all of his conscious thoughts. Now, that he was an officer and had a responsibility to a crew of three sailors, a new sense of ownership and responsibility began to develop. Eventually, he was involved in several rescues that involved stranded boaters, and small aircraft accidents at sea.

Joey loved the work and was good at it. Eventually he was promoted to Lieutenant Junior Grade, and later to Lieutenant where he was given command of his own MLB47. He never spoke of Charlie during this period, but never ceased to think about her. Of course, there were phone calls around Christmas time, but Charlie had been correct years earlier, when she told him he'd be too tired or busy to think about her. Now, that he had a crew of his own to account for, found little time with his new responsibilities.

One rainy day, Lieutenant Joe Hall received orders for transfer to a Coast Guard Station along coastal Maine. He made the necessary arrangements and called Charlie for a date in their old hometown of Johnsville the following weekend. He drove her to one of their favorite places and asked her to marry him and be a Coast Guard wife. He explained all the trials and tribulations, the impositions and interruption of unplanned rescues, and the Coast Guard's expectation of her as the wife of a Coast Guard officer. Charlie said yes, and the longtime couple was re-united and married five years after Joey's graduation from the academy.

Despite Joey's turbulent and disappointing early years, his persistence in something he desperately wanted to do paid off. He let nothing distract him from his goal or sway his interest. He challenged everything and anything that gave him the slightest feeling that might cause him to fail. He kept his focus despite disappointments and heartaches, and became an officer and captain of a United States Coast Guard vessel charged with saving lives at sea. The courage he learned as a boy and young man to persevere under the most difficult and trying circumstances molded the man he came to be.

Joey's past never followed him, but even if it had, the man was living proof that his early years only served to make him a stronger and more stable individual, not only physically, but also mentally.

Printed in the USA
CPSIA information can be obtained
at www.ICGtesting.com
LVHW020714091123
763476LV00003B/83

9 781663 255693